SARAH'S SURRENDER

— Land Rush Dreams 3 —

Vickie McDonough

SHILOH RUN  PRESS

An Imprint of Barbour Publishing, Inc.

Cover Design: Faceout Studio, www.faceoutstudio.com

Published by Shiloh Run Press, an imprint of Barbour Publishing, Inc., P.O. Box 719, Uhrichsville, Ohio 44683, www.shilohrunpress.com

Our mission is to publish and distribute inspirational products offering exceptional value and biblical encouragement to the masses.

 Member of the
Evangelical Christian
Publishers Association

Printed in the United States of America.

Chapter 1

What did you say?" Sarah Worley leaned back against the corral railing, staring at her longtime friend Luke McNeil. His vivid blue eyes sparkled, making even the cloudless sky seem dull.

He removed his hat, and the light breeze fanned his blond hair across his face. He sobered and cast an uncharacteristically apprehensive glance around the empty ranch yard then refocused on her. Luke took hold of Sarah's hand, sending odd tingles racing up her arm. "I said I want you to marry me. I think we should get hitched."

Luke had been the one who made her smile when she'd first arrived at the Coulter ranch over eight years ago and had felt so out of place with the loving family. He was a happy sort, always joking or teasing, but from the look in his eyes right now, he was dead serious. Sarah glanced toward the Coulters' two-story house, almost wishing Lara would call her to come in and help. She didn't want to hurt Luke but neither could she marry him. "I don't know what to say. This is so sudden."

"It's not sudden. I've been thinking about it for ages. Say you will. I can't imagine spending the rest of my life with anyone else."

"You wouldn't care that your children would be one-fourth Cherokee?" Heat rushed to her cheeks at such an intimate topic.

"Of course not, especially if they have your dark eyes." He waggled his brows and grinned in a manner that made her squirm.

Usually he could pull her out of her doldrums on the worst of days.

But not today.

She tugged her hand from his. "I care for you, Luke, but as a friend, not a beau. You've always been there for me, but you know I have no plans to marry."

His lips pursed as he rolled the brim of his hat. "But I thought—" He slapped on his slouch hat. "One of these days you're going to have to forgive your father and forget about what he did."

She *had* forgiven Pete Worley, but she could never forget how he used the women in the bordello he owned—that horrible place she lived for over a year when she was younger. She also couldn't forget how horribly he'd hurt Jo, the first person who ever truly helped her, other than her mother.

She grabbed Luke's sleeve when he started to walk away. "Luke, wait. You know my dearest dream is to have a home of my own. You've asked me to marry you, but you live in Gabe's bunkhouse. Have you considered that?"

He shrugged. "I've some money put back. Probably enough to buy a speck of property somewhere. I can build us a cabin. Maybe I should've ventured out on my own before now. Then I'd already have a house to offer you."

"If you had, you would have left years ago and our friendship would never have grown to what it is."

"I don't want just friendship, Sarah. I care deeply for you."

She reached out and touched his arm. "I care for you, too, and even though I'll be twenty-one soon, I'm not ready to get married. I feel like my life only started eight years ago when Jo brought me to her sister's ranch. I still have so much living to do."

He frowned. "We could do that livin' together if you weren't so stubborn. I can give you the home you've always wanted if you'd let me."

Her heart broke a little at disappointing him. She crossed her arms, lest he take her hand again. "I can't, Luke. I'm sorry."

He stared at her for a long moment, nodded, and then turned and strode into the barn.

Sarah blinked her stinging eyes. Luke was the best friend she'd ever had, and now she'd hurt him deeply. She thought of the times she'd been lonely or not feeling like she belonged in the Coulter home, not that Gabe and Lara had ever made her feel that way. It had been her own insecurities, partly because of the way some people in town eyed her dark complexion. She was a half-breed, and some folks would just as soon spit on her as talk to her.

Feeling more out of sorts than she had in a long while, she pushed away from the railing and headed toward the house. The lovely day had dimmed. Why did Luke have to go and ask her to marry him? Why hadn't she noticed he was getting serious? But why should she when she had such little experience with men? Could they still be friends, or had her refusal of him ruined that relationship?

The sad thing was, in a small part of her mind she could almost see them married. But she had her dreams, and one way or another, it was time she pursued them.

Luke leaned on the stall gate, staring at his palomino, Golden Boy. "I messed up."

The horse nodded as if agreeing then poked his head over the gate, hoping for a treat.

"Sorry, don't have any handouts today." He scratched the gelding's forehead. Why hadn't he waited to talk to Sarah? Maybe he should have courted her before blurting out that he wanted to marry her. He kicked the stall gate.

"Something wrong with Golden Boy?"

Luke glanced at his boss, Gabe Coulter. "Uh. . .no. I'm just frustrated about somethin'."

Gabe leaned one arm on the empty stall gate next to Golden Boy's. "Care to talk about it?"

Luke shrugged. He and Gabe had been friends longer than Gabe had loved his wife, Lara, but this seemed almost too personal to speak of. Still, he needed another man's perspective. "I asked Sarah to marry me, but she flat-out refused."

Gabe's eyebrows shot upward. "Well, I sure didn't expect that was your problem." He rubbed his jaw. "I find it hard to believe she'd refuse you. The two of you seem so close."

"Friends." Luke raised his hands in a helpless gesture then slapped them against his pants. "That's all we are, according to her."

"But you feel more than friendship, I'm guessing."

"I reckon. . .yeah. I thought so, at least." He scratched his hand across his heart as if that would stop it from hurting. "How's a man to know for sure if he's in"—he swatted a hand in the air—"love?"

"You must feel pretty certain about your affections for her to propose."

Luke shrugged. He lifted his head and watched the dust motes floating in the shafts of light that streaked through the cracks in the barn wall. He needed to fix those before winter set in.

"You know, Lara didn't want to have much to do with me at first."

"Yeah, I remember. How did you manage to win her over?"

"Persistence. I kept at it, and I sure am glad I did."

Luke thought of the three active children Lara had birthed since she married Gabe: Beth, Drew, and little Missy. It would have been a shame for them not to have been born. He couldn't shake the vision of a son of his own with Sarah's dark eyes and hair. Would that child ever have a chance at life?

He blew out a loud sigh at his sappy thoughts. "I'm thirty-one, Gabe. I'm grateful to have worked for you all these years, but if I ever hope to win Sarah's heart, I've gotta get a place of my own."

Gabe slapped Luke's shoulder. "I don't know how I'll get along without you, but I understand. A man's got to do what God's calling him to do. Let me know if there's any way I can help. And allow Sarah to consider your proposal. Don't press her for an answer. You may be ready for marriage, but her life was difficult before coming here. She may simply need more time."

He nodded. "I appreciate the advice." Luke opened the gate and stepped into the stall. He grabbed a curry brush off the shelf above the feed trough and began running it across Golden Boy's shoulder. The repetitive motion allowed him to think. Something Gabe had said nagged him. *"A man's got to do what God's calling him to do."*

He believed in God. Daniel, Lara's grandpa, had been a good influence on Luke's life before he passed on. He missed the old man, as he knew the rest of the family did. Daniel had often talked about God as if they were old buddies. Luke's life had been pretty good since he met up with Gabe. He liked being Gabe's foreman, but now he needed more.

Maybe it was time he talked to God and asked Him if He actually had plans for him—and if those plans included Sarah as his wife.

The brush paused. But what if God said no?

A week after Luke had proposed, Sarah reread the article in the Guthrie newspaper once more, her heart pounding faster with each paragraph her eyes scanned. This was it—the chance she'd been waiting for—*praying* for. July 29th was less than a month away—and there was so much she must do to prepare. She folded the paper and stared out the window of the home she'd lived in for close to a decade.

Would Gabe and Lara be upset when she told them she'd be leaving? They'd so generously opened their home to her when she showed up on their doorstep with Jo, Lara's younger sister. They had become her family. But she couldn't let that hold her back from reaching for her dream. The idea of leaving here was both frightening and exhilarating. Jo would probably encourage her to follow her heart, but Lara would be more cautious and protective—motherly.

Her gaze shifted toward the barn, as it often did. She wished she could have given Luke the answer he'd wanted, but she couldn't. Not yet. Maybe never. She'd never had a male friend like him, and leaving him behind would almost be harder than leaving Lara and the children. She was an older sister to the Coulter young'uns, even Michael, Lara's sixteen-year-old son by her first husband. Oh, how she would miss them.

Sighing, she turned and glanced around her room. It had been hers since shortly after she and Jo had arrived here. She loved this private oasis with its lacy curtains and comfortable furniture, but she longed for a *home* of her own—not just one room. It was time for her to move on. Time for her to keep the promise she'd made to her mother.

Dropping onto her bed, she remembered the tiny cabin she and her mother had shared. Distant relatives had helped provide food and water when her mother became ill, but Sarah was always hungry—except for the rare times her father stopped by with a mule-load of food or sent money. Her mother had told her to study hard and make her own way—not to be dependent on anyone so that she could be in charge of her destiny. Winning land would be the start of fulfilling that dream.

Her clock chimed, yanking Sarah from her thoughts. She hurried downstairs and donned her apron. She should have been down sooner to bring in the laundry and help Lara prepare supper, but she'd been praying once again about her decision. Excitement and nerves had tangled with her prayers. There were so many things she had to work out.

Lara looked over her shoulder and smiled as Sarah entered the kitchen. Her smile dimmed. "Are you feeling all right?"

Sarah nodded. "Yes, I was reading something and praying for

a bit. I apologize for not being down sooner."

Lara waved a dismissing hand in the air. "You don't owe me an explanation." She glanced at her daughters. "Don't peel those potatoes too thick, Beth."

"I'm not, Mama. But could you tell Missy to stop playin' with the peelings? She's makin' a mess." The eight-year-old sighed like a frustrated adult.

Sarah walked over to the table and hugged Missy. "Are you making a mess?"

The three-year-old giggled. "I makin' a house."

"Ma—a—a!" Beth rolled her eyes.

Lara crossed to the table. "Missy, if you play with those peelings, you'll be the one who has to clean them up."

The little girl looked at her pile then suddenly pushed the whole mess back toward her sister. "I done."

Lara's light green eyes twinkled as she glanced at Sarah. "I bet Sarah would appreciate your help taking down the laundry."

"Aw'wight." Missy slid from her chair, took hold of Sarah's hand, then glanced up at her with light green eyes, just like her mother's. "C'mon."

Sarah smiled and squeezed the girl's hand. "We need to wash your hands before you handle the clean clothes." She led the girl to the washtub, ladled in some fresh water from the bucket sitting next to it, and then cleaned and dried their hands. "Let's get the basket and the clothespin holder."

"I get it." Missy dashed across the kitchen and out the door to the side porch the men had recently added.

Sarah chuckled. "She sure is fast when she wants to be."

Beth snorted. "Don't I know. She likes to play with my doll, and no matter where I hide it, she finds it faster than you can say Jack Sprat."

"We need to make one for her to replace the dolly she lost. Then maybe she won't bother yours." Lara patted her daughter's shoulder.

"Can we start on it tonight?"

Sarah grinned as she exited the kitchen, looking for Missy. With a houseful of children, there was always something to chuckle about. Missy trotted under the flapping clothes on the line, pretending to be a horse, her favorite animal. Given the choice, the little tomboy would go to work with her father, as Michael did most days. Oh, how she'd miss this family when she was gone. Her days would be so lonely after the craziness of a large family, but achieving her dream would be worth it.

Sarah snagged the wicker basket off the porch and headed to the clothesline. She would have to add rope to her supply list so that she could create her own line for hanging laundry. There were so many things she needed to set up her own place. Though she'd saved the majority of the money her father had sent over the years, she now wondered if it would stretch as far as she needed it to. She reached for a clothespin. Was she making a big mistake?

Chapter 2

Sarah's hand shook as she spooned a bite of mashed turnips into her mouth. Would Gabe and Lara be upset when she finally shared the news of her decision? Would they think her ungrateful for all they'd done for her? Jack, Lara's brother and the local preacher, would probably try to dissuade her. He was like an older brother to her, and she highly valued his counsel. Maybe she should talk with him first.

The clink of silverware filled the room as eight people enjoyed their supper. Luke often joined the family for the evening meal, but his empty seat reminded her of their talk. Between bites, Missy jabbered to her pa about playing with the kittens in the barn with Beth, while Michael excitedly told his ma of the eagle he'd seen swoop down and snag a rabbit. Drew, a lively six-year-old with a sparkle in his brown eyes, stole a slice of meat off Beth's plate when her face was turned. Normally, Sarah would have smiled, but instead, she clenched the edge of her napkin, already missing the children's antics. This decision was the biggest one she'd made since choosing to run away from the bordello her father owned at the same time Jo did, eight years ago.

Lara glanced across the table and lifted a brow. "You're rather quiet tonight."

"I've got something I want to talk to you about."

The chatter instantly quieted, and almost everyone looked her way. Sarah's mouth went dry. Her leg started jiggling beneath the table. "I. . .meant. . .later."

"Say it now. We all wanna hear." Drew reached for another biscuit, but his ma snatched the plate away.

"Not until you finish your vegetables, young man."

"But, Ma–a–a, you know I hate turnips."

Lara eyed the boy as only a mother could.

"Do as your ma says." Gabe pointed his fork at his son.

Jack glanced down at his own plate, looking as if he were fighting a smile. His son Cody, only a few months younger than Drew, leaned against his pa's arm and looked up.

"I don't like turnips neither, Pa," he whispered loudly enough that everyone heard.

Beth giggled and ducked her head.

Jack glanced at the boy. "You eat what's put on your plate, son."

"But—"

Jack lifted his eyebrows, and the boy nodded. "Yes, sir." He picked up his spoon, shoved in a tiny bite of turnips, and grimaced. Then he grabbed his glass of milk and took a long swig. He glanced proudly at Drew. "It ain't so bad, if you drink your milk real fast afterwards."

With a serious expression, Drew nodded then mimicked his cousin's actions.

The adults shared private smiles.

Sarah sighed, glad that Drew's dislike of turnips had taken

everyone's attention off her and helped her to relax. There was nothing like children to lighten the mood.

After the meal, Sarah helped scrape the plates. The boys were sent to the barn to do their evening chores, while the girls went out to water the garden. Jack started to follow the boys, but Sarah hurried to his side and tugged on his sleeve. He paused, gazing down at her. "I'd like you to stay while I talk to Gabe and Lara, if you don't mind."

He nodded. "I reckon the boys will be all right on their own for a short while."

"This shouldn't take long." When she turned, Lara and Gabe were standing side by side near the counter, Gabe still holding his coffee cup. Lara looked a bit concerned.

Sarah glanced down and realized she was wringing her hands. She stuck one in her pocket and pulled out the newspaper ad then took a deep breath and blew it out quickly, hoping she didn't lose her nerve. "I've been doing a lot of thinking and praying for a while, and I have come to a decision." She held up the ragged page. "This article from the newspaper says the government is going to be opening up another section of Indian land—the Kiowa, Comanche, and Apache reservation land left over after the allotment to individual members of those tribes. More than likely, it's the last section that will be available in the Oklahoma Territory. It will be handled by a lottery instead of a land run." She drew in a breath as she read the curiosity in Gabe's eyes and worry in Lara's. "I've decided to go to El Reno to register and see if I can get some land of my own."

Gabe's eyebrows shot upward while Lara's mouth dropped open. He set his cup on the cupboard counter and wrapped an arm around his wife, as if knowing she needed comfort. Sarah hated to hurt the couple who had been so kind to her for so many years and had loved her as a younger sister. She struggled for something to say to soften the blow. "You know how much I love you both"—she cast a glance at Jack—"all of you. But I can't stay here forever. Your family is growing, and you'll need my room soon."

"We have plenty of space. There's no need for you to be concerned about that." Lara's eyes begged her to reconsider.

Sarah walked to the table and held on to the top of a ladder-back chair. "There's more to it than that. I'm sure you figured I'd be married by now, but. . ." She shrugged. "I feel it's time for me to get a place of my own. If I'm fortunate enough to win a homestead, I'll pick land near one of the new towns being established. I have most of the money my father sent me, which I will use to have a house built and get the things I need initially."

Lara stepped away from Gabe. "But what will you do until then? A woman can't live alone on the open prairie."

"I won't be alone. All the others who win claims will be nearby."

"But those will probably all be men. It wouldn't be safe for a woman alone." Lara spun around to face her husband. "Can you talk some sense into her?"

He shrugged. "I'm sorry, sweetheart, but Sarah has the right to do what she feels God is calling her to do. Besides, how can you fuss at her when you rode in the land run? The lottery is a much safer option."

"Gabe! I didn't have a choice—you know that. But Sarah does. She can't go alone. That's just foolhardy." She turned to

Jack. "Can't you be the voice of reason?"

Jack looked from one of them to another as if taking time to formulate his response. He stroked his chin, pursing his lips. "I guess it's time to admit that I've been thinking of doing the same thing."

Sarah's heart jolted at the exact moment Lara gasped.

"You can't be serious, Jack." Lara squeezed her forehead "What about Cody?"

"What about him? Things have been difficult on both of us since Cora died. I'm thinking a change would do us good. If we get land, we can settle there and start a ranch of our own. If not, we can stay and help Sarah for as long as she needs us, if that's all right with her."

She nodded, unable to hold back her smile. "I would love that—if you're certain that's what you want to do."

"I've been prayin' about it ever since I first heard about the lottery, and I'm startin' to believe it's what God wants me to do."

"What about the church? What will we do for a pastor?" Gabe turned to refill his coffee cup.

"Barry Addams would be a good one to take over. I've been meeting with him for two years and have taught him nearly all I know about God's Word. He's a good man who loves the Lord. He'd be a responsible leader for the time I'm gone. If I don't win a homestead, at least we'll have had a change of scenery for a bit. And if Cody and I don't return, I believe Barry would be willin' to consider a permanent position as pastor."

Lara tugged out a chair and sat down. "I feel like one of my children is leaving home. And I dread seeing you and Cody leave, Jack. We've loved having you here with us."

"We've enjoyed it, too, but things change, sis."

Sarah walked around the table, pulled out one of the chairs, and placed it so that she could face her dear friend, who was like a mother to her. She sat and took Lara's hands. "Please try to understand. This is something I feel compelled to do. I believe it's what God wants me to do."

Lara gazed at her with watery eyes. "You've prayed about this?"

"Yes. Ever since I first heard the land might be opened for settlement. El Reno is not that far away. The train already goes there, which is where I need to register."

"How far away is that?" Lara still didn't look convinced.

"Just west of Oklahoma City. A short train ride from here." Sarah smiled, hoping to relieve her friend's worries. "It's about the same length of a ride from here to El Reno as it is to where Jo lives in Perry."

Lara brushed her hand down the side of Sarah's cheek. "I still remember the quiet, reserved little girl you were when Jo first brought you to us—the girl who craved learning. You've grown into a lovely woman, whom I dearly love." She ducked her head a moment then looked up, her eyes watery. "I always thought you'd stay with us until you married."

Sarah blinked away the sting in her own eyes. "I thought that, too, but God has changed my mind. You and Gabe have had someone living with you ever since you married. It's time your family had this house to yourselves."

Gabe cleared his throat. "You know that doesn't matter to us. God has blessed us, and we're happy to share what we have with others. But if God truly has spoken to you, then you should listen. Sometimes He asks us to do hard things—things that don't make sense at the time." He stared at his wife, and Sarah wondered if he was remembering their past—how Gabe killed Lara's first husband in self-defense and then went on to track her down so he could return the money he'd won from her husband in a poker game. But that never actually happened because Lara wouldn't accept the money. Later, after riding in Oklahoma's first land rush, they fell in love and married.

It was such a romantic story that she nearly sighed. Did God have a special man out there for her? Luke's wide grin and sparkling blue eyes invaded her mind. She shook her head to rid it of his image. Jack was a handsome, God-fearing man, but he was far too old for her. And besides, he was like a brother, and he was still grieving his wife whose death had shaken them all. There was a time that she thought she'd never marry, after living in her father's bordello and seeing how horribly men treated women, but living in Gabe's house, with his example as well as Jack's and Luke's, she'd learned there were good men who loved and cared for women.

"Have you talked to Jo about this?" Lara asked.

"I've tried writing to her several times, but I've had trouble putting my thoughts to paper. I don't know why God is asking me to do this, only that He is. How can I explain it so she'll understand?"

Gabe chuckled. "You're selling Jo short. She'd probably be the first to encourage you to follow your dreams."

Sarah smiled. "You're right. She would. I just hate that this decision will take me farther away from her, since Perry is north of here and the lottery land is southwest."

Jack walked across the room, his boots thudding on the floor.

"That's true, but it's still not all that far away when you consider the railroad."

Lara squeezed her hand. "You're truly going to do this?"

Sarah smiled and nodded. "Yes, I am."

Jack admired the bright pinks and oranges on the horizon, created by the setting sun as he strode across the yard toward the barn. He'd been thinking and praying about leaving ever since Cora died in childbirth this past January. Both he and Cody had taken her death hard. Cody missed his ma, and he longed for his precious wife.

He'd been looking forward to having another child and raising the baby with Cora, but it wasn't to be. His time with her had been far shorter than he'd expected. He could still see Cora walking down the church aisle on their wedding day, looking jubilant and beautiful in her pale blue dress. He had almost missed the blessing of a wife because he'd been such a dunderhead and hadn't recognized that Cora cared for him. She'd been so happy that day, so filled with joy, as he had been. She'd pledged to love him until death parted them. Neither of them imagined death would part them so soon.

He leaned against the corral fence and stared at the horizon. He'd hoped they would grow old together, especially since he hadn't married until he was nearly thirty. But it wasn't to be. God had given him seven and a half blissful years with Cora and a wonderful son, but they'd lost three babies, including the one that had been born dead during the difficult childbirth that took Cora's life.

He gritted his teeth, still trying to understand. He loved children. He was a good father and would have been to any more children God blessed him with, so why hadn't the good Lord seen fit to spare his wife and baby?

"I didn't spare my own Son so that you could have eternal life."

Jack clenched the fence railing as the truth hit him. God *hadn't* spared His Son, and if He had, all men would still live in darkness. Who was he to question God? He gazed upward toward the darkening sky. "Thank You, Lord. I don't have all the answers. Don't know why You thought it was time to take Cora and our baby, but I will try to rest in Your arms. I miss her—and the daughter I never got to know."

Behind him, Jack heard a snicker. He turned and saw Cody and Drew standing just inside the barn's entrance. Their eyes widened and the duo ducked their heads when they noticed him looking their way. He pushed away from the corral and moved toward them. The boys shuffled their feet as he approached. "What have they done now, Lord?"

Drew leaned against Cody. "Who was your pa talkin' to?"

Cody exhaled a loud sigh and took on a mature posture. "He's talkin' to God again."

"Does he do that a lot?"

"Yep."

"I can hear you guys, you know."

Drew's eyes widened. "I didn't mean nothin', Uncle Jack."

He grinned and ruffled the boy's hair. "I know." He squatted on his heels to be on their eye level. "Cody knows you can talk to God anytime you need to, but do you?"

Drew shrugged and glanced down, toeing the dirt. "I reckon

so. Pa says that, too, but I just never saw you doin' it outside of church and blessing our meals."

"Maybe you'll see fit to talk to God one day, too."

Drew's dark brown eyes, the same color as his pa's, rounded again. "Ma makes me pray every night when I'm in bed. You reckon God knows everything I do, like I've heard you say when you preach?" He leaned in closer. "Even the bad stuff?"

Jack tried not to smile at the boy's whisper. "There's a verse in the Bible that says, 'The eyes of the Lord are in every place, beholdin' the evil and the good.' "

Drew scowled. "What's beholdin' mean?"

"It means God's watchin' us," Cody said, a proud look in his eyes.

"That's right, son. God sees everything you do, so you'd best think twice before disobeying or doing something you shouldn't."

Drew gulped and glanced over his shoulder into the barn.

Just what had the two young'uns been up to? "Is there somethin' you need to tell me?"

Drew ducked his head.

The whites of Cody's eyes showed for a second before he, too, looked down. "We. . .uh. . .locked Michael in the tack room."

Jack knew this wasn't a laughing matter, but he still wrestled back a grin. Boys will be boys. "What do you think you should do about that?"

Cody glanced at Drew. "Let him out, I reckon."

Jack stood. "That sounds like a wise idea. Go on and do that."

"Yes, sir," the boys said as they turned in unison and shuffled into the barn and to the door of the tack room. Cody reached for the lock.

"Son, let Drew do it."

"Yes, Pa." Cody stepped back.

"Why me?" Drew glanced at Jack.

"Because I suspect this was your idea, was it not?"

Drew pursed his lips then nodded. "How did you know?"

"I just did." Drew was usually the one to stir up the trouble and Cody followed along.

The boy twisted the lock they had slipped through the loop on the latch then opened the door. Light spilled from the small room, and the familiar odor of saddle soap wafted out the door.

Sixteen-year-old Michael's blond head popped up from where he sat polishing a saddle by lantern light. He grinned. "Howdy, Uncle Jack."

"How come you wasn't hollerin' and poundin' on the door?" Drew asked.

Michael grinned. "Because I knew that's what you wanted me to do. I figured I'd continue on with my chores since I couldn't go nowhere."

"Aw, no fair." Drew kicked the door frame.

"Was it fair for you to lock your brother in the tack room?"

"No, sir."

"I think it would be fair for you to finish polishin' that saddle for Michael."

Drew's gaze shot to his. "But—"

"Would you rather I tell Pa what you did?" Michael winked at Jack.

"No."

"Cody, you get in there and help, too. And you boys be careful with the lantern on." Jack stepped back so the boys could enter the small room.

Michael rose and stretched then stepped around the boys. "All that's left is the other side of the saddle. This one's done."

Jack wrapped his arm around his nephew, who'd be close to his own height in another year or two. "I'm proud that you kept a level head and were a good example to your brother and cousin."

Michael beamed, his blue-green eyes shining. "Thanks. I guess I should get to feeding the horses before the sun sets all the way."

Jack nodded and watched him go in the dimming light. He peeked at the younger boys, glad to see they were obeying. He sure would miss all of the young'uns when he and Cody left. He hadn't considered how hard that might be on his son. Drew and Cody were nearly inseparable. He needed to pray more and make sure he was doing the right thing and not running away again.

*

The railcar shimmied and the whistle screeched a long wail as the train pulled into the Perry depot. Sarah's stomach churned with excitement at seeing Jo and her family again. Jo and Baron were so tied to their general store that they rarely got to visit the ranch anymore, especially when Jamie, their oldest son was attending school.

She spotted Jo on the platform with her two youngest children and waved. Four-year-old Emma hopped up and down, waving one hand while holding her mama's skirt with the other. Jo held Matthew. The toddler stared wide-eyed at the noisy contraption. The train squealed and whooshed as it stopped, and the boy buried his face on Jo's shoulder.

Sarah smiled, shaking her head. How in the world had fierce-hearted Jo ended up with a timid son? He must take after his father, not that Baron was spineless, but he certainly had a milder temperament than Jo. Sarah rose, eager to see her good friend. If not for Jo, her life would have been drastically different. She might still be living in a den of sin, and her father might still be running that dreadful bordello instead of eking out a decent living as a cattle rancher.

When it came her time to exit, Sarah trotted down the steps and into Jo's open arms. She peeked at Matty as she hugged her friend. The boy offered a shy smile before turning his head away.

"Hug me, Aunt Sarah!" Emma tugged on her skirt.

Sarah put down her satchel and picked up the darling blond-haired, blue-eyed girl. She placed a loud smack on Emma's soft cheek. "I couldn't forget to hug you, sweetie. Look how much you've grown."

"I'm a big girl now."

"Yes, you are. And you're getting heavy." She gave the girl another squeeze then set her down and smiled at Matty. "And look at that boy. I can't believe he's already a year and a half."

"I know. He's growing fast." Jo shifted Matty to her other arm. "You look wonderful. How are things at the ranch?"

"Thank you, and everything is good."

"I was thrilled to get your telegram about your visit, but I was surprised since you were only here two months ago. Has something happened?" Jo's vivid blue eyes dimmed with concern.

"There are some things I need to talk to you about, and I wanted to do it in person."

"Like what?"

Sarah glanced around the busy depot. People still waited to board while those meeting friends and family were collecting their baggage and leaving.

"Forgive me." Jo squeezed Sarah's arm. "This isn't the place to chat. Let's get your baggage and head home."

Sarah let out a grateful sigh and picked up her satchel. "This is all I brought."

Jo quirked one blond eyebrow.

"Mama, can we stop for a treat?" Emma gazed up with a hopeful gleam in her eyes.

"Did you forget that we made gingerbread for Aunt Sarah?"

"Oh yeah." Emma spun around to face Sarah. "We fixed some ginnerbread."

"Yum! That's one of my favorite treats." She reached for the girl's hand. "Let's go home so we can eat some."

"Eat!" Matty nodded his white-blond head.

"This boy does like his food." Jo smiled as she patted her son's backside.

Sarah walked alongside her dear friend as they headed home. "It amazes me how much this town has grown since you first came here."

"I remember when it was virgin prairie with no buildings. It's hard to believe all the changes that have taken place in just eight years."

At the top of the depot steps, Sarah paused a moment to study the town. It consisted mainly of two-story buildings constructed of wood, brick, or stone. Buggies and horses with riders moved down every street. As she descended the stairs, her gaze shifted toward the part of Perry dubbed Hell's Half Acre, where a host of saloons and gambling houses existed. She was thankful that Baron and Jo lived on the opposite side of town. The seedier section reminded her too much of her father's former business. She glanced up at the sky, thanking God again for protecting her and getting her out of that dreadful situation.

Emma chatted up a storm as they walked. She smiled down at the darling.

"Clarence is assisting Baron at the store so I don't have to worry about going in today. I don't work nearly as much as I used to since the children keep me busy."

"That's wonderful. I'm happy to watch the children, though, if you need to work while I'm here."

"How long can you stay?" Jo glanced sideways at Sarah.

"Only a few days." She thought of all she had to do, most importantly getting to El Reno in time to register for the lottery.

Jo stopped and turned to face her. "Why such a short visit?"

"Let's get to the house. Then I'll explain. I'd prefer not to do it on the street."

Jo nodded, but it was obvious that she was curious. At the next corner, Jo turned left instead of right, which would have taken them down the street where Hillborne's Mercantile was located. Sarah thought back to the days when Jo and Baron had married. Shortly after that he'd ridden in the 1893 land run, often called the Cherokee Strip Land Run, and won a plot where they'd built their store. Later they bought a lot from a man who was returning to Arkansas and built a lovely home there. Each time she visited, Sarah had to fight back her feelings of jealousy. The two-story house with bay windows and a wide wraparound porch was just what she longed for. Would she ever have a home of her own?

It wasn't that she was ungrateful to live with Gabe and Lara in their big house, but she was ready to move on.

They rounded another corner, and Sarah's gaze landed on Jo's home. The lovely house was painted a soft yellow with white trim around the doors, windows, and porch railings. She exhaled a sigh, happy for her friend but unable to curtail the longing deep within her.

The noise of the business area softened as they moved into the residential part of town. Birds serenaded them from the trees that offered abundant shade overhead, and down the street a dog barked.

Someone who didn't know the history of the town would find it hard to believe that less than a decade ago this had all been virgin prairie. She, of all people, knew how fast change could come. One day she was tending her dying mother, and then the next, her father—whom she only remembered seeing a few times—showed up and took her home with him. Less than two years later, she ran away from him at the same time Jo did. It was the best choice she'd ever made.

They walked through the front door into the cool house, and Jo set Matty down. He toddled into the parlor where he plopped down next to a basket of blocks. Jo pressed her knuckles into the small of her back. "That boy is getting heavy."

Emma pulled her hand free from Sarah's and went to play with her brother. Sarah smiled, watching the two precious children. Jo tugged the satchel from her hand and set it on the bottom step of the staircase. "Let's have teatime while the children are occupied with their toys. I'm dying to hear your news."

"Where's Jamie?"

"He's playing with a neighbor boy. Mrs. Carpenter offered to watch him while I met your train." Jo lifted her brow. "So, tell me your news."

"Who said I had any?"

Jo smiled, her blues eyes twinkling. "I know you, remember? It's not your normal month to visit, and you wouldn't travel all this way unless you had a good reason."

"Can't I visit whenever I want?" Sarah tossed her a teasing look.

"Of course. You know you're welcome to move in with us, if you ever decide you want to." Jo wrapped her in a warm embrace. "I've missed you."

"Me, too." She swallowed the lump in her throat. Once she moved away, she would see Jo and her family much less.

Turning her stinging eyes away, lest Jo noticed, Sarah gazed around the pretty kitchen, gathering ideas for what she'd like for her future home. Jo's cabinets had been painted a fresh white and had round knobs. She had a small table in the kitchen but also a larger one in the adjacent dining room. For Sarah, a medium-sized kitchen with a table would be sufficient.

Jo set a pot of water on to boil then dropped onto a chair. "Before I check on the children, tell me why you're being so secretive."

"I'm not. I just didn't want to talk about things on the street."

"What things?" Jo sucked in a gasp and laid her hand on Sarah's arm. "Are you getting married?"

Sarah laughed. "I did receive a proposal, but I said no."

"You did? From who?"

"Luke."

Jo smacked the table with her palm. "I knew he was sweet on you."

Sarah looked away. "How come you never mentioned it?"

"I have! I told you several times that he was attracted to you, but you always laughed it off. Why in the world did you turn him down? He's a kind, honorable man. I know you've been attracted to him for years." She sat back and shook her head. "Luke must have been devastated."

"I hated hurting him, but you know how much I've longed for a home of my own. Luke is a good man, and I do care for him, but he lives in the bunkhouse."

"So? I'm sure he has money set back that he could use to get his own place. He's worked for Gabe for over ten years, and since he doesn't gamble, I'd suspect he has a goodly amount saved."

"He said as much, but I don't love him. At least I don't think I do."

Jo lifted her index finger. "Hold that thought for a moment. Let me check on the young'uns." She hurried from the room.

Sarah closed her eyes and blew out a breath. Telling Jo about Luke had been the easy part. Now she had to tell her she was moving.

Chapter 3

A knock sounded on the bedroom door. "Sarah, it's me."

"Come in." Sarah scooted over to allow Jo room to sit on the bed beside her and then continued running the brush through her hair.

Jo closed the door behind her. "Mind if I sit?"

"Of course not."

Jo plopped down onto the bed. "This reminds me of the days when we ran away from your father's place and first stayed at Lara's."

"Yes, it does." Sarah smiled at the memory. She'd been a frightened twelve-year-old. When Jo gave her the chance to leave the bordello with her, she'd grasped it and left right then. She'd never felt comfortable in her father's big house, especially since he made her stay away from the women who lived there and had locked her in her room when the men came visiting each evening. She'd been lonely and missing her mother when Jo gave her the opportunity she'd longed for.

"Why are you so quiet?"

Sarah shrugged and sent her friend a smile. "Just remembering those days."

"I'm sorry our talk earlier got interrupted by the children. And then Jamie was so excited to see you when he returned home. After that, Baron came home and I had to get supper on the table."

Sarah smiled. "I understand. Your life is a busy one. I can hardly believe you have three children."

"There are moments I long for the quiet of when I just had Jamie, but I wouldn't trade my life for anyone's."

"I'm glad you and Baron are happy. Who would have ever dreamed you'd end up marrying Mark's brother?" Sarah remembered the awful tales Jo had told her of how Baron's younger brother had deceived and beaten her, leaving Jo pregnant and alone. But God had restored the days the locust had destroyed and given her a godly husband who dearly loved her.

Jo laughed. "I'd have been the last to believe it, but I'm so glad I did. Baron's a good man."

Sarah thought about Luke. Had she made a terrible mistake in turning down his proposal? Would she look back one day and be sorry?

"You're thinking about Luke, aren't you?"

Sarah glanced up. "How did you know?"

Jo's eyes gleamed. "Because your mouth tilts up in a special smile when you're looking at him—the same one you had just now."

"I didn't realize anyone had noticed my feelings for him."

"So you do love him." Jo squeezed Sarah's arm. "I can tell you from experience that finding a good man who loves God *and* you is far more important than getting a house. There's something special between a man and woman who love one another deeply."

"I can't deny that I have an attraction to Luke, but I don't know if I love him enough to marry him."

"Well, it's certainly important to be sure."

Sarah nodded and laid her brush on the table beside the bed. She turned to face her dear friend. "That's really not the thing I needed to talk about."

"Oh?"

"No." She swallowed back her nervousness and squeezed her hands together. "I've decided to leave the ranch."

Jo's blue eyes widened. "Leave?" She reached for Sarah's hand. "Are you finally moving in with us?"

"No, it's not that." Excitement drove away her anxiety. "The government is opening more Indian lands, and I'm going to El Reno to register for the lottery."

"How exciting!" Jo clapped her hands then sobered. "But you can't go alone. It wouldn't be safe."

"Jack mentioned he had been thinking about going, too."

Jo leaned back against the bed's footboard. "Wow! I sure didn't expect that. What will you do if you don't get land?"

Sarah pursed her lips and lifted one shoulder. "Lara said I will always have a home with them, but I feel it's time for me to leave. I can't stay there forever."

"Come here. There's no reason for you to go clear on the other side of Oklahoma City."

"Thank you, but I have this craving to have my own place. I never have, you know."

Jo patted Sarah's hand. "Of course I understand. I felt the same way in the past. You could always purchase a home here in Perry. We could be neighbors."

"I would like that, but I feel pulled in a different direction."

"Have you prayed about this lottery thing?"

Sarah nodded. "Over and over and over. I can't help but believe this is what God is calling me to do. I know it doesn't make a lot of sense for a single woman to homestead on her own, but if God is calling me to do it, I have to trust that He'll help me and take care of me."

"You're so much more mature than I was at your age."

Sarah blinked. "I am?"

"Yes, and I'm proud of you. Is there any way that Baron and I can help?"

"There are many things that I'll need to purchase to set up my own place. I was hoping I could buy some supplies from y'all and maybe get a discount." She flashed Jo a toothy smile, hoping her friend would see she was half teasing but also half serious."

Jo squeezed Sarah's forearm. "That's the least we can do. Have you made a list?"

"A very long one."

"Good. Let me see it in the morning. Having set up a home from scratch—twice—I know pretty much everything you'll need, so I'll check your list and see what all you left off. We don't want you to get down there and end up not having something important."

"That's so generous of you."

"It's the least I can do for my little sister. We'll go to the store tomorrow and see if we have the things on your list in stock, and if not, I'll order them. That way if you do win land, they will be here, and I can get them ready and shipped quickly."

"That sounds perfect. Thank you."

"Anything for my little sister." Jo stood and gave Sarah a hug. "Make sure you have a gun. I know Luke taught you how to use one."

"He did, and I have to admit that I'm a fair shot."

"Good. I hope you never have to use a gun, but you need one just in case. Life in a brand-new town can be rough." Jo opened the door then turned back and waved. "See you in the morning. I'm excited for you."

Sarah reclined against the headboard. That had gone better than she expected. But then she knew Jo would be understanding and encouraging.

If only she didn't have doubts. Was she truly doing the right thing?

Jack offered Sarah his hand as she moved down the train steps to the El Reno depot platform and into the noisy crowd. He took her satchel, placing it in the same hand as he carried his own bag, and offered his free arm. "You'd better stay close to me," he hollered over the din.

"There sure are a lot of people here. I guess it's good you left Cody with Lara."

Jack nodded. "C'mon. Let's get away from this crowd."

He tugged her through the people waiting to board to the outer edge of the depot.

Sarah sucked in a gasp as she surveyed the busy town. Everywhere she looked, she saw people. "I never expected there would be so many folks here since registration doesn't start for two more days."

"Me neither." Jack pursued his lips. "Let's find our hotel and make sure they haven't given away our rooms. I telegraphed them last week to make a reservation, but I didn't realize so many folks would come early like this."

"What will we do if they don't have a room?"

Jack shrugged. "I don't know. Buy a tent, I reckon."

Sarah glanced at him to see if he was teasing, but his serious expression remained. She'd never camped out in a tent and would hate to do so among all these strangers.

Jack helped her down the steps. "If we should get separated, meet me at the Hotel El Reno. I'm sure there are plenty of folks who could point the way, but let's try hard to stay together."

Sarah smiled. "That sounds like a good plan."

As she allowed Jack to pull her through the crowds lining the front of the various stores and places of business, she wondered how she had thought she could have managed this on her own. There were some females among the horde of men but not many. And most of the men they passed turned her way, some with cheerful nods but others with lewd stares that made her want to hide behind Jack.

Someone bumped her, and she lost hold of Jack's arm and was knocked along with the people heading away from him. She stumbled but managed to grab hold of a post and held on. She thought she heard Jack calling her and looked back the way she'd come.

Suddenly Jack's head appeared above the others'. His frantic gaze searched one way and then the other. She raised one hand and waved, willing him to see her—and then he did. He held up his palm, indicating for her to stay where she was, so she took time to study the town. It wasn't much different than Guthrie. Mostly made up of one- and two-story wood, stone, or brick buildings. The wide streets allowed wagons to travel both directions easily.

"Well, howdy, ma'am. You're about the prettiest thing I've seen in ages."

Sarah spun around to find a gap-toothed old man two feet away. Standing at the very edge of the boardwalk, there was no place for her to go other than to step into the street. But a wagon pulled by two massive horses headed her way.

The man tipped his hat. "M'name's Elmer Doolittle, ma'am."

Sarah offered a smile, unsure what the man wanted. Was he just being friendly?

"Hey there, move along." Jack pushed his way past two tall men who frowned at him.

The old man's smile dipped. "You know this purty lady?"

Jack shot a worried look at her. "You all right?"

"I'm fine. This nice man was keeping me company."

"Then I'm in your debt, sir." Jack offered his hand. "I'm Jack Jensen, and this is Sarah Worley, my sister."

Mr. Doolittle smiled and shook it. "You oughtn't go off an leave a gal so purty all by herself."

"He didn't leave me. We got separated by accident."

"Easy enough to do with so many folks around." Elmer bounced his head, his pale blue eyes gleaming.

"You ready?" Jack asked her.

"Yes. Have a nice day, Mr. Doolittle."

He waved and shuffled off. Sarah watched him weave into the flow of people, hoping he didn't get knocked down. Then she turned her attention to Jack. "I'm sorry. One moment I had hold of you, and the next, I didn't."

"That's all right. I imagine once people get registered, most of them will leave town like we plan on doing and return the first day of the lottery."

Sarah latched onto Jack's arm again. "Why did you tell him I'm your sister?"

"Because in my mind you are. It doesn't matter that we have different parents." Jack's blue eyes held a smile.

"That's good, because I look up to you like I would a brother, if I had one."

"Just consider me yours." His ears turned red as he quickly looked away. "I mean, your brother."

Sarah bit back a smile. She knew what he meant. Jack was forty—almost double her age. While she loved him for the kind, caring man he was, she didn't love him in a romantic way and knew he felt the same. Jack had loved his wife dearly, and it had been such a sad time when Cora died this past winter. She'd prayed that Jack would one day find another woman to love—a woman who'd be a caring mother for Cody. She and Lara had mothered the quiet boy, but it wasn't the same as having a real ma.

Jack pulled her into an open door, and she blinked as her eyes adjusted to the dimmer lighting. It was quieter in here, although several people sat in the lobby chairs, chatting or reading the newspaper. On the back wall of the lobby was a registration counter, which Jack led her to. She studied the room as they waited their turn to check in. To her left, a pair of closed double doors with windows led to a large dining room. Through the glass, she saw two women setting tables in preparation for the noon meal. On the right side of the counter was a wide stairway leading up to the sleeping rooms. A burgundy carpet with a gold pattern covered the lobby floor, and a chandelier with dangling prisms decorated the walls with dancing lights. While it wasn't as fancy as some hotels she'd stayed in while on shopping trips with Jo and Lara, it looked to be a decent place to stay.

Jack moved forward. "Jack Jensen. I wired you a week ago requesting two rooms for three days."

The man frowned and flipped the page in the registration book. "Oh yes, I see you now, but I'm afraid we were only able to hold one room. But it does have two beds. We've been abnormally busy, as I'm sure you can see."

"What?" Jack rubbed the back of his neck and glanced at her. "I suppose that's better than nothing."

"Just sign here." The man fished a key off a board with a dozen hooks then handed one to Jack after he'd signed the book.

He took the key then backed away from the counter, blowing out a loud breath. "Let's go have a look."

They walked up the stairs to the second floor and down the hall to room 204. Jack opened the door then stepped back to allow her to enter first. Sarah swallowed the lump in her throat as she walked in and surveyed the room she'd be sleeping in for the next few days. As the clerk had said, there were two beds on either side of the small room. A wide dressing table with a mirror sat on the far wall between the headboards. Two windows on the western wall allowed in a good amount of light. In one corner, backing up to the hallway, was a dressing screen and a table with a bowl and pitcher of water. In the opposite corner sat a burgundy and gold wingback chair.

Jack placed her satchel on the bed to her left then walked to a window and lifted it. He cleared his throat and faced her. "You should be comfortable here."

"What about you?" She spun around, glancing at the two beds.

He shrugged. "I'll be fine. I can check the stores and see if one of them has an inexpensive tent."

"But you don't have any bedding."

"It won't be the first time I've slept on the ground."

She knew that his life hadn't been easy when he first left his sisters after their parents and then their grandmother had died. But he rarely talked about those days. She stared at the beds. Dare she voice her thought? It was quite improper, but she trusted Jack as much as she did Gabe or Luke. "That's silly, Jack. Why don't you stay here?"

His eyes widened. "That wouldn't be proper."

"I realize it's a bit unconventional, but I trust you with my life. I know you'll be a perfect gentleman."

He rubbed the back of his neck. "I suppose we could place that screen so it creates a divider. But I don't know. It still doesn't seem right."

"If you were my real brother, would you have a problem with it?"

He stared at his boots. "I don't guess I would. But although I look at you as my little sister, in truth you're not. I have to consider your reputation."

"Well, we don't have to decide right now."

"That's true. I probably should find out where we need to register."

"All right. I'll use the time to unpack and rest a bit. Fighting that crowd is tiring." Not to mention they'd risen early that morning in order to drive to Guthrie to catch the morning train.

"Keep the door locked while I'm gone."

She nodded and followed him to the door.

"I shouldn't be gone long. When I return, let's grab some lunch somewhere. I'll inquire as to what time the dining room opens and look for a café while I'm out."

"That sounds wonderful."

She locked the door then walked to the window and stared out. The people moving in all directions reminded her of the time she'd picnicked with Gabe, Lara, and the children, and their quilt had been overrun with busy ants.

Did she have a chance at getting land when competing against so many others?

Peace filled her worried heart. If it was God's will, she would win a lot.

And if not, then He would show her what to do.

Jack blew out a frustrated breath and dropped down onto the bench outside of the fifth general store he'd visited. After more than an hour of searching, he hadn't located one that had a tent available. Sold out. Every single one of them.

He'd also checked the other hotels in town but none had a vacancy. He didn't like sharing a room with Sarah—it didn't seem right—but he sure didn't care to spend the night on the ground without a tent, especially when there was lightning flashing on the horizon. Yeah, he'd done it before, but that was over half his lifetime ago. Back then he'd been a young buck, and it had been an adventure. Now, just the thought of it brought a twinge of pain to the small of his back.

Would it be wrong to share a room with Sarah when he knew he was an honest man?

"Well, there's a face I recognize."

Jack jerked his head up at the sound of Luke's voice. "I thought you'd decided not to come."

"Hardly. I left in the middle of the night and rode cross-country."

"Why didn't you take the train?" Jack slid over and Luke dropped down beside him.

"Wanted to save the money."

Lightning flashed, and a few seconds later, thunder rumbled in the distance.

"Looks like we're in for a storm. You got a room somewhere?"

Luke shook his head. "I figured I could get one once I got here. Didn't count on there bein' so many' people though." He yawned. "Where's Sarah?"

"In her room."

Luke cocked up one eyebrow. "How'd you manage to get rooms?"

"I wired ahead a week ago and made arrangements."

"Smart man." Luke flashed a grin and bumped Jack's shoulder. "How about you letting me share your room?"

"Can't. Because I only got one, and it's Sarah's."

"Oh." Luke leaned back and crossed his legs. "What are you gonna do?"

He wrestled with telling Luke about Sarah's suggestion to share the room, but he didn't see a way around it. "There are two beds in her room, and she offered the other one to me—"

Luke shot to his feet, bumping a man and nearly knocking him off the boardwalk. "Sorry," he grumbled. He turned his flashing blue eyes on Jack. "You can't share a room with Sarah."

"I didn't like the idea either, but she mentioned dividing the room with the dressing screen."

Luke turned down the heat of his fiery expression. "Still don't seem right, but I reckon she'd be safe with you."

"Thanks for the vote of confidence," Jack said with a thick dose of sarcasm. He couldn't begrudge Luke for wanting to protect Sarah. He knew the younger man had deep feelings for her. "As much as I don't like the idea of sharing her room, I also don't relish sleeping outside with a storm coming."

Luke plopped down beside him again. "Me neither. I brought a tent we can share, but if it hails, we'll be in a world of hurt."

Jack sat beside his friend for several minutes, watching the people pass by. A scraggly brown-and-white hound dog moseyed up to him and sniffed his boots. He nudged Jack's hand for a scratch and wagged his tail when Jack complied. Then the mutt sniffed Luke's pants and moved on. "Sure are a lot of folks here."

"Just like the land runs. Everyone is hopin' they'll get free property, but most will be disappointed." Luke scratched his belly. "I'm hungry. You wanna grab some grub?"

Jack nodded. "Sure. I need to find out where to register for the lottery first."

"I saw a poster somewhere that told where to get in line."

"Let's fetch Sarah and eat lunch. Then I want to find where the registration takes place so we can get there first thing in the morning." Jack stood and stretched.

"But we don't have to sign up for two more days."

"I know, but with this crowd, I'm sure the lines will be long. We'll probably have to be there all night."

Luke stood and yawned again. "Sure hope it doesn't rain tomorrow night."

Jack nudged him in the side. "Hey, you want to surprise Sarah? She doesn't know you're here."

Luke grinned. "That sounds like a grand idea."

Chapter 4

Sarah scowled and covered her ears. Why was someone hammering so early in the morning? She yawned and stretched then bolted upright in the bed. That wasn't hammering. Someone was knocking on her hotel room door.

"Sarah? It's Jack. You ready to get something to eat?"

"Um. . .yes. I need a few minutes though. Is the dining room downstairs open now?"

"I think so."

"Why don't you go on down and get a table?"

For a moment, Jack didn't respond, and she wondered if he'd heard her. "All right. See you downstairs."

She had planned to rest for a short while, not fall asleep. Sarah hurried to the chair on which she'd laid out her skirt and top. She pulled on her white blouse, glad she'd kept undergarments and shoes on, and then she slid her skirt over her head. She made quick work of pinning up her hair then grabbed her reticule and pulled open the door. Sarah's heart jolted and she emitted a squeal as she jumped back at the sight of a man leaning against her door frame. Luke? What was *he* doing here?

"Surprise, pretty lady!" His lips curled into his trademark grin, and he straightened.

Her heart pounded as if she'd run a race. The nerve of him to frighten her like that. Had he followed her here, hoping to change her mind about marrying him? If so, he was bound for disappointment. She crossed her arms over her chest. "What are you doing here?"

His grin dipped for a moment before he reinforced it. "That's not the greeting I expected."

She lifted her chin, refusing to be moved by his charm. "I sure didn't expect to find a man stuck to my doorjamb, either."

He yanked off his hat and curled the brim. "My apologies for scaring you. I didn't mean to do that. I was hopin' to surprise you."

"You certainly accomplished that, but you didn't answer my question." Had he followed her to El Reno? Did he think she was incapable of caring for herself, even with Jack here? If he thought she'd marry him because he chased after her, he would be sorely disappointed. It was time she was on her own. Gathering her composure, she stepped into the hall and locked her door.

"You know that I've wanted land for a long while. How could I pass up a chance at a free claim?"

She studied him to see if he had another agenda, but his clear blue eyes held only honesty. Maybe he hadn't followed her, but she still wished he hadn't come. She wanted a fresh start. Wanted to prove to herself and those who knew her that she was able to live on her own. Would Baron and Jo or Gabe and Lara show up next?

"Jack's waitin'. I reckon we should go downstairs." He offered his arm to her.

She wanted to ignore it, but there was no point in hurting his feelings. She looped her arm through his, hating the bolt of awareness that streaked through her. Why did she always feel that spark whenever they were close? When she'd held on to Jack's arm, she hadn't experienced it. Luke was a decade older than her but far closer to her age than Jack, so maybe that was the reason. Both men were handsome with striking blue eyes, although Jack's hair was brown where Luke's was blond.

As they descended the stairs to the lobby, a trio of young women looked their way. They were dressed in frilly, colorful day gowns. Were they looking at her? Sarah glanced at her dark blue skirt. Was it too far out of style? Her heart jolted. Or were they eyeballing her because she was a half-breed?

To her shame, she realized as she and Luke walked toward the dining room entrance that the women were gawking at *him*, not her. One smiled and ducked her head, cheeks turning ruby red, while the other two smiled and stared unabashedly. As they neared, a pretty blond fluttered her lashes at Luke. He tipped his hat at the trio then glanced at Sarah and smiled as if unaffected by their admiration. This wasn't the first time she'd been with Luke when women had ogled him. He was a tall, tanned, well-built cowboy, and a woman couldn't help staring at him. She certainly had a time or two.

She breathed in the fragrant aromas as they stepped into the dining room. The area held more than a dozen tables, all of which had people sitting at them. She searched for Jack and found him in the back corner of the room when he stood and waved. Luke guided her toward him, weaving between the tables.

As she neared the table for six, she noticed an older man and a woman who looked about her age sitting at the table with Jack. Both men rose as she and Luke stopped by the table.

Jack nodded at them. "The dining hall was full when I arrived, and Mr. Hawkins and his daughter graciously offered to share their table with us."

Sarah smiled at the pair, not missing the fact that the woman's gaze quickly passed over her to linger on Luke. "Thank you. It is kind of you to allow us to join you."

Jack held out a hand toward them. "This is Sarah Worley, my sister, and a friend of ours, Luke McNeil."

"Harold Hawkins, and this is my daughter, Nannette." The man's brown eyes gleamed with pride as he glanced at his daughter.

A shaft of jealously streaked through Sarah. Her father had been a scoundrel when he first took her from her dying mother, much to Sarah's objections. She had to give him credit for changing his life, but even so, they'd never been close. He'd sent her money and visited a few times over the years she lived with Gabe and Lara, but he'd always seemed uncomfortable there. As if it were the last place he wanted to be. The harsh way he had treated Jo was more than likely the reason. If not for her watching Gabe with his children and Jack with Cody, she wouldn't know what a loving father was like. She wasn't sure she'd ever marry, but if she did, she wanted a man who'd love their children and treat them as if they were special.

Luke shook Mr. Hawkins's hand then tipped his hat to the woman. "A pleasure to meet you both." He pulled out the chair next to Jack's for Sarah, and once she sat, he dropped down in the chair on her left.

Jack leaned forward, turning his head toward her and Luke.

"Mr. Hawkins is a newspaperman from Kansas City. He and his daughter have come to cover the lottery."

"Oh?" Sarah focused on Miss Hawkins. "Do you also work for the paper?"

Miss Hawkins covered her mouth and giggled. "Oh no. Father would never allow that, but I do transpose his notes." She leaned forward as if conveying a secret. "His handwriting is atrocious, and I'm the only one who can decipher it."

"Nannette," her father scolded, his cheeks red beneath his closely cropped beard.

"I do like to travel, too," the vivacious young woman continued, as if her father hadn't said a word. "So I usually jump at the chance to see new places." She cast a quick glance around the dining room. "Although I have to say, this is one of the more backward places we've been to."

Sarah tried to view the room through Nannette's eyes. She'd stayed in nicer hotels on the shopping trips she'd taken to bigger towns, but she failed to find fault with this one. The furniture was nice, and obviously the bed had been comfortable since she'd fallen asleep so quickly.

Luke cleared his throat. "It's admirable of you to help your father as you do."

Miss Hawkins's gaze latched onto Luke's, her eyes gleaming. "That's kind of you to say so, Mr. McNeil."

He shook his head. "Call me Luke. Everyone else does."

Sarah frowned. Luke never met a stranger, and he had no sense of propriety. Besides teaching Sarah to read and speak properly, Lara had taken plenty of time to teach Sarah what was proper and what wasn't. She knew manners and etiquette enough to know that you don't refer to someone you just met by his Christian name.

"And you must call me Nannette."

Her father cleared his throat as the waitress stopped at their table. "I do believe it's time to order."

They each relayed their requests, and then the waitress moved to another table.

"Do you plan to stay in town until the lottery?" Mr. Hawkins smoothed his mustache with a thick finger.

"No. We don't care to live in the hotel for several weeks. We're only staying long enough to get registered. Then we're returning to my brother-in-law's ranch, where we all live," Jack offered.

"I take it you're all staying in this hotel?" Mr. Hawkins asked.

Jack stirred some sugar into his coffee. "Not exactly. I had requested two rooms, but when we arrived, they'd only had one for us, so I gave it to Sarah."

She stared at her lap, greatly relieved he'd left out the part about possibly sharing the room.

"Oh, that's a shame." Miss Hawkins shifted her gaze from Jack to Luke again.

Sarah squirmed in her seat, uncomfortable with the woman's open admiration of her close friend.

Miss Hawkins batted her lashes as if she had dust in them. "So, where will you stay since the hotel is full?"

Luke shrugged and leaned back in his chair. "It won't be the first time we've slept under the stars."

After picking up her napkin, Miss Hawkins gave it a shake then placed it in her lap. "But if I'm not mistaken, we may get rain today."

Jack grinned. "The rain's good for washing off the dust."

Miss Hawkins frowned, but then her eyes lit up as if she'd thought of something. "Please excuse me while I ask Father a question." She leaned over and whispered something in his ear.

He lifted one eyebrow and studied his daughter for a moment. "If you're sure that's what you want to do, you have my permission."

A brilliant smile enveloped the pretty woman's face. "Thank you. I have the perfect solution." She turned to Sarah, sending a chill skittering up her spine. "You can stay with me, and Mr. Jensen and Luke can share the room you vacate."

An hour later, Sarah returned to her room with Jack and Luke following. She'd much rather have a room to herself than share with prissy Nannette. The woman's idea had merit though, especially with the storm clouds on the horizon and thunder in the distance, but she wouldn't admit it out loud. And she certainly couldn't begrudge her friends a bed for the night.

"Are you sure you don't mind sharing a room with Miss Hawkins?" Jack gazed at Sarah with apprehension filling his eyes.

Sarah smoothed out the blanket she'd lain on while resting and fluffed the pillow. Thankfully, she hadn't hung her nightgown on one of the pegs on the wall. "Of course. It's only for a few nights."

Luke leaned against the doorjamb. "We appreciate it. I don't mind sleepin' outdoors, but it's uncomfortable in the rain." He straightened. "I'll walk Sarah to Nannette's room then head back to the livery to get my gear."

Jack nodded. "I'll go with you. Still need to find out where the registration booths are."

Sarah packed her brush in her satchel and glanced around the room, reluctant to join Nannette. The woman had been kind, but Sarah hadn't liked the way she'd flirted with Luke—not that it was any of her business. But still. . . "That's all of my belongings."

Luke crossed the small room in three long-legged steps and took her bag. "You ready then?"

"Why don't we drop off my bag, and then I can accompany you and Jack to look for the booths."

"If you're sure you want to fight that crowd again."

She wasn't, but right now the crowd sounded better than spending the afternoon in Miss Hawkins's presence. "I'll be fine."

A few minutes later, they knocked on Miss Hawkins's room on the third floor. With the door at the end of the hall open and two large windows at half-mast near the stairway, a warm breeze attempted to cool the long hallway. But with the moisture in the air from the approaching storm, the breeze failed to stop the sweat trickling down Sarah's temple and spine.

Jack knocked on the door of room 303 and stepped back. Quick footsteps came their way, followed by the door opening.

Nannette beamed a smile as her gaze skittered past Jack and Sarah, landing on Luke. "Why, I didn't expect all three of you." She stepped aside. "Please, come in."

Sarah shot a peek at the men beside her. It had been stretching propriety for her to be in the hotel room with two men she knew and trusted with her life, but it was something altogether different for Miss Hawkins to invite them into hers.

Luke cast a quick glance at Jack then shook his head. "Thank you, but we have things we need to do. We're just dropping off Sarah's bag."

Nannette's disappointment was obvious. "Surely you could stay for a few minutes."

Jack cleared his throat. "I don't believe that would be proper, and we do need to be going."

"Very well." Nannette stared at Sarah, her gaze less than welcoming.

Sarah smiled and stepped into the room. This one was plush compared to the one downstairs. The dark cherry wood furniture gleamed and a wall-to-wall carpet covered the floor. The large bed sat to her left, with a sofa and two chairs on the right in front of a fireplace. Her gaze shifted back to the bed. Would she have to share that with Miss Hawkins?

She hadn't minded sharing a bed with Jo when they first arrived at the Coulter ranch, but she'd been only twelve then, and though she'd never admitted it, she'd been a bit afraid in the strange house with no one she knew except for Jo.

Sarah walked over to the sofa and placed her satchel on a small table that sat next to it. She'd sleep on the sofa before sharing with Miss Hawkins. Forcing a smile, she turned. "It was kind of you to offer your room to me so that Jack and Luke won't have to sleep outside tonight."

Nannette tittered and cooled her face with a decorative fan that looked as if it had come from somewhere overseas. "Nonsense. I couldn't very well allow your friends to get soaked tonight. There's plenty of room for two in this suite." She snapped her fan shut. "Oh! I know. I'll go with you on your errands. I'm so bored in this tiny town. It will give me something to do."

Sarah's heart sunk as Nannette rushed to the mirror, patted her hair, and pinched her cheeks. She should have expected this with the way Miss Hawkins was enchanted with Luke—and he hadn't even turned on the charm. He'd been much more restrained today than normal.

Nannette hurried out the door and latched onto Luke's arm. His gaze locked with Sarah's, and he rolled his eyes. Biting back a grin, she fled the room and closed the door, falling into step beside Jack. She blew out a sigh, eliciting a chuckle from him. Sarah frowned at him for noticing she was flustered, but he kept smiling. How could he find Miss Hawkins's blatant flirtation with Luke amusing?

A few blocks away from the hotel, they separated. Sarah and Jack turned right, while Luke and Nannette continued straight. Sarah peered over her shoulder at Luke and his leech until they disappeared from view into the crowd.

Jack chuckled again.

Sarah shot him a glare. "What are you laughing at?"

"Why does it bother you that Nannette is flirting with Luke?"

"Who said it does?"

Jack shook his head and appeared to be holding back another grin.

"What?"

"You turned Luke down flat when he asked you to marry him, but it annoys you when a pretty woman shows interest in him. That's mighty confusing behavior."

Sarah sucked in a gasp. "He told you that he proposed?"

"Yeah."

How many other people knew she'd refused Luke's offer of

marriage? Probably everyone at the ranch. "It's not that I mind a woman looking Luke's way, but it disgusts me how brazen Miss Hawkins is in her attempts to attract his attention. Has the woman no shame?"

"I think she's bored and sees Luke as a fun way to pass the time."

"I hope she doesn't hurt him." She sidled closer to Jack to skirt around a group of men standing in front of a barbershop. Several of the more rugged ones looked her way. The last man they passed had the audacity to wink at her.

"Luke's tougher than you give him credit for. And he won't succumb to Miss Hawkins's wiles."

"How can you be sure? She's a pretty woman, and it's obvious that she's smitten with Luke."

They sped up to cross a street in front of a slow-moving wagon pulled by a team of mules. At an alley, Jack tugged her to a stop. Sarah gazed up at him.

He stared at her for a moment with assessing eyes. Jack was a good man, and she'd never been afraid to be alone with him, so why did his stare make her want to squirm and look away?

"Sarah, you sound like a jealous woman. Are you certain you're not in love with Luke?"

She opened her mouth to reply but stumbled over her response. "I. . . No. . . How can a person truly know if they are in love?"

His jaw tightened, and he lifted his gaze, staring toward the street. "I almost missed out on my life with Cora because I was too shortsighted to see that I loved her."

"I'm not denying that I'm fond of Luke, but I also care for you and Gabe and Lara, Baron and Jo, and all of the children. But I don't want to spend the rest of my life *living* with all of you. I want something I've never had before—a home of my own. Luke can't give me that."

"So, if Luke had his own home, would you have said yes?"

Sarah's cheeks warmed. He made what she felt for Luke sound cheap. "I don't know. Perhaps. But it wouldn't only be because of the house. And besides, he doesn't have one, so it's irrelevant."

"It sounds like a house is more important to you than Luke, so you were probably wise in turning him down. He's a good man and deserves to be with a woman who loves him more than anything."

"I didn't make my decision lightly, Jack. You know my background—what my father did. I've seen the worst in men."

"Yes, but that should have no bearing on you now. You've met a number of good men who are trustworthy, and you have to know that Luke isn't the same kind of man as those who frequented your father's brothel."

"Of course I know that. Why are we even having this conversation now?"

He rubbed the back of his neck. "Luke's one of my closest friends, and I want what's best for him—and for you, too. I know you pretty well, Sarah, and I think maybe you care for him much more than you realize."

"Well, if that's true, then God will have to show me. I've prayed and prayed, and I feel that trying for a piece of land is God's will for me now."

Jack nodded. "All right. I can't argue with that." He held out his elbow. "Shall we finish our task and find the registration booths?"

Sarah nodded and looped her hand around his arm. She

respected Jack and knew from the stories he'd told about his early days before marrying Cora that what he'd said about nearly missing out on being a husband and father was true.

As they stepped back onto the busy walkway, she realized she was shaking. Had she truly heard God correctly?

Or should she have said yes to Luke?

Chapter 5

July 10, the first day of the lottery registration

Sarah stood in the women's line to register, so excited she found it hard to stand still. Luke stood beside her, waiting patiently. "Really, Luke. You don't have to stand here and wait on me. I'm sure I'll be safe." She gazed at the line of about thirty women who were farther back than she. "Most of these women are alone, and besides, I would hate to discover that I caused you to miss your opportunity to register."

Luke shook his head. "Not much chance of that happening with Jack saving me a spot. Did you see those long lines outside the Kerfoot Hotel? I'll be surprised if we get to register before suppertime."

"I read that the registration booths close at four."

He shrugged one shoulder. "If I miss out on signing up today, there's always tomorrow."

"Jack and I plan to leave tomorrow—unless he doesn't make it through the line today." She could hardly wait to escape the room she shared with chatty Miss Hawkins. She wasn't used to women babbling and preening constantly. Lara and Jo talked, but if there was nothing important to say, they had no problem working alongside one another in silence. Though, more often than not, the children normally kept them entertained.

Sarah glanced down the line of two dozen women in front of her. Most looked older than she and had wiggly children playing nearby. From reading the rules of the lottery in the newspaper, she knew that for a woman to register, she had to be head of her home, so Sarah assumed most of them were widows that had never remarried.

She turned back to Luke. "With so many people still arriving on the trains, the lines are likely to be longer tomorrow. It kind of makes me wonder if we should have traveled to Lawton. Surely there can't be as many people there as there are here." She puffed out a sigh. "It's too bad you can't register at this booth. I'm grateful to not have to stand out in the hot sun all day, but it seems a shame to dedicate a whole booth just to women when the men's lines are so long."

Luke removed his hat, revealing his thick blond hair, forked his fingers through it, and then returned his hat to his head. "I'm glad someone had the foresight to think up the idea. Women shouldn't oughta have to stand in the sun all day listenin' to crude men or watchin' their games of chance."

Sarah smiled and nudged Luke in the side with her elbow. "That's mighty noble thinking."

Luke straightened, flashing his trademark grin. His sparkling sky-blue eyes were the prettiest she'd ever seen on a man. "Haven't you noticed? I'm a noble kind of guy. That's why I'm standing here with you when I could be enjoyin' Jack's company."

Chuckling, Sarah shook her head. "You and I both know Jack isn't a big talker, except when he's preaching—or debating something." Sobering, she turned away from Luke and watched a group of children playing tag. Jack had been plenty talkative yesterday when he shared his concern over her feelings for Luke. His thought-provoking comments—as well as Nannette's twenty or thirty questions about Luke—had kept her awake until well past the midnight hour. She covered her mouth to hide a yawn.

"Hey, look. They've opened the door. With so few ladies in front of you, it shouldn't take long for you to get registered. Did you remember to bring your papers?"

"Yes, I have them in my reticule." Excitement poured through her. If she won a claim, her dream would come true. Between now and July 29th, the first day of the lottery, she needed to find out how much building a house would cost and to see if she could have some men lined up to start, should God bless her with land. She blew out a breath. There was so much she'd have to do in a short time. So many supplies to purchase and then have shipped. And where would she stay while the house was being raised?

A little over an hour later, they stepped forward as another woman entered the small building, leaving only three women between her and the registration booth. Sarah bounced on her toes, grinning at Luke. His solemn expression cooled her excitement as effectively as if he'd thrown a bucket of frigid water on her. "What's wrong?"

He stared off in the distance. "I'm just thinkin' of the day I'll have to ride off and leave you here alone." A muscle ticked in his cheek, as he assessed her with cool blue eyes. "Are you sure this is what you want to do? Have you considered what living alone with no one you trust nearby will be like?"

Sarah crossed her arms. "Of course I have. And yes, this is what I want to do."

"A home doesn't mean much when you don't have anyone to share it with."

Maybe not to him, but then he had been on his own for half his life. He chose to work for Gabe and live in the bunkhouse. Besides, a house was a woman's place—her nest. As much as she loved living with the Coulters, it was no longer enough. She stepped forward again as another woman left the booth, all smiles.

Sarah's insides jiggled, and her limbs felt weak as she stepped up to the booth. And then the last woman in front of her moved away, revealing a thin man with wire-framed glasses and a skinny white mustache.

He eyed her up and down. "You got yer papers? You don't look twenty-one to me."

"I can assure you I am. I have an affidavit signed by my father and a judge from Oklahoma City, certifying my birthdate." She unfolded the valuable document and handed it to him. He squinted as he examined it.

"As you can see, I recently had my twenty-first birthday." She cast an anxious glance at Luke then straightened, standing a bit taller.

The man took an interminable amount of time scanning the paper, even looking at the back, which was blank. Finally, he cleared his throat and slid a card toward her. "You're not married to this fellow, are you?"

Sarah's cheeks felt instantly hot. "No, sir. He's my good friend and escorted me here."

The man nodded. "All right then. Everything looks in order. Just fill this out."

Smiling, she penned her name, the place she currently lived, her weight, height, and age. Then she passed it back.

The man read over her information then nodded. "You're all set, Miss Worley. Good luck to you."

"Thank you." Excited to finally be registered, Sarah clapped her hands and smiled at Luke.

He returned her smile, never able to stay upset for long. "So, you want to go get a slice of pie to celebrate?"

"At ten thirty in the morning?"

He shrugged. "Anytime's a good time for pie."

The man behind the counter cackled. "I agree, sonny. If I wasn't stuck here, I'd join you. Rhubarb's my favorite."

The lady next in line cleared her throat.

Sarah took the hint and tugged Luke around the corner. "Let's check on Jack and see how far he's moved up the line first."

Luke nodded, and they headed for the Kerfoot Hotel, one of the six places that men could sign up for the lottery. Sarah couldn't quit smiling. She'd finally taken the first big step in getting a home. Now if only God would answer her prayer to win a homestead.

Monday, July 29
First day of the lottery

Eager for the drawing of names to begin, Sarah could hardly stand still. But moving around was nearly impossible with the large crush of thousands of people surrounding the drawing tent on the grounds of the Irving School. The large group had been standing there all morning, and not a single name had yet been drawn. She shifted her feet, trying to get some relief from their aching. What was the delay? Yes, the lottery was a massive undertaking, but things had seemed so organized.

She read in the newspaper that over 165,000 people had registered in both El Reno and Lawton. Her excitement dimmed whenever she thought of those numbers. With so many people, did she have any chance at all of getting land?

She stood on her tiptoes, peeking between hats worn by both the men and the few women present, hoping to get a view of the men in the open-sided tent. Jack, Luke, and she had walked around the thirty-two-square-foot tent on a raised platform.

Earlier that morning, envelopes containing the names of registered applicants had been placed in two rotating bins that were ten feet long and two and one-half feet wide and tall. All of the names of the people who registered in El Reno were in one bin, and the other rotating bin held the Lawton registrants. With the containers being so large to permit a thorough mixing of the envelopes, fairness was ensured. There would be no mad land rush with people getting hurt or killed this time.

Jack slipped in beside her after squeezing through the crowd to get lunch for them, but Sarah had little appetite. He rummaged through the small basket he held and passed sandwiches to her and Luke.

Both men gobbled theirs down, but Sarah barely ate a fourth of hers. She rarely had much hunger after being out in the summer heat, and today her stomach churned from anxiousness and concern over all that was at stake.

Luke nudged her. "You'd better eat or you'll never make it out here all day."

She glanced at the thick ham and cheese sandwich she held. Sweat ran in rivulets down various parts of her body. If the summer heat and cloudless sky weren't bad enough, the crush of warm, often smelly bodies was more than enough to steal her appetite. Still, she forced another bite into her mouth. The last thing she wanted was to grow faint and have to leave.

She managed to get down half the sandwich before she wrapped it up in the paper it had come in and returned it to the basket. Jack offered her a canteen, and she gulped down the cool water. Wetting her handkerchief, she wiped her face and the back of her neck, enjoying the brief relief it brought.

"There are some apples, in case we get hungry later," Jack said.

A man on the stage let out an ear-piercing whistle, and all eyes turned toward him. "All right, folks, we're ready to get this shindig started," said Ben Heyler, the man chosen to draw the first name.

" 'Bout time," a man behind her yelled. "It's already one thirty. You're burnin' daylight."

Mr. Heyler ignored the comment as he moved to the El Reno bin, which another man had been turning for the past ten minutes, mixing up the envelopes. He opened one of the small doors and placed his hand inside, withdrawing an envelope. He handed it to Colonel Dyer, the commissioner, who passed it to Chief Clerk Macy. He stamped the envelope and wrote number one on it, making it official, and then handed it back to Colonel Dyer. An ear-numbing cheer rose up from the crowd.

He walked to the front of the platform and raised his hand

for order, and an instant hush settled over the crowd. "Stephen A. Holcomb, Pauls Valley, Indian Territory, wins the first claim."

A cheer unlike anything Sarah had ever heard rang out all around her. She covered her ears. Luke grinned and joined in, whooping. The winner was pushed to the front so everyone could see him, and the crowd yelled for several minutes. As delighted as they were acting, you'd think everyone's name had been drawn. Twenty-four more names were pulled from the El Reno bin, and then the men moved to the Lawton one. The second name drawn from it was Mattie Beal—the first woman whose name had been called.

Sarah looked at Jack and then Luke. "I'm so glad a woman finally won."

Luke winked at her. "You've got as good a chance as anyone." His smile dipped as if that fact bothered him.

She didn't like knowing he was unhappy with her decision to enter the lottery. It hurt to think he was displeased. But would he still feel that way if they both were fortunate to win?

Another name was drawn, and murmurs filtered through the crowd.

"Hey, that name was already drawn," someone yelled.

The men on stage congregated together. The man in charge of the winners looked through the envelopes and pulled one out. After the men conferred for several more minutes, Colonel Dyer moved to the front again.

He raised his hands for quiet. "It appears we have a duplicate entry. Kermit Eldridge's name was the seventeenth name drawn from the El Reno wheel. We've compared all the info on the registration cards, and it appears he entered more than once, thus he is disqualified and his winning lot is forfeited. The next name drawn will replace him. Anyone else found with duplicate entries will also be disqualified."

"That sure was a foolish thing to do." Jack removed his hat and fanned his face. He shook his head. "Imagine winning land only to have to forfeit it because you cheated."

Sarah tugged a fan from her reticule, snapped it open, and waved it in front of her face. Oh, for the shade of a cloud or two. "It's good that the officials are keeping things fair and honest."

Luke gazed at her, concern on his handsome face. "If you want to go back to your room to rest, we'll let you know if they call your name."

"Thank you, but I'm all right for now. It would be nice to walk around, but I don't want to lose my spot."

Luke flashed a saucy grin. "If you need to rest, you could lay your head on my shoulder and take a nap."

Jack chuckled.

Sarah gasped, glancing around to see if anyone had overheard him. "Luke McNeil, wipe that grin off your face."

The afternoon hours dragged by at the speed of a turtle. More and more names were drawn, and with each one, Sarah saw her chance at getting land fade. There were only thirteen thousand homesteads—enough for only a fraction of the people who registered.

At six that evening, after one thousand names had been drawn, five hundred from each district, the drawings halted, and the sides of the tent were lowered. Disappointed people, many exhausted from not eating or drinking anything, dropped to the ground all around Sarah. She looked at them with concern then blew out a sigh.

"Well, that's that." Jack rolled his shoulders and rubbed his neck. "Don't be too disappointed. I read that tomorrow they'll be drawing twenty-five hundred names. I reckon we oughta get some supper."

"I want to wash and get off my feet." Sarah limped along with Luke holding her arm as if to support her. She was too tired and disappointed to resist.

It took them fifteen minutes to weave through the thousands on the streets to their hotel, which was only a few blocks from the school. Finally, they stepped into the lobby.

"Would you like to go on upstairs?" Luke offered. "I can bring you a supper tray."

His thoughtfulness for her comfort, even after he'd stood alongside her all day, touched a place deep within her.

Jack swatted his hand toward the dining hall. "I'll grab us a table before the place is packed out."

"Good idea. Be there in a minute." Luke turned his attention back to Sarah. He lifted his hand and ran the backs of his fingers across her cheek. "Your face looks sunburned."

She raised her hand to her cheek, feeling the warmth emanating from it. Even with her darker complexion due to the Indian blood, she'd gotten too much sun. Although she'd tried to keep her head down and out of the afternoon sun, she obviously failed. "After I wash the dust off, I'll put some facial cream on it."

He smiled, his eyes conveying his affections. "Good idea, although I think the added color is becoming. Make sure to drink lots of water tonight." He gestured toward the stairs. "C'mon, I'll walk you to your room."

"That's not necessary."

"I want to make sure you don't have any problems. This is a nice hotel, but there are a number of shady people in town."

Knowing any argument she offered would be rejected, she started up the stairs. Her feet ached more now than she could remember. Finally, they reached her room on the third floor.

Luke leaned against the wall next to her door, as if he too were exhausted. "So, what would you like to eat?"

Sarah shrugged. "I don't even feel hungry—just tired. You know what I like. Why don't you surprise me?"

His lips twisted in an ornery grin. "I like surprises."

Before she could react, he leaned down and placed his lips on hers, stealing her first kiss. Warm sensations she'd never experienced surged through her, but then anger took over. She pushed away. "What do you think you're doing?"

"Surprising you." He winked then strutted away, whistling as he headed for the stairs.

"Why, the nerve of that man." All manner of emotions raced through her, most disturbing was delight at having her first kiss. But then she thought how it had been stolen, and her temper soared.

Sarah turned to go into the room and gasped.

Nannette stood at the open door, her face white.

Chapter 6

On the second day of the lottery, Sarah, Luke, and Nannette walked down the street toward the Irving School. Nannette had risen early to join them for breakfast and babbled on about the excitement of the first day of drawings. When Luke first met Sarah at her room to escort her to breakfast, he'd been surprised to find Nannette up so early and ready to leave. He'd hoped to enjoy a quiet breakfast with Sarah—longed to see if he could convince her that she needed him in her life. But Nannette had quickly lassoed his plans, hog-tying them into a boring conversation. She explained her long absence from the room she and Sarah shared the night before was because she'd been transcribing her father's notes so that he could send in his report of the day's activities.

Was that true? As he'd turned to leave Sarah last night, he'd caught a glimpse of Nannette's shocked expression at witnessing him kissing Sarah. He had no desire to hurt Nannette, but neither was he interested in a relationship with her, and it was important that she knew that Sarah had already stolen his heart. He hadn't flirted with Nannette or offered any encouragement of a relationship with her, but evidently she wasn't one to give up easily. In fact, she seemed even more determined to win his affections.

He guided the women to a cleaner path on the street, avoiding a pile of manure. Breakfast certainly hadn't gone as he'd planned, but dining with two beautiful women had made him the envy of some in the room. Nannette's pretty features turned many men's heads, but he only had eyes for a quiet, dark-haired beauty. He loved the way Sarah's black eyes sparked when she teased him or came up with a sudden idea. Her dark brown hair was lighter than the black hair most full-blooded Indians had, and not a single freckle marred her perfect skin. He slapped his hand against the stair railing. What a chump he was—being sweet on a woman who'd rejected him.

He tried to think of something—anything—other than his feelings for Sarah. It wasn't easy when she walked beside him. At least the weather was cooler this morning, although it wouldn't last long under the warm Oklahoma sun. Last night there'd been a brief downpour, but it would only make the day more humid.

He looked over the crowd already gathered around the lottery tent. "Jack was smart to head up to the site early."

Sarah nodded. "I suppose if one was at the front of the crowd, the heat later in the day might not be as sweltering as it was in the midst of so many people."

Luke noticed Jack waving his arm. "There he is, over on the left in front of that doctor's office."

"Why is he so far from the tent? I was hoping we'd be up close today." Disappointment laced Sarah's voice.

"You won't be able to see a thing from there." Nannette flounced her head, lips curled.

"Hold your horses, ladies. Jack must have a good reason for choosing that spot."

They climbed the steps to the boardwalk and squeezed through the crowd to get to Jack. His broad smile alerted Luke that he'd been successful in his mission.

"Morning, ladies." Jack tipped his hat then bowed, holding his hand out toward a vacant spot on the bench.

Sarah gasped. "What a wonderful idea. And the roof overhead will block the afternoon sun. I'm sorry I questioned your choice."

Nannette scowled at a man as she squeezed past him. "I'd still rather be up closer. You can probably hear from this spot, but I doubt you'll see much."

"There ain't all that much to see. Just men pulling envelopes from the bins." Luke grinned. "Have a seat, ladies, before someone else snags such a prime spot."

Sarah smiled at him, gathering her skirts and claiming the place at the end of the bench. Nannette was left to squeeze in between Sarah and a well-dressed man, who looked pleased with the situation.

"This is nice. Thank you, Jack, for getting out so early and having the foresight to find a perfect observation spot like this. We can even see over the heads of the crowd to the men in the tent." Sarah gazed at the clear view of the lottery tent. "I can see so much better than yesterday."

"If we moved to the front, that wouldn't be an issue." Nannette scooted closer to Sarah, eyeing the grinning man beside her.

"I doubt those men standing closest to the tent would be too happy if we butted in front of them."

Nannette pulled her fan from her handbag and snapped it

open, giving Sarah a snide look. "Obviously, you don't know how to handle a man. All you have to do is sweet-talk them and they quickly come around to your way of thinking."

Luke glanced at Jack and rolled his eyes. His friend grinned. To Luke's way of thinking, he was glad Sarah wasn't the flirty type. Nannette might make cow eyes at him and hang on his arm, but her flirtations didn't affect him. Another woman had already staked a claim on his heart—she just didn't know how much yet. Somehow he had to find a way to show her the depths of his love.

He wished he could talk to Jack about it, but broaching the subject was difficult and not something easy for a man to talk about.

A cheer rang out from the crowd, drawing his attention to the tent. Several men were rolling up the sides. A clock somewhere rang out nine chimes. Apparently the lottery would start on time today.

Luke leaned against the wall of the doctor's office, settling in for another long, boring day. He'd much rather be currying a horse, riding fence, or even branding instead of standing all day burning daylight. But this was his last chance to get free land and to offer Sarah the home she longed for. If he had a nice house, would she consider marrying him?

Maybe.

Maybe not.

He blew out a long breath, drew out his knife, and started cleaning his fingernails. It was better than doing nothing.

Colonel Dyer read out the name of the first winner, and cheers resounded as a gray-haired man squeezed through the horde and made his way onstage. He took a bow, raising more cheers.

"Cleaning fingernails in public is not exactly gentlemanly behavior." Jack chuckled.

"Can't help if I'm bored."

"You don't have to stand here all day. Go on. I'll let you know if you win."

He shook his head. "Naw. I reckon I'll wait. I want to be here in case Sarah wins."

Jack leaned in closer. "I imagine you're hoping she doesn't."

Luke gazed at him for a long while then glanced at Sarah, glad to see her in conversation with Nannette. "I don't exactly know how I feel. She wants a place of her own. I want to see her dreams come true, but. . ."

"You want to be a part of those dreams."

His jaw tightened as he nodded. But he was afraid that he wasn't part of Sarah's dreams. He cast another quick glance at Sarah, glad she was focused on Nannette's animated story. "What if she doesn't feel the same?"

Jack rolled his head around, popping his neck. "You need to pray. Make sure that it's God's will for her and you to be together, and if it is, trust Him to make that happen."

Luke listened to another man's name being called out. Jack almost always turned a topic to God. There was a time Luke hadn't given God much thought, but having been around Gabe, Jack, and Lara's grandpa, three God-fearing men, for so long, his ideas on faith and God had changed. He wasn't the strongest believer, but he did believe. He leaned a foot against the wall behind him and pocketed his knife. Now was as good a time as any to pray.

He gazed up at the sky. A few small clouds floated by like fluffy dandelion puffs. *Lord, I know I haven't talked to You much, but I aim to do better. Jack's sermons have settled in and made me realize I need You in my life. I'd also like to have Sarah—the woman I love—by my side, but I need You to help her see that she needs me— that is, if it's all right with You.*

"Well, well," Colonel Dyer said, "the next winner is a lady— Miss Sarah Worley of Guthrie."

Sarah squealed. She jumped up and grabbed Luke's arm. "I won! I won!"

She rushed down the steps. Jack cast him an odd look then followed her.

"How about that?" Nannette watched Sarah and Jack make their way to the tent.

Luke couldn't move. Couldn't suck in a breath. He felt as if a horse sat on his chest. If Sarah had land and a home, what need did she have for him?

⌒

Pure joy bubbled through Sarah in a way she'd never before encountered. Her dream was finally coming true. She thanked God all the way to the stage. She couldn't stop smiling and glanced over her shoulder to share her joy with Luke, but Jack was the one following her. Luke was nowhere to be seen. A smidgeon of her delight dimmed, but nothing could ruin this day. She tried to see what had happened to him, but the crowd blocked her view of the doctor's porch.

At the stage, Jack helped her up the steps, and then Colonel Dyer took her hand, assisting her onto the platform. "Congratulations, Miss Worley. You're one of a handful of women to have won a homestead."

"Thank you, sir. I'm so excited and honored." She almost said she couldn't believe her name had been called, but God had led her here, so why should she be surprised?

"If you'll go over to the table there, Chief Clerk Macy will inform you which day you need to return to the land office to select your lot."

"Thank you." Sarah smiled at Jack. They crossed to the table where Chief Clerk Macy sat.

"Congratulations, Miss Worley. The assignments of land will begin on August 6th, but only one hundred twenty-five homesteads will be assigned each day. Everyone whose name was drawn before yours will get to choose before you will. The land office will be closed on Sunday, the tenth, so you'll need to be here on Monday, August 11th to pick your homestead off the map that shows which ones are still available. Since you're number 512, you'll be twelfth in line. If you don't show up before the office closes that day, you will forfeit your claim. There are no exceptions to that rule. Do you understand?"

"Yes, sir. I'll be here."

"Good." He handed her a paper stating her name and winning number 512 then nodded. "Congratulations, Miss Worley. Have a nice day."

"I already have." Sarah beamed at him as she took the paper. Cheers rang out for another winner. The plan was to draw many more winners today, so the officials were keeping a quick pace. As Jack escorted her down the stairs, several men congratulated her.

Jack leaned down. "Now that you're a landowner, you'll probably get gobs of marriage proposals."

She swatted his arm, receiving a chuckle for her efforts.

She searched for Luke and found him. He stood in the same spot he'd been in earlier, watching her approach, but he didn't look very happy. Was he jealous she'd won a homestead and he hadn't? Or did he think she shouldn't be living on her own? It was true that she never had. Of course, there would be adjustments, but for the first time in her life, she was the one who would make the decision where she would live. And that felt grand!

She climbed the few steps to the boardwalk platform, and Luke was there, offering his hand. She accepted it then stopped in front of him. Her heartbeat galloped as she slowly lifted her gaze to his—and there was the smile she longed to see.

"Sorry. I think I was shocked into a stupor when your name was called. I mean, the odds of it were so slim."

So, he never thought she had a chance?

"Congratulations." Luke smiled, and then his gaze darted toward the crowd surrounding her and he stepped back.

Several men squeezed in to congratulate her then moved back to where they'd been standing.

"Oh, this is so exciting!" Nannette rushed forward and took hold of Sarah's hand. "Do you know which town site you want to live near?"

"I'm hoping for a homestead in the Anadarko vicinity, since it's the closest to Guthrie."

Jack stopped at the top of the stairs. "Those towns are nearly a hundred miles from one another."

Sarah frowned. That sounded so far from her loved ones, but she was a pioneer, forging a home in a new land, and like other pioneers, she had to make sacrifices to get what she wanted. "But the train goes most of the way. I'm just not sure if it reaches those new towns yet."

"Always the optimist." Luke winked over Nannette's head.

"It's better than being a pessimist." Sarah shot him a teasing grin.

"So, now that you have your land, shall we go back to the hotel?" Nannette waved her frilly fan in front of her face, her toe tapping on the boardwalk.

Sarah glanced at Luke and Jack. She might have won her land, but they hadn't. She should stay to support them. "I think I'll hang around here for a while. I'm hoping Jack and Luke both get land, too." She wasn't opposed to having friends close by as long as she got her home.

Nannette snapped her fan shut. "Well, I for one am ready for tea, and I simply must get out of this sun. I don't dare go home with freckles. Mother would have a conniption fit." She batted her lashes at Luke. "Would you care to escort me?"

Sarah recognized the tic in Luke's cheek—the one that appeared whenever something bothered him, but he was too much of a gentleman to refuse. He smiled and offered his arm. "Of course. Shall we?"

Nannette made a great show of blushing and taking his arm, then shooting a victorious gleam at Sarah. For the briefest of moments, she longed for a cow flop to hurl at Nannette. Instead, she waved and took her seat on the bench again.

Jack chuckled and squatted down on his heels. "You'd better watch her. She's bound and determined to win Luke's heart."

"Why would that matter to me? If he wants that shallow, rich woman, he can have her."

Jack stared at her for a long moment. "I don't believe for a second that you mean that." He wagged his index finger in her face—a rare thing for the peace-loving pastor. "Just beware. . . A man's heart is sensitive. He can only handle so much spurning before he turns his sights on someone else." Jack rose and leaned against the building, facing the tent once again.

She looked in the direction Luke had gone. She wasn't jealous of Nannette's blatant attempts to woo Luke. She just didn't like that kind of behavior. It was beneath a proper woman. In fact, it reminded her of how the ladies of the night who'd worked for her father had acted when flaunting themselves to garner the attention of the men who visited the bordello. Shameless.

She'd always be grateful to Jo for helping her get away from that horrid place. It was certainly no place for a girl of twelve to have been living.

Glancing at the paper she still held in her hand, she considered how much her life had changed—and would change again soon. She was a landowner, or would be once the paperwork was completed. She already knew the style of house she would have built—a simple two-story clapboard painted white with dark blue trim. With a picket fence around the front yard.

Leaning her head against the wall, she sighed and gazed up. *Thank You, Lord, for making my dream come true.*

Luke stomped across the street, glad to be away from that crowd of people packed closer than new bullets in a box. Glad to be away from Sarah. Could she not see how much he cared? How he was worried sick about her living alone? Concerned how she'd make ends meet with no job or steady income?

Nannette jerked on his arm. "You're not listening to a word I said. I declare, where in the world are you, Luke?"

The last place he wanted to be, that was for sure. "Just thinkin', I reckon."

"Well, stop thinking and listen. I asked you to explain to me why a pretty woman like Sarah wants land so bad. I don't for a moment understand why any woman would want to live all by herself on the prairie—or wherever her land is."

Luke couldn't share Sarah's secrets, but maybe he could pacify Nannette so she wouldn't harass Sarah later on. "It's not so much the land she wants as it is a home—and to fulfill a promise she made to her mother. Owning a homestead will enable her to build a house that belongs only to her. She's never had that before."

"What has she been living in? A tepee?" She released a loud huff and tossed out her hands. "Hasn't she been living in a house all her life? Why is that so important? I mean, most women would want to live in a town with people to visit, decent evening entertainment, and stores where they can purchase the things they need. Why doesn't she buy a house in a town that's already built?"

He assisted her up the steps and into the near-empty hotel lobby. "I reckon I can understand wanting to build on virgin land that no man has ever touched before. There's an excitement in it."

"I can see a man wanting to do that, but not a woman. So. . .what will you do if you don't get a homestead?"

Good question. Could he ride off and leave Sarah alone? He shrugged. "Haven't decided yet. I can always go back to Gabe's ranch, where I worked before, but I'm not getting any younger.

I'm ready for a place of my own."

Nannette cocked her head, and her lips tilted in a beguiling smile. "Why don't you come to Kansas City? I'm sure there's a farm for sale that you could buy."

"I'm a rancher, not a turnip planter."

She pushed out her lips in a pout he was sure most men would find intriguing. "Oh pooh. I don't see that there's all that much difference. One milks a cow while the other chases them around. Besides, if you came to Kansas City, we could get to know one another better. Wouldn't you like that?" She fluttered her lashes as if she had something in her eye. "Father might even be able to help you get a respectable job."

Luke frowned. Ranching was a perfectly respectable job. And he wasn't about to work at some place where he had to wear a suit and shiny shoes. He was more than happy with his dusty boots and cowboy gear. He tipped his hat to her. "I'd best be gettin' back. I sure wouldn't want to miss out on hearin' my name called."

Her frown deepened. "I thought we might get some tea and chat for a while."

He shook his head, gently pried her hand loose from his arm, and backed away. "Mornin', Miss Hawkins."

"Lu–uke, wait."

He spun around so fast he nearly knocked down a couple entering the lobby from the dining room. "Sorry."

He couldn't get away fast enough. Why was it the woman he longed for wanted little to do with him, and the woman who grated on his nerves like fingernails on a chalkboard was nearly begging him to move to her town? He shook his head, unable to make a lick of sense out of it. Why did he have to lose his heart to Sarah?

He strode down the street. He'd always been happy and content being a cowboy and working for Gabe—at least he had most of his grown-up years. But now he wanted more, and that included a black-eyed woman who stirred his heart like no other. He had to find a way to win her over.

He paused then gazed at the town's businesses. Women were fond of jewelry and frilly baubles. Sarah rarely ever bought anything special like jewelry, but maybe if he got something nice for her, she'd realize the depth of his love.

He changed directions, crossed the street, and stopped outside of McElmore's Jewelers, gazing at the sparkly display of rings, bracelets, and necklaces in the windows. Jingling the coins in his pocket, he stared at the fancy gold, silver, and platinum creations, wondering if he had enough to buy one and still pay for his half of the hotel bill and food he'd eat before returning to the ranch. He hadn't expected to need a passel of cash in El Reno, so he hadn't brought all that much with him. His eyes landed on a gold flower with an onyx jewel in the center. The black-eyed Susans that grew all over the ranch reminded him of Sarah's eyes. The gold flower in the window did, too. His decision made, he stepped into the store.

Chapter 7

Jack leaned against the wall as another name was drawn—not his. He had a feeling in his gut that he wouldn't get land. That he wasn't in El Reno for himself but merely to escort Sarah. He wasn't sure what he'd do if he *did* win a homestead. He certainly wasn't a farmer. He could ranch, but he didn't have the funds needed to buy stock or to build a house and barn.

The more he thought and prayed about things, the stronger he felt that he'd be returning to his church—eventually. He felt sure, though, that he needed to help Sarah first. Maybe when she returned to claim her homestead, he could come and bring Cody. The boy would think it an adventure to live in a tent and cook by campfire. His heart fluttered as he thought of his son.

How different things would have been if Cora and their baby had lived. He wouldn't be here, for one. He'd be home, holding his little daughter and kissing his wife, telling her how good she'd done in giving him little Emily. He remembered the night they'd decided on names for their baby, just a week before Cora—he swallowed back the tightness in his throat—died.

He shook away that sad thought and grasped for a happy one. Cora had laughed so hard at the silly names he'd thrown out, like Marusha Mephibolitz, that she'd had to get up and go to the outhouse. When she returned, he warmed her cold feet, and they had settled for Christopher for a son or Emily if the new baby was a girl.

Glancing around to see if anyone noticed his eyes watering, he lifted up his arm and swiped them with his sleeve. He sure missed Cora. Missed her welcoming smile when he returned after a hard day's work. Missed lying in bed, holding her close and talking about their day. Why hadn't God saved her?

He blew out a loud breath, and Sarah glanced up, smiling. He returned her smile, not wanting to cause her to worry. She was a kindhearted woman who would make Luke a good wife, if she ever realized that she loved him. He just hoped Luke would have the patience needed to wait until she did.

Shifting his stance, he gazed toward the hotel. Luke was on his way back without Miss Hawkins. She sure was one chatty lady. How did a man live with a woman who talked so much? He certainly didn't know.

His gaze traveled over the massive crowd of people. Several thousand, he'd guess. More people than he'd ever seen gathered in one spot. For the most part, they'd been an orderly group. Few troublemakers causing problems, although he had seen a number of swindlers trying to entice folks into their games of chance. He prayed for the people that he felt prompted to. Just as with the land run, so many would be heartbroken when they didn't win land.

"Excuse me, please." A short woman in a dark blue calico dress pushed through the crowd. The babe she carried lay limp in her arm, its face pale. "Let me pass. I must get to the doctor."

As she drew near, Jack opened the door and stepped back to allow her to enter.

She mumbled a thank-you and hurried past him.

Jack closed the door, saying a prayer for the woman and her child. He knew the pain she would face if her baby died. *Please, Father, spare the child. Give the woman strength and grace.*

Luke squeezed past the people in front of the doctor's office, joining Jack and Sarah again. There was an unexpected gleam in the man's eyes. Jack figured his friend would be discouraged since Sarah had won a claim and he hadn't, especially since Luke had seemed so stunned when Sarah's name was called. What had that been about? Luke wasn't the type to be jealous, but maybe getting land meant more to him than Jack realized. He *had* worked for Gabe for a long while—more than twelve years.

Maybe Luke was just relieved to be free of Miss Hawkins. She didn't let much space come between her and Luke whenever she was around. Luke's gaze dropped to Sarah, but Jack couldn't see her reaction since he stood slightly behind her.

Sarah had a good head on her shoulders, but she'd never lived alone, as far as he knew. How would she manage when the time came for him to leave? He hoped Luke would get land so he'd be in the same vicinity as Sarah, although unless his name was drawn soon, they might get claims that were miles and miles apart—and that would not help her.

His jaw tightened as he thought again of the day he'd have

to leave. She was like a sister to him, and he felt compelled to make sure she was safe. Since Sarah had won land, God must have something planned that Jack wasn't privy to. Though the idea of a homestead excited him at first, he'd realized how hard it would be for Cody to leave his cousins. Right before Sarah won her claim, he'd pretty much decided that the three of them would come to the lottery but go home empty-handed.

"Yee-haw!" Luke shouted, pumping his fist in the air.

Lost in thought as he'd been, Jack jumped at his friend's caterwauling. Sarah bounced up from the bench and hugged Luke. The crowd turned their way as Luke flashed him a gigantic grin and headed for the stage.

Sarah grabbed Jack's arm and shook it. "Can you believe it? Luke won a homestead too!"

He smiled at her and nodded, wondering how he missed hearing Luke's name called. He'd certainly been wrong about them winning land, but he felt a peace wash over him knowing Luke and Sarah would be close together. The last number he remembered Colonel Dyer calling had been 547. That meant after Sarah picked her homestead, only thirty-five people would get to choose before Luke got his chance. Jack leaned back against the wall. *You don't owe me anything, Lord. You know that better than me, but I'd sure appreciate it if You'd work things out so that Luke and Sarah could get land close to one another. It would greatly ease my concerns about her safety.*

With cheers resounding all around, Luke ran up the tent steps then jumped about, waving his clenched fists in the air like a boxer who had just won a fight. Jack couldn't help smiling at his friend's excitement and enthusiasm.

August 6, Anadarko town site

Two things Dr. Carson Worth despised were crowds and noise, but they were in overabundance today. He supposed he'd have to get used to both since he'd decided to buy a town lot and resume his medical practice. He wiped a trickle of sweat that slid down the side of his face. He'd miss the quiet, wide-open spaces of the Texas plains where he'd herded cattle for the past year, but God had made it clear that he was a doctor, not a cowboy.

He shifted his stance a foot to the right, stepping back into the shade offered by one of the few trees in the area that had been designated for the Anadarko courthouse. Popping open his pocket watch, he checked the time. Two minutes to nine. Good. The auction for town lots would soon be under way. He returned his watch to his vest pocket and tugged his list of lot selections out. The ones he'd chosen were mostly along the edges of the new town of Anadarko as far away from railroad tracks as possible in the small area. Trains created a ruckus, spilled soot everywhere, and brought with them the noise of many people congregated in a small area: three things recovering patients didn't need.

A cheer rang out all around him, and he focused his gaze on the men standing in front of the land office. Excitement raced through Carson, surprising him. He prided himself in being a levelheaded man, and few things other than medical books and a successful surgery made his heart race. The memory of his father's sudden demise reminded him of the main reason he was in this virgin town, but he shoved that unpleasant thought away. Today was a time for new beginnings not past nightmares.

"All right. Listen up, folks." A tall man with a wide mustache pushed his hat back on his head, revealing his pale forehead. It looked odd compared to the leathery tan of the rest of his face. "This here auction is for three hundred and twenty acres of town lots. Residential lots are fifty feet wide, and business ones are twenty-five feet. The proceeds of this sale will go to improving streets, building bridges over the Washita River and other places, as well as the construction of the county courthouse. You can purchase one business lot and one residential one, and that's it. You cain't buy two business ones. Is that clear?" He scanned the crowd as if searching for dissenters. "I didn't make the rules, but I will enforce them. All right, now. Let's get this show under way."

The throng roared its agreement, and Carson found himself uncharacteristically letting loose and joining in. This was an historical day, one that would set the future of many of those in the crowd. More, though, would go away disappointed. He didn't intend to be one of those. All he needed was a business lot since he planned to have a two-story building erected. He would live upstairs so he could be close to patients who needed to stay overnight.

Fierce bidding began for the first lot—not one of his selected ones.

"Twenty-five dollars," a man in front of him shouted.

"Thirty!" A woman in a blue-flowered sunbonnet waved her hand in the air.

"Fifty!"

He watched with interest as the amount rose to seventy dollars—quite an astounding amount for a lot on the barren prairie. He couldn't decide if he should bid on the first of his chosen lots or wait until the end. If he waited, the selling price may be lower because those with more money would have already gotten their land, but then again, prices could rise as there were fewer and fewer lots left and people grew more desperate. No, better to go for the first and hope he got it. He had confidence he would because God had led him here for the purpose of reestablishing his practice. It was just a matter of which lot and how much. The less he had to pay meant more funds for purchasing needed supplies and medicines, so he needed to be frugal.

The auctioneer hollered out one of the lot numbers on his paper, and Carson's heartbeat shot up as it had the first time he'd sliced into a live person with a scalpel. He was tempted to shout out a bid but chose instead to watch and wait. If he called out too soon, it could cost him.

"Twenty!"

"Twenty-five!"

"Forty!"

The bids continued, and with each one, his pulse raced like a runaway train. Sweat poured down his face, but he feared wiping it and having the auctioneer mistake the action for a bid. At least the light breeze helped cool him. The bidding slowed as did the increment of each one.

"Sixty-two."

"—three."

"Sixty-four," A man up front yelled. When no one countered him, he cast a proud grin around the crowd.

If he didn't know it was impossible, Carson felt sure his heart would pound clear out of his chest and take wing. Now or never. His hand shot up, just as the auctioneer pointed his finger toward the man up front. "Sixty-five!"

The auctioneer had his mouth open but swiveled his finger toward Carson. "We have a bid for sixty-five. Any others?"

The man up front glared at Carson, then his shoulders slumped. Carson tasted victory.

"Sold!" The auctioneer directed his gaze at Carson while the loser yanked off his hat, slapping it against his trousers. "Congratulations, sir. Make your way up front and pay for your lot."

Unmitigated delight surged through him at his success. He blew out a loud breath and cast a quick glance heavenward, knowing that in truth the success had been God's, not his. Amid slaps on his shoulders and choruses of "Congratulations" coming from all directions, he nodded his thanks over and over as he squeezed through the horde to claim his land.

⌒

The train shuddered as it pulled out of the El Reno depot, taking Sarah, Jack, and Luke back to Guthrie. Sarah relaxed against the seat, watching the town slowly go by, unable to believe how much her life was about to change.

Sarah glanced at Jack, who sat across the aisle, arms crossed with his hat over his face as he attempted to rest. She felt bad that his name hadn't been drawn, but he seemed at peace with that and eager to return to his son.

Luke was another thing. She was happy he would finally own land and could realize his dream of being a rancher, but a part of her resented that he wanted to get land close to hers. On the other hand, having someone she knew nearby would be nice. She glanced at him and caught him staring.

He winked, creating strange sensations in her stomach. She looked at the closest passengers to see if anyone noticed his antics. Luke shot a glance in Jack's direction then straightened in his seat and cleared his voice. He leaned sideways, tugging a small package from his pocket. "I had hoped to find some time alone in El Reno to give you this, but that never happened."

Her heart flip-flopped. What if it was a ring? Surely he wouldn't buy one after she'd turned down his proposal. "What is it?"

He held out the tiny package tied with a blue ribbon. "It's just a little something to celebrate your getting a homestead."

"Lu–uke, you didn't need to get me a gift." He'd given her flowers and small things he'd made before but never a wrapped, store-bought present.

He shrugged. "I know, but I wanted to."

She accepted the package. "Thank you. That was very kind of you."

"Open it before you thank me. You might not like it."

The image of a ring jumped into her mind again. Surely he wouldn't give her something like that in a public setting. It would make the rest of the ride home awkward. Her cheeks burned. With a shaky hand, she untied the bow on the unexpected gift. She unwrapped the paper, setting it and the blue ribbon on the seat beside her. She held her breath as she tugged off the lid, revealing a beautiful gold flower with a black stone in the center—a black-eyed Susan. She sucked in a breath then gazed at Luke's hesitant expression. "It's lovely."

Luke ducked his head, looking uncharacteristically shy. "It

reminded me of black-eyed Susans—and those remind me of your pretty eyes."

Her gaze shot to his, her heart pounding. He thought her black, colorless eyes were pretty? She wasn't one to wish for things that were impossible, but there had been times she'd longed for pretty blue eyes like his. There'd been a few times he'd said her eyes reminded him of the bright yellow flowers with the big dark center, but she'd thought he'd been teasing her. "This is gold. Why would you get me something so expensive?"

He shrugged one shoulder, looking more relaxed. "Your life will change now that you have land, and I wanted you to have something special to remember the day you won your homestead."

"Luke, I don't know what to say."

"Don't say nothin'. Just put it on."

She lifted the flower, examining the details. Instead of a chain, the flower hung from a yellow ribbon.

"I. . .uh. . .didn't have enough money with me to buy the chain. I hope that's all right."

She laid a hand on his arm. "It's perfect. I love it just like this." The chain would have been too much. She didn't wear fancy clothes or jewelry. In fact, the only other necklace she owned was a silver cross that Gabe and Lara had given her on her twentieth birthday last year.

She handed the necklace to Luke. "Would you please tie it on?"

"If I don't drop it." His tanned complexion darkened in a rare blush. "Turn around."

She did as asked, not expecting the tingling on her neck that his gentle touch brought as he lifted the hair that had come loose from her bun.

He fiddled for a moment then patted her shoulder. "All done."

She turned on the seat to face him, fingering the flower. "How does it look?"

His eyes flicked down for a second then lifted to her face. He raised his hand, lightly brushing his knuckle down her cheek. "Beautiful. More beautiful than a whole field of flowers."

Rattled, she smiled at him then turned, glancing across the aisle at Jack, who still rested. Had he overheard, or was he really asleep? Across the aisle, the other passengers were engaged in conversation.

She settled back, attempting to study the new list of supplies—things she'd added since visiting Jo and giving her the original list. There were so many things she needed to purchase, and she only had so much money. Having the house built would be her biggest expense. She'd asked around for recommendations of reliable men to build her house, and she finally made a deal with a man—Mr. Peterson—who had four grown sons who worked with him. The man had even said his wife was willing to come along and cook for the family for a small additional fee that Sarah was happy to pay.

Her cooking skills weren't bad, but she'd never had to prepare a meal on an open fire, especially for a herd of hardworking, hungry men. And she more than welcomed the idea of another woman being present while the Peterson men were on her property.

She stared out the window at the landscape whizzing by and realized that she was fingering the necklace. The ribbon was too short to allow her to see it without a mirror, but it warmed her heart, knowing it was there. What a kind thing for Luke to do. But why had he done it?

Yes, he'd asked her to marry him and had even kissed her once, but he had never spoken any words of affection. His proposal almost sounded like one of the business deals he made when selling Gabe's horses to a customer. In fact, at first she thought he'd been joking, like he often did. Could he actually have deep feelings for her?

How was a woman to know? Half of her life had been spent with just her mother. She'd seen her parents together only a few times, but they'd argued each time. There had been no affection between them, but there must have been at one time. Her mother had always been quiet and never talked about Pete Worley. Had she loved him?

He was a handsome man, although she'd hated the business he ran. Hated living at the bordello even though she hadn't been there all that long. Most nights she'd been locked in her room to protect her from her father's clients. What kind of father put his daughter in such a situation? She'd been frightened at first and missing her mother. She should have been there to take care of her when she was dying, but her mother hadn't wanted her to witness her death.

After running away with Jo and moving in with Gabe and Lara, she'd witnessed for the first time a healthy relationship between a man and woman. She'd seen a couple truly in love, a love that grew stronger over twelve years of marriage and the raising of four children.

She peeked sideways at Luke, who'd followed Jack's example and was resting with his arms crossed on his chest and his hat hiding his handsome face. He was her dearest friend, and she couldn't deny that she cared for him. She'd always admired the way he deftly handled a wild horse, gentling it slowly until he had earned the animal's trust. She trusted Luke with her life, but did she love him? How was a woman to know?

Though Luke was nothing like her father, she couldn't help wondering if she were to marry him, would he leave her one day as her father had left her mother?

On the morning of August 11, Sarah stood near the front of the line of men who'd arrived at the El Reno Land Office to claim land. There were a couple of other women near the end of the line. Sarah shifted her feet, wishing Jack had come along, but he had taken Cody to the livery to shop for a buckboard for her.

In the days since they'd returned to Gabe's ranch, she had pored over a map of the land openings, along with Luke, Jack, and Gabe, picking out several choice pieces with good water sources near Anadarko. She prayed that one of them would still be available when it was her turn to choose a homestead.

She turned and looked to where Luke stood a ways back. His gaze latched on hers, and he waved. She'd finally come to realize that living near someone she knew was wise. One never knew when she would need help, and being close to him meant that she wouldn't be completely alone on her new land. She had fought the idea, wanting to be independent and self-sufficient, before realizing the wisdom of it. Lara had quietly mentioned more than once how she would worry about Sarah's safety, and knowing Luke was near would help to ease her concern. So for her friend's sake—and her own—she'd agreed to work with Luke and try to find land near each other.

But there were thirty-five claim winners between her and Luke. If they all wanted to be near Anadarko and a water source, the land near hers might all be claimed before Luke got a chance to pick his homestead. At first she'd prayed he wouldn't pick land near hers, but now she muttered a prayer that he would. The thought of living in a tent all by herself on the wild prairie had kept her awake several nights until after midnight.

Over an hour after the land office opened and the line started moving, she stepped inside. Two men stood behind a counter, the one on the left beside several stacks of papers and a ledger book, and the other standing near a map that hung on the wall where people looking in the window could see it.

"Good morning, ma'am." The man by the papers, wearing a black suit with a string tie nodded at her. "I'm John Simons, and this is Mr. Meed. And what is your name?"

"Sarah Jane Worley." She slid the paper with her information toward him. "My claim number is 512."

He checked the ledger and several other papers, causing Sarah's heartbeat to pick up speed. What if a mistake had been made? She wished Luke was here in case she had a problem, but he needed to keep his place in the line.

Finally, Mr. Simons nodded. "Everything is in order. Move on over to Mr. Meed and pick out your homestead, Miss Worley."

Excitement unlike she'd known before made her hands sweat and her limbs weak. Mr. Meed eyed her then smiled. "Haven't seen too many women pass through. Congratulations."

"Thank you, sir." Sarah stared at the map, trying to make sense of the Xes.

"Do you know which town site you want to live near?"

"Anadarko, if there's still land available."

Mr. Meed scratched his chest. "There's plenty of sites still open. The land's been split into three counties: Caddo, Comanche, and Kiowa. A county seat has been established in each one at Anadarko, Lawton, and Hobart. All of the homesteads immediately surrounding Anadarko have already been taken, so just look over the map and see what you want. You get one hundred sixty acres, in the shape of an L, T, Z, a mile strip, or a square."

Sarah opened her list of claims, most of which lined the Washita River, and searched for them on the map. Several had already been chosen. What made things difficult were the odd shapes of some of the homesteads. Why in the world would someone want one shaped like a Z or even a T? She preferred a square plot.

The man was correct in that all the homesteads butting up to the town site had been picked, but there were several plots next to those still available. A large section of land north of the Washita had been reserved for the Riverside Indian school. She pointed to a lot between the river and the town. "Is that a pond there?"

Mr. Meed leaned over, squinting at the map. "Yes'm. Appears to be a small one, and you can see here" —he tapped the map— "that the river crosses that patch of land, too."

She nodded but looked at lots closer to town. On the north end of Anadarko, there was a homestead in the shape of an L butting up to the town that had been claimed. If she chose the plot next to it, she'd have a short ride across her neighbor's homestead to reach town, and a reliable water source. It seemed the perfect spot. And besides, there was plenty of available land for Luke to the north of hers, if someone didn't beat him to it. She bounced on her tiptoes, unable to hold back her excitement, and tapped the spot on the map. "I would like that one right there—in a square shape."

Mr. Meed studied the map then drew a square along the land belonging to a Mr. David Robertson and then placed an X inside of it then wrote her name across the square. Mr. Robertson's L-shaped land partially hugged two sides of hers. She hoped he was a friendly sort.

Mr. Meed sorted through a stack of papers on a table along the back wall and pulled one out. He wrote her name, the date, and the location of her homestead on a document. "Sign here, Miss Worley." He blew on the paper and then presented it to her with a smile. "Congratulations on owning a homestead."

Chapter 8

Luke tapped his hand against his pant leg, keeping his eyes glued on the land office door. What was taking Sarah so long? Had she been able to get land close to the Anadarko town site as she wanted? He muttered another prayer—something he was getting in the habit of doing—that she would get the land she desired. The closer the homestead was to town, the safer she would be. At least that's how he figured it.

The thought of her in the middle of nowhere, days from a town, sent a chill up his spine. What if she got hurt? Or what if a group of troublesome rabble-rousers attacked her place? She knew how to shoot, but he wasn't sure she would, even to save her life.

The relentless sun heated his back and shoulders, sending trickles of sweat down his temple and spine. What he wouldn't give for a cloud or breeze or even a tree to stand under. He yanked off his hat and ran his fingers through his sweaty hair. Doing nothing grated on his nerves. This time of day he ought to be working, not just standing around.

He shifted his gaze back to the doorway. Sarah should be out any minute. As grateful as he was that his name had been drawn close in number to Sarah's, there were still thirty-five people ahead of him. If they all chose land near Anadarko, his homestead might end up being miles from hers. He blew out a sigh.

His heart bolted as Sarah stepped outside, smiling widely. Her gaze shot past the other men to him, but a man near the front of the line stopped her. Several others gathered around. She talked to them for a few minutes then stepped aside. The men tipped their hats then huddled together. Luke relaxed as she headed toward him, looking prouder than he'd ever seen.

Holding a paper in one hand, she stopped in front of him, beaming a smile that quickened his pulse. "Can you believe it? I'm a landowner." Her grin was contagious.

"I'm happy for you. I know it's a dream come true."

"Oh, it is." She leaned forward and embraced him in a quick hug.

He rested one hand on her arm, relishing the rare moment. "So, were you able to get a homestead in one of the areas you wanted?"

Her black eyes gleamed with delight. "I did. There's only one homestead between mine and the northern boundary of the Anadarko town site, and that one is L-shaped. That means I'll only have to ride across a narrow strip to get to town."

Thank You, God. "That's perfect. So there were plenty of lots still available in that area?"

"At this time there are, at least on the northern and western sides. Most of the claims to the south and east of the town site had already been taken. It will all depend on what the people in line choose." She turned and gazed at the long stretch of men in front of him.

Most wore the work clothes of a farmer or cowboy, but there were also men dressed in fancy suits. A few even sported accents he didn't recognize.

"There is a big section of land north of the river reserved for a school for Indian children."

That bit of news seemed to please her, but it could make it harder for him to get land near hers.

"Hey, squaw," a man behind Luke hollered. "How come you got land? Didn't you get an allotment from the government?"

Sarah stiffened, and Luke spun around, fists clenched. The men in line right behind him had turned around, probably looking at the lout who'd uttered the comment. Luke set his sights on the bearded man in ragged overalls glaring at Sarah. Planning on teaching the man some manners, Luke took a step toward him, but a hand on his arm stopped him.

"Let it go, Luke. It's a fair question."

Luke turned to face Sarah. "But it was rude and uncalled for."

"True, but getting in a fight won't settle anything."

"It would make me feel good to defend your honor."

"Knowing that you would is enough for me."

He smiled but then cast a glare at the man that told him he'd better keep his trap shut. Luke blew out a sigh then stepped between Sarah and the man, blocking his view of her. "What did those men at the front of the line want?"

"They asked me which town site had the most available land around it."

"What did you tell them?"

"I said Hobart and Lawton." Her eyes twinkled. "You didn't

think I'd tell them Anadarko, did you?"

"Only if it was the truth."

"You don't think *I'd* tell a falsehood." She straightened, her eyebrows lifted in a show of indignation.

Luke chuckled.

"Fortunately, what I told them just happened to be the truth. Both locations are farther south and closer to the Texas border."

"Good to know." He had no desire for land that far away. In truth, his land would mean little to him if it wasn't near hers. He supposed he could always sell it like some city slickers from the East who entered the lottery solely for that purpose had done. What was the point of having a ranch if Sarah wasn't there to share it?

She fanned her face with her land deed. Sweat trickled down her cheek, and she wiped it with her handkerchief.

He didn't like seeing her discomfort. "Why don't you go back to the hotel and get out of the sun?"

"I thought I'd wait until you got your land."

"It may be noon before I get to the front. No sense standin' around until then."

She looked over her shoulder in the direction of the hotel then hunched one shoulder. "I don't mind waiting."

He took her by the shoulders. "I appreciate that, but it's hotter than Lara's frying skillet out here. Go back and relax where it's cooler. I'm sure there's things you need to be doing."

She nibbled her lower lip. "Are you sure you don't mind? I've had trouble sleeping the past few nights. I wouldn't mind resting for a bit."

"Go." He turned her around. "I'll come find you when I'm

done, and we can get some lunch."

"All right." She waved at him as she walked away.

If she'd give him a chance, he'd work hard to make things easier for her.

"That your gal?" The man behind him asked. "She's quite a looker."

Luke stiffened and turned but saw only friendly curiosity in the man's gaze. "She'd be my wife, if she'd have me."

The man's eyebrows lifted. "Turned you down, did she?"

"The first time I asked her to marry me she did, but I intend to ask again." He just wasn't sure when. What if she said no the second time?

"I've been married eleven years—best years of my life." The stranger rubbed his hand across his beard. "Thing is, you gotta let a woman know you care for her, just like you did by sending her back to the hotel. Show her that you love her, and keep doin' things that tell her you care. She'll figure it out."

Luke nodded his appreciation for the man's insight. He'd have to figure out other ways to express his affection. He'd been pleased to see that she was wearing the necklace he'd given her. The pretty thing had cost him quite a bit, but it was worth it to see Sarah's eyes light up and to watch her finger the flower when she was deep in thought.

Two hours later, he stepped into the land office, handed the man at the counter his card with his information, and then stood in front of the map of claims. His gaze shot straight to Anadarko, and his gut tightened. He saw the L-shaped homestead Sarah had mentioned and her claim, but all the land surrounding them—and the river—for miles had already been taken.

Sarah's pounding heart nearly burst from her chest as Jack drove the wagon onto her property for the first time. Gently rolling grasslands spread out before her with enough trees to offer relief from the heat of summer but not so many that they'd have to be cleared before she could build her house or plant a garden. Yellow and white wildflowers braved the hot, dry weather, dotting her field with beauty. Just imagine, one hundred sixty acres, and it was all hers. "Isn't it the most beautiful spot on God's earth?"

"It don't look much different than any other land we crossed to get here." Cody leaned forward, studying the homestead.

Jack chuckled. "That's true, son. It looks much the same as Gabe's land or most of the prairie we drove through, but Sarah owns this patch of property, and that makes it special to her."

She flashed a smile at Jack. "That's true."

"How come you want to live here? There ain't even a house." Cody shook his head as if he thought her crazy.

Jack guided the horses toward a line of trees, which Sarah suspected followed the Washita River. "I'll have a house soon enough. The builders will begin on it tomorrow." Excitement zinged through her whole body.

"But it's so far from home. And there's no one to play with." Cody yawned and leaned against his father's arm.

Sarah smiled to herself. Leave it to a child to keep her feet on the ground.

"Land near Gabe's ranch costs a lot now. Sarah got this homestead for free. Remember how I told you she won it in a drawing?"

The boy nodded. "I'm hungry."

Jack stopped the wagon near the glistening river. "This looks like the perfect place to eat lunch."

Sarah feared she was too excited to eat. She shinnied down the wagon's wheel and hurried toward the water's edge. It was vital to her survival. At this spot, the river looked to be about twenty-five-feet wide. The steep banks would make getting to the water more difficult, but they would protect her land from flooding. "I wonder how deep it is."

Jack drew alongside her, holding Cody's hand. "My guess would be four to ten feet, but there's only one way to tell."

"Can we go swimmin'?" Cody leaned toward the river. "How come the water is so brown?"

"Silt from the muddy banks is part of the reason." Jack tugged him back. "I don't know that we'll have time to swim today. We've got lots to do."

Sarah reached into the back of the buckboard for the basket that held the lunch she'd ordered from the hotel dining room. "Since Cody is hungry, let's go ahead and eat. After that, we can finish our tour of the homestead so I can determine where to have the house built."

Jack took the basket from her, and they walked to the nearest tree. Sarah thought about the muddy water. She wasn't too inclined to drink it. "Is that water even drinkable?"

"All water is drinkable, but it could make you sick." Jack stared toward the river. "You'll probably need to have a well dug. In the meantime, we can buy a barrel and collect rainwater."

She hadn't previously considered that she'd have to hire someone to dig a well. She'd have to wait until after the house was done to see how much money she had left. Though she'd saved most of the money her father had sent her the past eight years, paying to have a house built and buying all the supplies needed to stock it were quickly depleting her funds.

Luke had mentioned he might be able to loan her some money if hers ran low, but she was determined not to borrow any. The only dark cloud on the day had come when he told her that he needed to stay in Anadarko instead of joining her and Jack today. She followed Jack back to the wagon. "What do you think Luke is doing?"

"Business, that's all he told me."

"But what kind of business could he have? I know he was very disappointed in getting land so far from mine."

Jack shot her a teasing grin. "I guess if you wanted to know so bad you should have asked him."

She made a face at him, resisting the childish urge to stick out her tongue. She hadn't seen much of Luke since they'd returned from El Reno. In fact, she'd wondered if he was avoiding her. He'd made several trips to Guthrie before coming to Anadarko. She knew him enough to know he was up to something, but she had no idea what it was.

Cody ran ahead of them, carrying the blanket Sarah had pulled from the railcar, which held many of the items for her house. More would arrive later, like the pretty parlor furniture and dining table Jo had ordered after they'd scoured catalogs for hours. She couldn't wait until the house was done and everything was in place. After several nights of sleeping on a cot in a tent during their drive from El Reno to Anadarko, with the prospect of many more until the house was done, she longed for a real bed.

They settled down next to the slow-moving river and dined

on pork sandwiches, hardboiled eggs, apples, and peach pie. "I was surprised to see so many wooden structures already in town."

Jack nodded and handed Cody a hardboiled egg. "There are still a bunch of tents, but people are anxious and want to get their homes and places of business built before winter sets in."

Using her napkin, Sarah dabbed at a trickle of sweat running down her cheek. "It's hard to imagine cold weather is just a few months away when it's so hot now."

"True. We don't normally get much snow here, but I have seen a few inches as early as October."

"I remember that snowfall. I'm glad, though, that the weather warmed up after the snow melted. I don't enjoy long, cold winters." Sarah bit into her sandwich, determined to eat at least half of it. In spite of her excitement, she'd need her strength to do all that had to be done by nightfall. She would pray tonight that winter didn't come early this year. She and all the other homesteaders would need to plant gardens as soon as possible, and that required a few months of good weather in order to reap some fall vegetables. Without them, winter's eating might be slim pickings.

She was grateful now for all those hours of planting and weeding the garden, side by side with Lara, and relearning about cultivating seeds, something her mother had taught her before she had become sick. She hoped she'd be able to grow all the fruits and vegetables that Lara had. She yawned as she watched Jack rub Cody's back. When the boy went to sleep, they could leave him resting on the shaded blanket while they searched the land and decided where to place her house.

She quietly packed up their leftovers from their meal then walked along the banks of the river, looking for a place where the banks were less steep. Jack unhitched the horses from the wagon, watered them, and then hobbled them in a grassy patch. Then he untied the saddle horses, including the beautiful dappled gray mare named Dottie that Gabe and Lara had given her as a combination birthday and going-away gift. Sarah turned back toward the wagon, eager to see the rest of her land.

An hour later, they'd circled the property. They crossed the river at a shallow spot to inspect the small bit of land she owned on the far side of the Washita. As they reached the final bit of land, Sarah blinked at the field of tall plants waving in the light breeze. "Is that corn?"

"Looks like it." Jack dismounted and walked toward the plants. He reached up and broke off an ear with brown silks and waved it. "It is, and it looks ripe for the picking."

Sarah dismounted and walked over to him. "But how did it get here? Who planted it?"

He shrugged. "I suppose it could have been squatters or possibly Indians. I heard there's been some confusion with the Indians not understanding the boundaries of their land allotments. Or it's possible that the people who planted this field were squatters the army chased off right before the land was opened."

"Since this is my land now, wouldn't I have the right to harvest the corn?"

"I don't see why not. If you'd been fortunate to find a house on your land, you wouldn't hesitate to live in it, would you?"

Sarah gazed at the field of corn, hardly able to believe her good fortune. She'd only just arrived, and God was blessing her already. "You're right. I would use it—but only after I had cleaned it thoroughly."

Jack rubbed the back of his neck. "As much of a blessing as this is, it will also cause more work. The corn needs to be harvested soon."

Sarah walked over to a stalk and wrangled off an ear. "Let's get enough for supper and some for tomorrow. Once the builders have arrived and have started on the house, then I can think about the corn."

Jack nodded. "Good idea, but let's pick it quickly. I want to get back and check on Cody."

With Jack focused on picking corn, Sarah pulled off one of her petticoats to use to carry her bounty back. She gazed up at the sky, smiling. "Thank You, Lord, for this unexpected treat. Please bless this land and my endeavors here."

Jack's ears reddened when Sarah handed him the petticoat with her single ear in it.

She shrugged, feeling her own cheeks warm. "It was all I could think of in a pinch."

He smiled, scratching his ear. "Smart thinkin'."

As they crossed the river again and headed back to their horses, Sarah scanned her land. Pride surged through her. The only sounds to be heard were their footsteps crushing through the thick grass, the insects buzzing around them, and the grass swishing in the light breeze. She was eager to see what the future held for her in this peaceful place.

"Pa! Pa!" Cody's scream rent the quiet.

Sarah's heart jolted.

Jack stiffened, dropped the corn, and ran for his horse. He leaped onto its back, turned, and shot her a frantic glance.

She motioned at him. "Go!"

Luke shook Mr. Swinney's hand. "Thank you for purchasing my homestead, sir. I hope you'll be happy and successful on that section of land."

The man smiled a wide, gap-toothed grin, his hazel eyes shining. "Thank you for selling it. I can't imagine why you'd want to, but it's a dream come true for me and my family. I'd thought I had missed any chance at getting a homestead."

Luke pursed his lips and nodded, hoping he'd made the right decision. He'd prayed and had wrestled with his thoughts ever since winning his claim. As much as he wanted land, he longed to be near Sarah more. And if that meant selling his homestead, so be it. Now if only the second part of his plan would work out.

He signed his deed, relinquishing ownership, and handed it to Mr. Swinney. "Make sure you get that registered with the land office in El Reno so it's official."

The man nodded. "Gonna get my family settled on the land today; then I'll leave for El Reno tomorrow."

"I wish you good fortune."

The man tipped his hat. "You too, young man. I hope things work out like you're wantin'."

So do I. Luke blew out a loud breath. He'd been a landowner for a few weeks, although he'd never even set foot on his property. He headed for the town square where the courthouse would be built one day. He'd read in the newspaper that the money earned from the sale of town lots at the public auction on August 6 would be used to construct the courthouse and other town features.

All around him, hundreds of tents had been erected, and a number of wooden buildings were in various stages of completion.

All manner of storeowners were already doing business. He passed an elderly couple selling clothing. Another man hawked guns and ammunition, and a tall, thin man with a handlebar mustache offered shaves and haircuts. It boggled his mind how this land had been virgin prairie only a few weeks ago, and now it was a bustling town of thousands of people. The chatter of voices had replaced nature's peaceful quiet.

He turned down a street and saw the town square up ahead. While eating lunch at a tent café, he'd overheard talk that people wanting to sell their town lots had tacked notices to the trees in the town square. A number of people from other states had entered the lottery in hopes of winning land they could turn around and sell, thus lining their pockets. Fine by him.

He'd made two hundred fifty dollars selling his homestead. Surely a much smaller town lot would cost less than that. If he could get one on the north end of town, he'd be less than half a mile from the edge of Sarah's property. A smile tugged at his lips. He'd always planned to become a rancher like Gabe. He even had his own herd of more than fifty head that ran on Gabe's land, but now the idea of owning a livery had taken root. The more he thought about it, the better he liked it. He could still work with horses, and he'd be helping others by selling and renting quality stock and buggies. He'd just have to get used to living in a town again. It was something he hadn't done since he was a boy. He'd miss Gabe's family and the quiet of the prairie, but he'd be near Sarah.

As he drew close to the town square, he spied the half dozen trees shading the grassy area that was empty of any tents. Several pieces of paper tacked to the trunks fluttered on the warm breeze.

The first notice he checked was for a business lot on the southern end of town. Next was a residential lot and then one for a business and residential lots in the center of town. The price for the last one—three hundred fifty dollars—lifted his eyebrows clear to his hairline. He blew out a whistle.

He might have to live in his livery until he started making some money, but he'd lived in worse places. Rubbing the back of his neck, he headed to the next tree. It probably was a good idea to live on the premises anyway since he'd have valuable horses, tack, and equipment at the livery. At least until he and Sarah married.

"Howdy." A well-dressed man smoothed down a wrinkled page at the second tree and scanned the info.

"Afternoon." Luke slowed to a stop several feet from the man, waiting for him to move on.

"You looking for land?"

He nodded. "You too?"

"Yes. I'm looking for a good place to open a hardware store." The man's brown eyes darkened and he shook his head. "I fully meant to arrive in time for the auction of the town lots, but my nine-year-old daughter took ill, and I didn't want to leave her to travel out of town."

"I hope she's doing better."

The man smiled. "She is, thank the good Lord. My name is Reggie Best."

"Luke McNeil." He shook the man's hand. "I'm thinking of starting a livery—if I can find the right place for it on the north end of town." He studied both notices then moved to a third tree—the last with papers attached.

Mr. Best headed to the first tree Luke had checked and tugged on one of the papers. "Well now, I do believe I'm in luck."

"That's good." Luke checked the last tree and sighed. Nothing. He walked back to Mr. Best to see which ad had caught his eye. It was the expensive one with both a business and residential lot.

The man smiled and started to walk off. "I'll be looking for men to work for me. Got a house and place of business that need to be built. Would you happen to be looking for work?"

Luke shrugged, not ready to give up on his own dream. "I've done some building, but I've mostly herded cows and horses."

"How long did you stay at your last place of employment?"

"Over twelve years. I only left there to register for the lottery."

Mr. Best frowned, looping his thumbs through the lapels of his brown frock coat. "That must be somewhat close to half of your life."

"That's not far from the truth. I was lucky to get a job with a good, responsible man that had a vision to build a ranch. I helped him do it."

Mr. Best nodded. "I could use a good man like you, if you're looking for employment."

Luke glanced at the trees where the notices hung. If he bided his time, he might be able to find a lot for sale near Sarah. It wouldn't hurt to add to his funds, because if he was successful, he'd have to build a livery, buy several wagons and buggies, as well as tack. At least he had the stock he'd need. He brushed the back of his hand along his jaw. Maybe this job was God's providence.

Chapter 9

Jack kicked his horse into a gallop, his gaze scanning the field where he'd left his son. Two large wagons had stopped near Sarah's buckboard, and several men stood next to them. He gritted his teeth, willing his horse to run faster—and praying he wouldn't stumble in a hole.

He was glad he'd taken the time to load his gun this morning and yanked it free of the holster. He pointed it toward the men as he drew near, reined his horse to a sudden stop, and then dismounted. His gaze landed on each man, then shot to his son, who sat on the blanket. A heavyset woman sat on the edge of the blanket, her arm around a medium-sized dog. Cody spied him, jumped to his feet, and ran to him. Jack snagged his son in midair as the boy leaped up.

A large, bearded man in overalls walked toward him, hands in the air. "You don't need that gun. We didn't hurt the boy. I reckon we scared him. He was sound asleep when my dog Rascal trotted right up to him and licked him on the cheek. Shocked the sleep right out of the poor kid."

Keeping his gun trained on the man, Jack shifted Cody higher on his hip and glanced at the younger men, all of whom looked to be related. "Who are y'all? And what are you doin' here?"

One of the younger men helped the woman to her feet. "We're the Peterson family, and we're lookin' for a Miss Sarah Worley. Is this her land?"

Jack's gaze zipped from the woman to the younger men, none of whom looked threatening. In fact, they all seemed quite relaxed in spite of the fact he still held his gun on them.

The black-and-white dog crept toward Jack, stopping five feet away. His black eyes seemed focused on Cody. Whining, the dog eased forward, sniffing Jack's boots, completely oblivious to the gun aimed at his master.

Hoofbeats sounded behind him, but he didn't move. Sarah dismounted and rushed to his side, pressing his gun hand toward the ground. "Put that thing away. This is the family I hired to build my house."

Feeling like a fool, he holstered his gun then got a better grip on his son. At six, Cody was already getting heavy. "You all right?"

Cody nodded and laid his head on Jack's shoulder. "I got scared when I woke up and saw that dog. I thought it was a wolf and he was gonna eat me."

Sarah walked up to Mr. and Mrs. Peterson. "Thank you for coming, but I wasn't expecting you until tomorrow."

"We start work in the morning, so we needed to arrive today to get our camp set up. Where would you like us?"

Sarah looked at Jack as if asking for his help. He walked toward her and held out his hand to Mr. Peterson. "I'm Jack Jensen, Sarah's brother—of sorts. Sorry for the misunderstanding. I reckon I jumped to conclusions when I heard my boy yellin'."

Mr. Peterson shook his hand so hard he thought he'd drop Cody. "Perfectly understandable. I'd'a done the same thing."

Mrs. Peterson moved over to her sons and waved her hand. "These here are our boys. Amos, he's the oldest at twenty-seven." She swatted a chubby fist at the blond man with a red beard then turned toward the two dark-haired men. "These are our twins, Zeke and Zach. They're both twenty-five." Her eyes narrowed as she cocked her head, smiling. "And this is my baby, Johnny."

The youngest man scowled. "I'm twenty-one, Ma. I ain't no baby."

She tweaked his cheek. "You'll always be *my* baby."

Johnny sighed and rolled his eyes, while the man's brothers chuckled.

Zeke—or was it Zach— walked over to stand next to Sarah, but his gaze rested on Jack. "How can you be her 'sort of' brother? Either you are or you ain't."

Sarah covered her mouth, hiding a snicker. "His family is my adopted family. So that makes him *sort of* my brother. You see?"

"I care for Sarah as much as I do my two sisters by birth."

Cody wiggled. "Can I pet the dog?"

By now the animal had flopped on its back, practically begging to play with the boy.

"All right, but stay where you can see me. Don't wander off."

"Yes, Pa." He slid to the ground then stooped down and scratched Rascal's belly. The dog wagged its tail, hopped up, and licked Cody's face.

The other twin sidled up beside his brother and gazed at Sarah. "So, he ain't your beau then?"

Sarah's cheeks darkened. "No, he isn't."

"That's true," Jack said, struggling to keep a straight expression. "But don't forget I still have a gun."

The twins' eyes widened.

"C'mon and get to work, you two," Amos shouted.

Mr. Peterson ambled over as the twins drifted away. "Have you decided where you want to put your house, Miss Worley?"

"We were out looking over the land right before you arrived, but I can't decide. The river is that way. I don't want to get too far from it."

"If I was you, I'd have a well dug. That river is mighty silty."

Sarah nodded. "That's what Jack said."

"He was right. What about the house then?"

Sarah turned and studied her land. For a brief moment, a shaft of jealousy speared Jack before he pushed it away. God had spoken clearly that he was to be a preacher, not a landowner, at least for now, but it wasn't clear yet if he was supposed to go back to his old church on Gabe's land or start a new one in Anadarko. God would tell him when the time came. Right now he planned to keep his promise to Lara and make sure Sarah had a snug house built and was safely settled before he decided what was next for him and Cody.

Sarah walked away with Mr. Peterson, pointing out various places to put her house, and the gazes of the man's three youngest sons followed. All were of marrying age. Jack blew out a sigh. Luke had better hurry up and get out here before he lost Sarah.

Carson strolled through his brand-new, fresh-smelling building, feeling a surge of pride. When the townsfolk had learned he was a doctor, many halted work on their own businesses and houses to help get his place done quickly. They all knew that a doctor could mean the difference between life or death and had seemed happy to pitch in and help.

He removed his spectacles, tugged a clean handkerchief from his pocket, and after blowing a puff of breath on the lens, he cleaned the dust from them. He returned them to his face then crossed his arms, leaning against the open back door, and stared out. He hadn't gotten land right on the edge of town but almost. Only a row of lots separated him from the open land.

The only sad thought to darken the day was that his father wasn't here to witness Carson's first practice—one that was his alone. He'd grown up learning medicine by his father's side and by assisting his father in procedures. He'd furthered his education in college and had the good fortune to work for six months at the brand-new Johns Hopkins Hospital before he returned to Indian Territory to work alongside his pa. But then one horrible event shattered all his dreams.

He shook his head, scattering the disturbing thoughts. This was a day to celebrate, not dwell on things that couldn't be changed. Hammers rang out overhead as the workers continued their attempt to finish the roof today as promised. Needing something to do, he grabbed the broom he'd purchased from one of the tent vendors and swept the floor for the third time.

The August heat made closing the windows impossible, and thus dust constantly blew through them. Maybe things would improve once all of the town's building had been completed, but that day was a long way off.

He tugged out his pocket watch and checked the time. The

train bringing many of his supplies was due to arrive at two. He'd be able to move in his furniture and equipment, unpack his supplies, and get everything organized in the next few days. Then he'd open up shop. With all the building going on, there were bound to be some mishaps, not that he wished that on anyone, but it was a fact of life, and he wanted to be ready to give the best care possible.

Grabbing the satchel that held his clothing and personal toiletries, he crossed to the back of the building and jogged up the stairs to the two rooms that made up his private quarters. He would put his bed in the rear one and set up a small parlor and kitchen at the front of the building. It wasn't much, but it was a whole lot better than the noisy bunkhouse he'd once slept in or when he'd camped outside on the trail last year. The only thing that concerned him was whether his future wife would be happy here.

Setting the satchel in a relatively clean corner, he laughed and shook his head. "What wife?"

Carson walked downstairs, putting a buffer between him and the pounding overhead. It was a futile effort to wonder if his future wife would like his apartment when there was no such woman on the horizon. But now that he finally had a place of his own, maybe it was time to pray for God to bring him a wife.

The aroma of frying bacon drew Sarah from her tent. She should have been up an hour ago, but between attempting to sleep on the unfamiliar cot and the excitement of finally seeing her house built, she'd tossed and turned until the early hours before dawn. Standing, she stretched the kinks from her back and tugged off her nightgown. She made quick work of dressing.

Mrs. Peterson was probably a much better cook than she was. She hoped Jack and Luke would be satisfied with her cooking and not abandon her and join the Petersons. Once her house was up and the stove in place, things would be different, but she had rarely cooked over a campfire.

As she brushed her hair, she smiled at the sound of sawing. In her mind, she saw her folk Victorian–style home rising up on the prairie with its square angles and large porch. She'd ordered decorative brackets for under the eaves, scrolled porch spindles, and gingerbread gable trim from a company in Illinois. The color was another issue. She had settled on white with blue trim, but now that the house was being built, she wasn't so sure. She pushed the pins into her hair and tried to imagine the completed house in several different shades. Yellow was her favorite color, but she was leaning toward a light green with dark green and ecru-colored trim.

"Sarah? You still in there?" Luke called.

"Coming." She rose from the chair Jack had placed in her tent and shoved back the tent flap. "Good morning."

"Morning. I thought you were going to sleep the day away."

"Very funny. I imagine you're just hungry and wanting me to get started on breakfast."

"I was hungry for a glimpse of you." His blue eyes blazed, revealing the truth in his statement.

Her heart fluttered and cheeks warmed. "Lu–uke. Don't say such things."

"Why not? It's true."

"Someone might overhear you." She tied her tent flap shut.

"I don't care if they do, especially those Peterson brothers. I don't like the way some of them were eyeing you last night, like a man who'd been on the trail and got his first glimpse of a saloon."

She shook her head, laughing softly. "You sure know how to charm a woman."

"Glad to know my efforts are working."

She fingered her black-eyed Susan necklace and stared at him, not knowing what to say. Even though she'd turned down his proposal, he seemed to have doubled his efforts to woo her. Why couldn't he take no and leave it at that? She didn't want to have to push him away or distance herself. His friendship meant too much. "How did things go in town?" she asked, more than a little curious what he's been doing. "You got here so late last night that we didn't get to talk much."

He smiled, revealing his straight white teeth. He really did have an intriguing smile. "I sold my land. Got more than I'd hoped for it, too."

"You sold your land?" Sarah stared at him, wondering what had gotten in to him. "Why in the world would you do that?"

"Because it's farther than I want to be from you. I've decided to buy a lot in town and open a livery."

She started toward the Petersons' camp, not sure about Luke's surprising news. It would be nice to have him closer, but then again she wanted her independence. She needed a cup of coffee. "And did you find a town lot to purchase?"

He fell into step beside her. "Not yet, but I did get a job."

"A job?"

"Yep. Gonna work for a Mr. Best. He's starting up a hardware store."

She paused and searched his eyes. "Why would you want to work at a place like that?"

He shrugged. "I might as well be making some money while looking for a lot to buy."

"But I thought you planned to work on my house."

"I can't work for Mr. Best until his building is up. Besides, you hired a bunch of men to help you, so I didn't think you needed me. If you do, I can work on it in the evenings."

She resumed walking and smiled at Mrs. Peterson, even though her excitement had dimmed. Luke had never actually told her he'd help build her house, but she'd assumed he would want to. She couldn't fault him, though, for working. He'd need all the money he could get to start a business. Still, she'd miss seeing him during the day.

"Mornin'," Mrs. Peterson called out. She poured a cup of coffee and held it out to her.

She gladly accepted the warm cup. "Thank you."

Mrs. Peterson glanced up at Luke as she bent to stir a massive cast iron skillet filled with eggs. "You wanna'nother cup?"

"No, ma'am. It was mighty good though."

"I reckon you're wantin' breakfast. Be ready in a few minutes."

Sarah stared at the stack of bacon, plates of biscuits, and huge bowl of peaches. The Peterson family sure liked to eat. "Would you please let me know when you're finished, and I'll start on our breakfast."

Mrs. Peterson straightened, wrapped her hand in her apron, and then picked up the heavy skillet and carried it to the wagon's tailgate, which had become a sideboard.

Sarah's stomach grumbled. She'd just planned on making a

stack of pancakes. She longed to run up the hill and see what the men had gotten done, but that was silly since they'd only just started on her house an hour ago.

Grabbing two plates off the stack on the tailgate, Mrs. Peterson turned and then walked toward her and Luke. She stuck out the plates. "No need for you to cook. I've made plenty. He'p yourself before my men get here and eat everythin' in sight."

"Are you sure? That's very kind of you." Sarah glanced at Luke and wiggled her eyebrows as she passed him a tin plate.

"I halfta cook, so there's no sense in us both doin' it. I wouldn't mind if you wanted to contribute to the food stocks and help a bit, though."

"I'm happy to do so. Should I go tell your family now the food's ready?"

"No need." The woman waddled to the front of the wagon where she'd hung a large iron triangle and ran a rod around inside it, setting off a clamor. "They'll be here in a jiffy. You'd better dish up."

Luke handed his plate to Mrs. Peterson. "You go first."

The woman blushed under her already pink cheeks. "Aren't you the gentleman." She accepted his offering and winked at Sarah. "You'd better lasso and hog-tie this'n before he gets away. He's a keeper."

Luke straightened and puffed out his chest as he grinned at Sarah. "D'you hear that? I'm a keeper."

She teasingly nudged his side with her elbow, hoping to deflate his ego, and then she stepped in front of him and dished up her plate. "Be that as it may, I beat you to the food."

He took another plate, leaned against her shoulder, and

sniffed, sending odd tingles racing through her at his nearness. If she turned, she'd be only an inch or two from his cheek. She sidestepped and placed a biscuit on her plate then a small spoon of peaches. "Where's Jack and Cody? I haven't seen them."

Luke laid a half dozen slices of bacon on his plate. "He took Cody down to the creek to wash up. The boy wet himself last night."

"I wonder if it was the excitement of sleeping in a tent or something else. As far as I know he hasn't done that in a while."

"Don't know."

"I hope they get back in time to eat. I wonder if I should fix them a plate."

"You go right ahead and do that," Mrs. Peterson said. "But do it fast. Here come my men."

Sarah glanced over her shoulder then handed her plate to Luke and stepped around him, grabbing two more plates. By the time she'd filled them, a herd of Petersons had galloped into camp. The twins smiled at her, tipping their hats in unison. Had they planned that or did they always do things at the same time?

Johnny stopped next to the wagon and smiled at her. "You gonna eat all that?" With his fair hair and hazel eyes, he looked more like Amos than the twins. Mrs. Peterson had warned her that her youngest three boys—as she called the big, strapping men— were looking to marry. Amos had a wife and two daughters living in El Reno. Because the youngest was only four months old, they hadn't come on this trip.

Sarah sat next to Luke on the end of a bench someone had moved near the campfire. Had he purposely sat in the middle so one of the other men wouldn't sit beside her? If so, it was a considerate thing for him to do. She laid the two plates on the far end of the bench, liking how he watched out for her and protected her, but did she care enough to marry him? Although she'd turned him down, the idea kept rising to the top of her thoughts like cream in a milk bucket.

Maybe after her house was built she'd feel differently.

Three days after the start of construction, Sarah sat in the buggy next to Luke and stretched her gaze towards town. When she returned, she hoped to see the skeleton of her house rising from the foundation. She was glad she had made arrangements in advance for the Petersons to purchase and bring the wood for the house. With all the construction happening in Anadarko, she might have had a long wait to get her hands on any precut lumber.

As much as she enjoyed watching the progress, she needed this trip to town. She hadn't planned well enough for the meals she'd expected to share with Jack, Luke, and Cody and needed to lay in some more supplies. It had been a blessing when Zelma—as Mrs. Peterson had asked her to call her—had invited her to join them for meals. Sarah smiled, proud of herself for learning the art of cooking on an open fire, but she still needed more provisions for her and her men. Bacon and fresh eggs were on her list as well as some smoked meat, potatoes, and fresh vegetables, if any were to be had.

The sound of hammering greeted them as they drove into Anadarko. She glanced behind her to see Cody playing in the back with some wooden animals his pa had carved for him last year. With her watching his son, Jack was free to help with the house and not worry about him.

"Your pancakes were real good." Luke smiled.

"Thank you. I'm so glad Zelma offered to let us eat with them. I've learned a lot from her." She chuckled. "Zelma has told me several times, 'Hungry men are unhappy men.'"

Luke flicked a glance at her. "I figured as much. I had my mind prepared that all we'd get to eat was pancakes. Pancakes for breakfast, lunch, and supper—and not nearly as good as this morning's were."

"Very funny." She nudged him in the side, not wanting to admit how close to the truth he was. "Zelma said the key to good pancakes is buttermilk. So, what are you going to do while I shop?"

"Check and see if there are any new notices posted of lots for sale."

"Have you tried looking in a newspaper?"

He turned the wagon, guiding it down another street. "No, but that's a great idea, if I can find one."

"Do you know where any general stores are? I haven't spent enough time here to locate one."

He nodded. "I saw a sign for one yesterday. It's up ahead."

He guided the horses to the side of East Oklahoma Street in front of the Anadarko General Store—a store in a tent—then stopped and set the brake. He jumped down and hurried around to help her descend the wagon. She bent and reached for his shoulders as he cupped her around the waist then easily lifted her to the ground. They locked eyes, and she smiled her thanks, momentarily stunned by the affection in his gaze. Then he stepped back, breaking the brief moment. Rattled, she turned to Cody. "Ready to do some shopping?"

The boy looked less than enthused.

"You want me to take him?"

Cody's blue eyes brightened and he jumped up. "Yeah, can I go with Luke?"

His excitement to join Luke instead of her was a disappointment, but it would allow her to focus on her task and finish quicker. She loved going into a store and smelling all of the fresh scents and seeing the new fabrics and what all was available. "Of course, if that's what you prefer."

The boy shrugged, looking serious. "Shopping is for ladies."

Luke chuckled, and she shot him a glare. "Men shop for things, too. In fact, Luke is shopping for land, but it's fine for you to accompany him."

"Yippee!" He leaped from the wagon, forcing Luke to adjust his stance and catch him in midair.

"I shouldn't be too long. If I'm not here when you get finished" —she waved her hand in the air— "check the stores nearby. I won't go far, but I'd like to see what's available here in case I forgot to order something I need for the house."

Luke tipped his hat to her, and he and Cody headed down the street. Anyone who didn't know them would assume Luke was the boy's father. He'd make a good father—a fun one—someday. She swallowed a lump in her throat at the thought then turned her attention to shopping. Nothing like a long shopping list to get a woman's thoughts off of a man.

At the store she paused at the entryway to inhale the scents of spices, coffee, leather, and so many other things. As she wandered the aisles of the tent, she checked to see what the place had to offer, as well as the prices. She'd read in the newspaper that in some start-up towns, storeowners were charging inflated prices, but this one seemed to be fair.

After studying the list of smoked meat available that was posted at the counter, she ordered a large ham and two slabs of bacon.

The clerk, a man she'd guess was in his fifties, marked it on a piece of paper then looked up. "A woman traded me some full-grown hens this morning if you're in the market for some."

She tapped her lip, thinking. Plucking a hen wasn't her favorite task, but they made for good eating. "I hadn't thought to buy any until my henhouse was built, but they would taste good for supper. Do you have a cage for them?"

"Got some wooden crates with enough holes for air but not so many that they could escape."

"Good. I'll take six then, and just enough feed to last a week." That way they could enjoy another chicken meal later in the week. Three hens for tonight and three for next time. "Do you have any fresh eggs or milk?"

He removed his wire-framed spectacles and wiped them with a rag he pulled from under the counter. "Got a couple dozen eggs that came in this morning, but I'm plumb outta milk."

"Do you have three dozen?"

"Just barely."

"Good. I'll take them, too, and a hunk of that cheese behind you."

The man nodded then walked into the back of the store. Sarah strolled the aisles, making sure there wasn't something she'd forgotten. It amazed her that with the town being so new, the storeowner had had time to get all these supplies sent to Anadarko and set up so quickly. She paused at the canned foods, carried several cans of applesauce, peaches, and apples to the counter, then returned for some green beans. She much preferred them fresh, but canned would do in a pinch.

She needed to show Zelma her cornfield, and she probably should water it and pick the new ears that were ready. Muttering a prayer for God to bless the people who'd planted it, she walked to the bins that held the fresh food. If she got more ears than she could use, she could bring them and trade for other things.

The store had a supply of carrots, onions, and turnips. After carrying what she wanted to the counter, she added a bushel of potatoes to her list.

"I should've introduced myself," the clerk said as he strode back into the store, carrying her ham and bacon in a box. "My name's Theodore Moore. My wife, Betty, helps me at times, but she's doing the washing today."

"A pleasure to meet you, sir. I'm Sarah Worley. I've got a homestead not far from town."

"Is there a Mr. Worley?"

Her cheeks warmed. "No, there isn't."

He rubbed his chin. "I heard some females won land, but you're the first I've met. Mighty brave of you to set up housekeeping in such a rugged place."

She smiled. This part of the territory didn't seem all that much rougher than where Gabe and Lara lived, except that she had no home, well, or other basics she needed, but they would come in time. "Here's the list of the rest of the things I need. Could I leave it while I visit some other stores?"

"Sure can. I'll have it ready in a short while, providing I don't get overly busy with customers."

"Thank you. I'll return shortly." She smiled and walked out the door. Looking to her left and then her right, she wondered where to go next. She couldn't afford to buy much, only things absolutely necessary, but that didn't mean she couldn't browse. She took a step to her right and noticed a handsome, well-dressed man and a young boy walking toward her. The man smiled and tipped his hat, but the boy stopped suddenly, staring at her with wide eyes and open mouth. Suddenly his eyes sparked and he ran toward her. "Mama!"

Chapter 10

Sarah braced herself as the boy collided with her skirts and hugged her. She lifted her stunned eyes to his father's. The man hadn't moved a step, and the color had fled his tanned face. His confused gaze locked with hers.

Not knowing what to do, she reached down and patted the boy's head. He'd held on to her as if she actually were his mother and he hadn't seen her in weeks. Where was his mother? Why would he think she was her?

The man finally escaped his stupor, walked over to them, and then knelt beside the boy, pain etched on his handsome face. "Phillip, you know this woman isn't your mother."

He grasped her tighter. "She is. She is!"

The man gently laid his hand on the boy's shoulder then attempted to pull him away.

"No!" The child jerked free and buried his face deeper in Sarah's skirt.

The man stood, removed his hat, and ran his fingers through his dark, neatly cropped hair. He opened his mouth then shut it and turned his head, staring into the distance as if he could find the words there to explain his son's odd behavior.

"I'm Sarah Worley." She smiled when he looked at her again.

He cleared his throat. "My deepest apologies, Miss Worley. I'm Stephen Barlow, and this is my son, Phillip."

Sarah glanced at a bench in front of the store. "Maybe we could sit for a minute and clear things up?"

He nodded. "Of course. Come on, Phillip. Let's have a seat on this bench."

"Is she coming too?"

Sarah smiled at the boy. "Yes, I am."

He wiped his dark eyes then took hold of her hand, stealing a piece of Sarah's heart. Again, Mr. Barlow flashed an apology.

"It's fine. Honestly, I don't mind."

"You're very kind, Miss—or is it Mrs.—Worley?"

Sarah sat, and Phillip scrambled up next to her, leaving his father standing. Not wanting to stare up at the tall man, she scooted over, pulling Phillip with her. Judging by his small size, she guessed he was a little younger than Cody, around five years old. "It's Miss Worley."

Mr. Barlow sat on the very edge of the bench. His right knee bounced. He flicked a quick glance at his son, who leaned against her arm, his left thumb in his mouth. The man's lips pursed in obvious concern, probably for his son as well as her. "I. . ." He cleared his throat. "My wife, Rosalia. . ." He looked away again then sighed loudly. "She died almost two months ago."

Phillip started humming and swinging one foot.

"She had gone back east to visit her parents and suddenly took sick. I've taken Phillip back there, but he's having a difficult time believing she will not be returning."

The poor child. She ran her hand down Phillip's cheek as he gazed up at her adoringly. This wasn't good. Surely he could tell she wasn't truly his mother. She glanced up at Mr. Barlow and mouthed, "What do we do?"

He shook his head and shrugged. "This never happened before."

Holding her hand gently against Phillip's ear, she whispered, "Do I truly look like your wife?"

Mr. Barlow's dark brown eyes warmed. "Actually, you do. Her eyes weren't black like yours, but they were brown, although I'd say her hair was a shade or two darker—and curlier. Rosalia was almost full-blooded Italian. Very beautiful. . .as you are."

Uncomfortable for the first time, she glanced down the street, hoping to see Luke returning. How was she going to untangle herself from Phillip without wounding the poor boy emotionally? He'd been through so much already.

Mr. Barlow held his hat in front of him. "May I ask what you're doing here in Anadarko? Do you have family that won a claim or bought land in the auction?"

She smiled again. "Actually, *I* won a claim. It's not far from town."

His mouth dropped open, but he quickly recovered from his surprise. "Congratulations. You sure don't look like a farmer or rancher. What do you plan to do with all that land?"

"I haven't decided yet. My first order of business is to get my house built."

He lifted one eyebrow. "Surely you're not constructing it yourself?"

Sarah shook her head. "I know my limitations, sir. I hired a

131

crew to work on it." She glanced down at Phillip. His leg had stilled, and he felt heavy against her arm. "I do believe your son has fallen asleep."

Mr. Barlow heaved another sigh. "He's had trouble sleeping since Rosalia's death. He wakes up screaming quite frequently. He hasn't adjusted to living in a tent here, but I don't want to send him home with my aunt, who cares for him while I'm working. I can't leave, either. I'm the engineer tasked with overseeing the construction of the depot."

Her heart ached for the father and son. "I will pray for you both."

"Thank you. That's very kind of you." He stood and bent down. "Let's hope he doesn't awaken until you make your getaway."

"What will you tell him?"

He lifted his gaze to her, and her heart pounded at the intensity in them. It had to be because he was only inches away. She could feel his warm breath on her face. "The truth," he said softly. "But if you would consider joining us for a meal in the tent for railroad workers, I'd be truly grateful."

A meal? Was he asking for Phillip's well-being or his own? "To what end, sir?"

"To help my son, Miss Worley. I believe seeing you again will help him adjust to his mother being gone, and knowing that he will see you again will make my discussion with him go much easier. It was our good fortune to cross paths with you today."

She searched his gaze, looking for an ulterior motive. Surely a man who'd so recently lost his wife wouldn't be looking for another one. He seemed like a nice gentleman, but she learned from her own father that men could easily wear masks when they wanted to impress someone. Knowing they would meet in a public place and that Phillip would be there eased her concern. Maybe she should bring Cody along so the boys could play with one another. "All right. For Phillip's sake, I'll meet you for lunch this Friday at one, providing your aunt will be there."

Stephen Barlow's eyes twinkled, and a smile lifted one side of his mouth. Her heartbeat kicked up its pace. He certainly was a fine-looking man. He finally nodded and picked up his son. "For Phillip's sake."

"You're in for a surprise, Zelma." Sarah helped the older woman down the incline to the river. "Cody, you stay there until I can help you."

"I can cross by myself," the boy shouted.

"No, you wait."

"I wouldn't mind a soak in the water," Zelma said as she stepped to another flat rock, "if I didn't know I'd just get sweaty all over again later."

"Be careful crossing on these rocks. It's not deep here, but the surface of the rocks is a bit slippery because of the moss on them."

"All righty. Don't worry about me. A dunkin' won't hurt a thing."

It wasn't the dunking Sarah was concerned with but rather that the heavyset woman might twist her ankle or hurt some other part of her body if she fell. There was no way she could get Zelma out by herself.

She blew out a pent breath as they drew near to the farside. With a not-so-graceful leap, they made it onto the other bank of the river. "Be right back." She crossed the river again, thankful for the low water level, snagged Cody's hand, and then returned to the other side. What she needed was a bridge, especially if she decided to plant corn in this plot of land next spring. Tonight she'd tally up her money and see if she could afford to hire the Petersons to build one while they were here.

They walked about ten feet when Zelma stopped suddenly. "Land sakes! Is that a corn patch?"

Sarah smiled. "Surprise! Didn't you wonder where the corn came from that we ate the other night?"

"I just assumed you traded for it in town." Zelma turned toward her, eyes still wide. "How did it get here?"

"Someone planted it."

Hands on hips, Zelma narrowed her gaze, giving her the look she gave her sons when they didn't do something she'd told them to do. "I know that, but *who* planted it?"

"Pa said it was In'juns." Cody looked up to Sarah, his eyes wide, as if he thought he'd upset her. "Uh. . .not like you, Sarah, but wild In'juns."

Sarah smiled and ruffled his hair. "I knew what you meant. Jack thinks it was probably Kiowa or Apache who thought this land was part of their allotment. I guess there was some confusion about where the land was that belonged to the Indians and the land for the lottery. Thus a few lucky settlers arrived to find planted fields on their homesteads." Shall we see if there are any ears left? Much of it has been picked, but I hope we'll find a few stragglers that ripened late."

"That's wonderful for you, but I feel bad for those who did the work and don't get to reap the harvest." Zelma lifted the edge of her apron and wiped the sweat from her face.

"I do, too, but I believe they reaped the largest part of the harvest. Since I have no idea who the people are who planted it, I guess we'll enjoy the corn and pray that God will bless the hands that made it possible."

"Amen. Sounds like a right good idea to me. Let's get pickin'. My mouth is waterin' for some more of that sweet juiciness."

"Mine, too!" Cody shouted.

Sarah took his hand. "Let me show you how to tell when the corn is ready to be picked. "You see this fringy tassel? When it's all brown, it's ready. If it still has yellow or green in it, then don't pick it." She showed him how to pull down then lift up to break off the ear. Then she handed it to him. "You'll be our stacker. Go lay this on the ground over there, and we'll start a pile."

He jogged to the grass at the edge of the cornfield, set down the ear, and then hurried back to her, eager to help. He was such a good boy. Sarah muttered a prayer for God to bring Jack a good woman to mother the boy. Her thoughts swiveled to Phillip, and she prayed for comfort and peace for the sad child.

Half an hour later, they'd made their way through the field. "It looks like we'll probably only get one more picking before the corn gives out."

Zelma nodded, pressing her fist into the middle of her back as they walked back to their pile of corn. "I think you're right. The field needs waterin'."

"I should have thought to bring a bucket."

"I'll go get one." Cody bounced on his toes.

"That's a wonderful idea. We can work on getting the corn across the river until you get back. I should have thought to bring something to haul the corn in, but I didn't really expect to find this much."

She helped Cody back across the water. "When you return, don't try to cross by yourself."

"I won't." The boy waved as he ran up the hill. Once on the other side, he'd be in view of the others, so she didn't follow him.

"He's a pleasant little boy." Zelma swished her hand in the river then scooped up a drink of the brown water.

Sarah was thirsty, too, but she preferred to drink from the barrel of rainwater she'd collected. "Cody is a good boy."

"Could I ask what happened to his ma?"

Sarah dropped down beside Zelma at the water's edge, relishing the canopy of shade overhead. She removed her bonnet, allowing the gentle breeze to cool her sweaty head. "Cora died last January in childbirth, along with her baby."

Zelma nodded. "It happens, far too often for my likin'."

Sarah closed her eyes, remembering the awful day. "It was terribly sad."

"It's the way of things out west. I lost two daughters and my youngest son when they was all small. The girls died of a fever, and my boy got a cut that didn't never heal. It was such a small cut, I didn't worry about it." She sighed and looked away. "It was my fault Petey died."

Sarah laid her hand around Zelma's shoulders. "Don't think that. It wasn't your fault. There's no way you could have known the cut was such a bad one."

"When you lose a child, a piece of your heart dies."

Sarah thought about how glum Jack had been those first months after losing Cora and the baby. It *was* as if part of him had died. Thankfully, he believed in God, and the heavenly Father had brought him comfort and healing. Having Cody had helped, too. She couldn't imagine the hurt of losing a child. What had her mother felt when Sarah's father took her away? Had she experienced a deep sense of loss? Or was she relieved that Sarah wouldn't be alone after her death? Did her mother know what kind of place her father was taking her to? Part of her was glad she hadn't witnessed her mother's death, but another part wished she'd been there so her mother hadn't had to die alone. But at only twelve, she'd had no say in the matter. Her father had ignored her cries to stay.

"My boys are all sweet on you. Well, all 'cept Amos, 'cause he's married. Sure would be nice if you was to marry one of 'em."

Sarah's gaze zipped to Zelma's. "Uh. . .I don't know what to say. I have to tell you that I honestly don't know if I'll ever marry."

Zelma blinked her eyes several times as if trying to make sense of Sarah's comment. "Why ever not? A pretty gal like you deserves to find a good man and be happy. I didn't think my boys had much chance with you because of the way that good-lookin' Luke stares at you. I figured he already owned your heart."

Sarah stared at the slow-moving water. The sun glistened off it as it bubbled across the rocks. "I do care for Luke. He's my best friend next to Lara and Jo, but like I said, I don't know if I will marry."

Clicking her tongue, Zelma shook her head as if it were the oddest thing she'd ever heard. "A good man can make a woman very happy. And I can't begin to explain the joy of holdin' your brand-spankin'-new child in your arms and seeing the way your husband's eyes light up when he looks at you and the babe."

A deep longing to experience that very thing spiraled through Sarah, surprising her. She'd never thought much about being a mother, although the idea of having a child of her own was appealing. But she could never have that child unless she married. For some reason, the idea of doing so didn't seem as awful as it once did.

In Gabe and Jack, she'd learned that men could love their women and be kind, caring, and protective. Luke had taught her that men could be fun and make you laugh. Those sure weren't things she'd learned from her father. Although, to be fair, she had to give Pete Worley some credit. After finding her when she ran away and allowing her to live with the Coulters, he'd sold his bordello and moved onto a small ranch. She'd never been close to the man who'd taken her from her mother, but she was grateful for the way he'd supported her financially the past eight years and made the dream of owning her own home a reality.

The idea of marrying and living with a man had some merit, but she wasn't sure she was ready. For now, she was happy living on her land and dreaming of moving into her house.

Luke's smiling face barged into her thoughts, followed by Stephen Barlow's troubled one. She'd never actually prayed about marriage. Could it be that God wanted her to consider it more than she previously had? She blew out a sigh, drawing a curious glance from Zelma.

She supposed she could at least pray about it.

What could it hurt?

⌒

Luke reined Golden Boy down the hill to the banks of the river. Jack rode up beside him and stopped, allowing his horse to drink, too. "You reckon this is a branch of the Washita River?"

Jack stared for a moment then shook his head. "Naw. My guess would be it's the Canadian."

"We've ridden that far north?" They'd hoped to find some game, but the pickings had been slim so far.

"Might be a good idea to get Sarah a dog."

Luke gave his friend a long look. "Where'd that thought come from?"

Jack shrugged. "I'm surprised you didn't think of it first. Once we're gone, she'll be alone. A dog would be good protection and could warn her of trouble coming her way."

The thought of Sarah in trouble made his gut churn. He clenched his teeth, blowing long breaths out his nose. "I don't want to think about that."

"What? Gettin' a dog?"

"No. Sarah in trouble."

Jack rubbed the back of his neck. "It's kind of hard not to with her living alone like she plans. I've met a few of her neighbors, and they seem like decent folk, but I worry about her living by herself."

"How come women are so stubborn?"

Jack barked a laugh that made Golden Boy jerk his head. "You'll be the richest man in the world if you can find the answer to that question, my friend."

"Why can't she see that I care for her?" Luke didn't like talking about his feelings, but Jack was his friend and easy to confide in. And if he didn't talk to someone, he feared he'd go loco one day, worrying about Sarah.

"Have you ever come right out and told her?"

"I asked her to marry me. Isn't that plain enough?"

Jack shook his head. "Not to a woman. They need to know you love them. That you'll always be there to protect them, listen to their troubles, and allow them to cry on your shoulder while you keep your trap shut, when all you want to do is flee the cabin and go herdin' cattle or huntin'."

Luke nudged Golden Boy forward. "Dealin' with women folks sure is complicated."

"That's certainly an understatement."

"You think you'll ever get married again?"

After a moment, Jack shrugged. "I guess I would if God sent me another good woman. I hate for Cody to grow up without a ma, and besides, I wouldn't mind havin' a few more young'uns."

"That would be nice. I hope it happens." Luke knew how broken up his friend had been over losing his wife and baby. It was good to hear him thinking of moving on, especially for his son's sake.

He studied the shallow valley they'd ridden into, searching for food. Over the years he'd given little thought to marriage and having children, but ever since he'd had his thirtieth birthday, something had shifted inside him. He had a longing to settle down, a desire to marry Sarah and raise a family. Too bad she wasn't interested in the same thing. All she cared about was her house.

Well, she'd soon have it, and then he'd have a huge decision if he still hadn't found a lot in town to buy. He wasn't cut out to be a deliveryman or to work in a hardware store for long. He needed to be outside, enjoying God's creation. He feared the day would come when he'd have to ride off and leave Sarah here.

How in the world was he going to do that?

Jack shot a look his way. "Have you noticed how those three Peterson men watch Sarah? If you're not careful, one of them might steal her away."

Luke grunted. He'd noticed the looks, and they made his blood boil. "You think those fellows have more on their minds than lookin' at a pretty woman?"

"Could be. They're all close to Sarah's age. The twins are older, but Johnny is about the same as her."

"So?"

"It'd be my guess they're looking for a woman to settle down with."

"Well, it won't be Sarah. Not if I have anything to say about it."

"Just don't drag your feet too long." Jack yanked his rifle out of his scabbard, cocked it, and fired. A fat turkey dropped to the ground about fifty feet from them.

Luke had been so caught up in his thoughts of Sarah that he'd forgotten he was supposed to be hunting. How was it a woman could control a man's mind, even when she was nowhere near him?

Chapter 11

I don't like this one bit. Who is this Stephen Barlow that he thinks he can order you to have lunch with him?" Luke sidled a sharp glance at Sarah that made it hard not to squirm.

"It wasn't like that."

"Then how was it? A woman doesn't eat lunch with a man she just met, especially by herself."

Luke's overprotectiveness was both endearing and annoying. "I'm meeting him for his son's sake. It has nothing to do with Mr. Barlow."

Luke guided the team into town. Both animals shook their heads and stretched their necks. Sarah reached over and squeezed his tight fist. "Relax, you're upsetting the horses."

He slumped in the seat. "Sorry."

"I told you what happened. How Phillip thought I was his mother. I don't understand why meeting with him and his father has you tied up in knots."

"It ain't right for a woman to meet a man alone when she doesn't know him. How do you know you can trust him?"

"Would you feel better if you tagged along?"

His relieved gaze shot to hers. "Yes."

She nibbled her lip, wishing she hadn't mentioned that. "I'm sorry, but I don't think that would be wise. And besides, Mr. Barlow's aunt will be there."

"Why don't you want me along?"

"It's not that, Luke. I'm only going because of Phillip. The poor boy has been through so much in losing his mother and not being able to accept she's gone for good. Then he saw me and thought she'd returned. He was so happy then. I don't want to hurt him."

Luke steered the wagon to the side and stopped. "How would me going along bother the boy? I can see his pa not liking it, though."

She frowned. "What's that supposed to mean?"

"It means he's a lonely man who's found a woman similar-looking enough to his dead wife that his son thinks you're her. I can easily see him wanting to solve his son's problems by keepin' you around."

"Oh for heaven's sake." She bolted to her feet and proceeded to climb down—not nearly as easy a thing to do gracefully as when Luke lifted her to the ground. Her irritation with him grew. Who made him her protector? She was a grown woman and able to make her own decisions. "I'm going to lunch—alone."

When he opened his mouth, she held up one hand. "Don't say a word." Then she spun and left him standing where he was. She could feel his gaze on her back, but she didn't slow her steps.

Ever since they'd left the ranch, Luke had stuck closer than a sandbur, and she was getting tired of it. Even the closest of friends crossed the line sometimes—and Luke had just done that.

She'd be glad when her house was done and he and Jack returned home. At least she hoped Luke would go back to the ranch. She couldn't stand the thought of him hovering around her all the time if he happened to buy a lot and live here. She would have no peace.

As she drew near the area where the depot was being constructed, her steps slowed. Hammering and sawing drowned out the noise of the town. Several tents sat on the far side of the tracks, so she headed that way. A group of men entered the largest tent, which was surrounded by numerous other ones. It must be the one where the railroad crew ate. She started for it.

"Miss Worley!"

Slowing her steps, she turned toward the voice. "Mr. Barlow."

He hurried to her side and offered his arm. "May I assist you?"

"Thank you, but that isn't necessary."

"Very well." He held out his hand, indicating for her to follow a path to the left—away from the large tent.

"Where are we going?"

"To get Phillip at my tent, and then we'll eat by the river. It's much preferable to the awful noise of the food tent. We wouldn't be able to hear one another talk, and besides, the men would all be late getting back to work because they wouldn't be able to take their eyes off of you." His dark eyes twinkled, but she saw no guile in them.

Although she'd prefer to dine in public, at least they would be outside for all to see. So what harm could come from it? "All right."

They passed close to fifty two-man tents and then turned onto a trail leading to a larger one staked in a grove of trees. Behind it was a smaller tent but bigger than the two-man ones. Phillip paced out front. He looked up, spied them, and broke into a run. "They're here!"

An older woman with gray hair stepped through the tent opening and gazed their way. She frowned when Phillip rushed up to her and fell against Sarah's skirts, hugging her. Sarah patted the boy's head, unsure of what to say to him. Had his father explained she wasn't his mother?

The older woman approached. Mr. Barlow smiled at her. "This is my aunt, Miss Esther Barlow. She's caring for Phillip while we're here in Anadarko."

Sarah smiled. "A pleasure to meet you Miss Barlow."

The woman nodded but didn't return the greeting. She stood back watching them.

Mr. Barlow cleared his throat. "Phillip, would you please show Miss Worley where we'll be eating?"

"Yes, Pa." The boy stepped back and took hold of Sarah's hand. "It's this way."

She allowed him to lead her down a faint path, through a copse of trees, to the river's edge. An already set table covered in a white tablecloth and pretty dishes with a blue floral pattern sat on a level piece of ground, only fifteen feet from the banks of the winding Washita River. "Why, this is lovely."

Mr. Barlow pulled out a chair for her. "I'm glad you think so. We prefer to dine here when the weather cooperates rather than in the hot tent with men who've been working hard outside all day—if you catch my meaning."

Miss Barlow approached the table, her features pinched. "Honestly, Stephen. That is not appropriate table conversation."

He gave a quick bow then pulled out a seat for her across from Sarah. "My apologies, Aunt Esther. I was merely explaining to Miss Worley."

"I'm certain she is able to understand without you going into details."

Sarah turned her gaze on Phillip as he climbed into the chair on her right. "Do you like eating outside?"

He nodded. "Yes. I like it a lot. One time I saw a fish jump out of the water."

"You did? I bet that was exciting."

Miss Barlow harrumphed and laid her napkin in her lap.

Sarah resisted sighing. If the woman growled at every comment she made, this would be a long, unpleasant meal. Mr. Barlow lifted a basket off his chair and pulled out a platter of fried chicken, mashed turnips, green beans, and corn bread.

"There's pie for those who finish their food." His gaze was directed at his son.

"But I don't like turnips, Pa."

"Shh. . .don't complain." Miss Barlow tapped Phillip rather roughly on the arm.

He ducked his head and folded his hands, resting them on his lap. "Yes, ma'am."

Sarah halfway wished she'd allowed Luke to join them, but there wouldn't have been enough room. At least he probably could have wrangled a smile from Miss Barlow.

A gentle breeze swished the oak trees overhead, creating a dancing dappled pattern on the tablecloth. The water on her right flowed so quietly she could barely hear it.

"There, now." Mr. Barlow said as he set a crock of butter on the table. "I believe that's all of the meal. Shall we eat?"

Phillip, napkin tucked into the front of his shirt, rose onto his knees and passed his plate to his aunt as if he did the same thing at every meal. Instead of filling it, she handed it to Mr. Barlow, who added a bit of each item then leaned over and set the plate in front of his son. "Shall I dish up your plate or would you prefer to do it yourself, Miss Worley?"

She'd expected someone to bless the food before filling the plates, but no one had suggested it. "Please, go ahead, but don't give me too much."

He nodded. "It would be my pleasure." As he filled her plate, Aunt Esther grabbed her own and proceeded to stock it quite sufficiently. Evidently the woman liked to eat—or perhaps this meal was a bit fancier than the ones they normally enjoyed.

While Mr. Barlow took care of his own plate, Sarah ducked her head and asked God to bless her meal and their conversation today.

Mr. Barlow sat down and bit into a crunchy thigh then muttered, "Mmm. . . This tastes wonderful. We don't get chicken often."

"I recently purchased some hens and am looking forward to eating it again," Sarah said.

Aunt Esther dabbed her mouth and caught Sarah's eye. "Stephen says you won a homestead. Do you live there by yourself?"

"I will eventually, but right now, Jack, who is my adopted brother, is staying with me, along with his six-year-old son, Cody, and a friend." She decided it was best not to mention that her "friend" was another man. She had the feeling Aunt Esther wouldn't approve. "Mr. and Mrs. Peterson and their sons are also staying on my property while they build my house."

Aunt Esther clucked her tongue. "Young ladies are too forward these days. I can't imagine living on a homestead."

Mr. Barlow grinned and rolled his eyes, forcing Sarah to focus on her plate to avoid smiling. "I bet you never imagined you'd be living in a tent in a brand-new town, Aunt Esther."

The woman lifted her chin, staring at her nephew. "I wouldn't be if you had any sense. You should have left Phillip at home with your nanny."

"But I want to be here with Papa."

"And so you are. Eat your turnips, son."

Frowning, Phillip took a minuscule bite of the tablespoon of mashed turnips, licked the end of the spoon, and shuddered. Once again, she found herself fighting a smile. He reminded her of a tame version of Drew. Gabe and Lara had their hands full with that boy.

A wave of nostalgia washed over her. She'd never been away from the Coulter children for so long. She'd held each one with the exception of Michael on the day they'd been born, and they'd been so much a part of her life. She thought of them as her nieces and nephews, even though they weren't.

"Where do you hail from, Miss Worley?"

She looked at Aunt Esther. "The Oklahoma City area. I've lived on a ranch near Guthrie for the past eight years." What would the woman say if she knew Sarah had been born in the Indian Territory? No doubt she'd flee to her tent with her hands on her forehead in fear that Sarah would scalp her.

It mattered little to most white people that the Cherokee

tribe was one of the Five Civilized Tribes. Wouldn't the woman be surprised to learn that Sarah's ancestors had been lawyers who owned a huge plantation in Georgia before they'd been forced to abandon it by the government and travel on foot to Indian Territory?

Thankfully, the meal passed quickly and in relative silence with Mr. Barlow asking a question now and then and Phillip saying something. Finally, the dessert was finished, and Sarah was more than ready to leave. She failed to see how her being here had helped the boy, other than that he seemed to enjoy her presence.

Mr. Barlow placed his napkin beside his plate and leaned back in his chair. "Aunt Esther, would you please take Phillip for a walk so I can talk with Miss Worley privately?"

Puckering her lips, his aunt nodded. "Of course."

He rose and helped her from her chair. She cast a strange look at Sarah then snapped her fingers at Phillip. "Come along, boy. Don't dawdle."

"But I want to stay." His eyes glistened with unshed tears.

"Not today. Your father has business to discuss."

Phillip slid from his chair on Sarah's side rather than on his aunt's. "Will you come back again?"

Sarah's heart ached for him, but she had to be truthful. "I don't know."

"Phillip. Come." Aunt Esther snapped her fingers.

He fell against Sarah, giving her a hug, then rushed to his aunt's side. As they walked away, Phillip wiped his eyes and looked back at her over his shoulder. She waved at him, earning a smile. When they were out of earshot, she looked at Mr. Barlow. "So, what did you want to talk to me about?"

He steepled his fingers over his chest and glanced toward his son and aunt then back at her. "I'd like to hire you to spend time with Phillip."

⌒

"Spend time with Phillip? I don't understand." Sarah's heart raced. She glanced over to where Aunt Esther and Phillip walked, hoping they'd come back this way soon. It was inappropriate for her to be alone with the boy's father, especially since she barely knew him.

Mr. Barlow rubbed his hand across his chin. "As you well know, Phillip is attached to you."

"I beg to differ. He doesn't even know me."

"You remind him of his mother."

"But you did tell him that I'm not her, correct?"

A sad expression passed over Mr. Barlow's face for a moment. He must have loved his wife dearly. "I did. He didn't want to believe me, but Aunt Esther persuaded him to see the truth."

Sarah wondered just how the aunt managed that with a five-year-old.

"I've thought about it, and I think it would help Phillip to adjust to his mother's passing if you and he spent some time together."

Sarah shook her head. "I don't think that's wise. He'll only grow more attached if I do."

Mr. Barlow sighed and tapped his well-manicured fingernails on the tabletop. "I'm willing to pay you handsomely. My son's peace of mind is very important to me."

"What would you want me to do?"

He shrugged. "Read to him, maybe play a game or take him for a walk. Aunt Esther watches him as best she can, but it would do her good to have a break in the middle of the day."

"So, you'd want me to come after lunchtime?"

"If you would be agreeable to that."

"Every day?"

"No, of course not. Maybe two or three times a week. Would that work for you?"

She fiddled with the fringe on her napkin, which she'd placed on the table. "I honestly don't know. I don't have a regular schedule yet. I help Mrs. Peterson with the meals for the men building my house, but once it's done and they leave, I'll be setting up my home."

"Do you live far from town?"

She shook her head, not wanting to be specific about the location of her homestead. "No. Not all that far."

"So it wouldn't be a hardship to come to town on a regular basis?"

"It's hard for me to say since I don't know what all I'll be doing after my house is done. But *if* I decide to watch Phillip, it wouldn't be a hardship to get to town."

He nodded. "Good. So, is it settled?"

She turned and stood. "No, I'm afraid it isn't. I need some time to consider it and pray over the matter."

He rose, towering over her. "I see. I can pay you more, if that makes a difference."

"It's not about the money."

"Very well. Would you let me know when you've made a decision?"

"Yes, of course. I should be going."

"Let me escort you back through the tents."

"I would appreciate that." With her mind arguing between saying yes and turning him down, she kept pace with him. What could it hurt to spend time with Phillip? Wouldn't his father be working? And as long as Aunt Esther left them alone, the time would be pleasant. Still, she wouldn't give him an answer until she prayed about it and maybe even talked to Jack.

She knew well what Luke would have to say about the matter.

Luke kicked at a rock in the road, sending it skittering into the hoof of a horse slumbering at a hitching post. The horse crow hopped then looked back his way. "Sorry," he muttered.

He had half a mind to follow Sarah and see what this fellow she was meeting with looked like, but he didn't want to earn her ire. She was smart, but in many ways she was also naive. You'd think someone who'd lived in a brothel would have seen the worst in people and would be more cautious. But no, she just scurried off to meet this stranger because he had a little boy she was worried about.

He blew out a loud sigh. Might as well check the notices and see if any new ones had been posted. He shuffled toward the town square, feeling rather melancholy—not something he was used to experiencing.

Most of the time he worked from sunup to sundown, tending cattle, riding fence, and dealing with issues on Gabe's ranch. Working on Sarah's house had kept him busy part of the time, but it also left too much time to think—and stew over whether Sarah would ever come to care for him as he did her. And men weren't meant to stew. They were made for action. Gettin' things done.

"Lord, I need a lot to buy." Then he'd have plenty of work building his livery. He searched the trees, but all the notices had been removed.

An elderly man in cowboy gear hobbled his way. "Hey, there, young fella. If'n you're lookin' for them notices about lots for sale, try the land office."

Luke nodded at the man. "Much obliged."

He grinned and scratched his whiskery cheek. "Glad to he'p."

Shifting directions, Luke made a beeline for the land office. Today there was no line, so he walked through the open door.

A man looked up from the other side of the counter. "Can I help you?"

"I'm lookin' for the notices of lots for sale."

He pointed his thumb toward the wall to Luke's right. "Over there. But I'm fairly sure all but one or two of them have been sold."

He frowned. "Why are the notices still up if someone bought the lots?"

The man shrugged. "People forget to let us know about the sale."

Luke sighed and stared at the pieces of paper tacked to the wall. The wind blew through the open window, curling them. He flattened one, read it, and then several others. He remembered them all from before and doubted the land was still available. As he read the final notice, he sucked in a breath. The ad was one he hadn't seen before, and the lot was along the western side of town. He'd hoped for one on the northern boundary, but this one would work. He read the contact name: Mr. Herbert Brownlee. He tugged the paper off the wall and spun around. "You know where I can find Mr. Herbert Brownlee?"

"I think he owns the shoe store that opened up shop two streets to the east."

"I appreciate the information." He turned to leave.

"Wait a minute. Let me have that notice back."

Luke spun, settling a big grin on his face. "No need. I intend to buy this hunk of land."

The man narrowed his eyes at him. "If you end up not buying it, bring that back."

"Will do." Luke nodded, although he knew he wouldn't be back. He dropped his gaze to the advertisement. This was exactly what he'd been waiting on. Maybe he wouldn't have to work in Mr. Best's hardware store after all.

Excited for the first time since the lottery, he skirted around two wagons loaded with someone's belongings and hurried down the two streets the land agent had mentioned. Then he searched for the shoe shop. With most of the businesses still being in tents, they all looked the same unless they had a big sign or until you got right up on them and could peek inside. He passed one tent that was closed and continued checking the others as he came to them. When he reached the end of the street, he turned around and headed up the other side, hoping he'd simply missed the shoe store. He reached the beginning of the street and stopped, looking around.

The sounds of building echoed all around him. It wouldn't be long and people would be working from their brand-new buildings. And his would be one of them—if he could find Mr. Brownlee.

He turned in a circle, wondering where to check next.

"Can I help you find somethin', mister?" A man stood outside his tent, cutting stalks of broomcorn on a wooden table.

Luke crossed the street to talk to the broom maker. "I hope so. I'm lookin' for Herbert Brownlee, owner of a shoe shop."

The gray-haired man pointed a clump of broomcorn toward the tents in the middle of the street. "Down there. It's the tent that's closed."

"Closed! At midmornin'?"

The man lifted one shoulder. "There's no tellin' a baby when to come, whether it be midnight or midday."

Luke groaned. "I don't suppose you know when he'll open up again, do you?'

"Hard to say. Might depend on how his woman is doin'."

"If you see him again, will you tell him that Luke McNeil is interested in the lot he has for sale and to not sell it to anyone else until I return?"

"It ain't him that's sellin' it but his brother. That gent rode in on the train, took one look around, then told his brother he was leaving and to sell his lot."

Luke rubbed the back of his neck, hoping to relieve the tension of the ache building in his head. "How do you know all of this?"

The man grinned, revealing a wide gap between his two front teeth. "Kind of hard not to when they was standin' in the street, hollerin' at one other."

Luke glanced up to see where the sun was. He needed to head back to where he and Sarah were to meet. "I'll ride into town later and see if he's back. If he isn't, I'd appreciate it if you'd let him know of my interest when you next see him."

"I can do that. Hey, you don't need a broom, do ya? Business has been a bit slow."

Luke started walking. "Not today but maybe when I get settled."

He hated being so close to owning his town lot and still so far away. It was rotten luck that Mr. Brownlee had been gone. He returned to the meeting place and stood in the shade of a tall oak.

A frazzled looking man in a white shirt with black trousers and a black string tie and odd cap rushed past him and into the gun shop. He was close enough to hear the man call out, "Anyone in here named Luke McNeil?"

His heart bucked. What could the stranger want with him? Had something happened to Sarah? He pushed off from the tree, heading straight to the man. "I'm McNeil."

The wiry man spun around, looking relieved, and hurried toward him. "Do you know someone named Gabe?"

Luke nodded, wondering how the man knew his good friend. "I do."

The man glanced at the paper he carried—a telegram, if Luke wasn't mistaken. "What's his last name?"

Luke stiffened. "Why do you want to know?"

"Got a telegram from him, and I'm just making sure you're who you say you are."

"Coulter. His name is Gabe Coulter."

Nodding, the man looked at the paper again. "And where does he hail from."

"He has a ranch near Guthrie."

Continuing to nod, the man relaxed. "I suppose you are Mr. McNeil. Here." He shoved the telegram Luke's way.

Luke took it and placed a coin in the clerk's hand. Telegrams generally meant bad news. What had happened at the ranch that Gabe had to wire him about it?"

He unfolded the wrinkled paper.

GABE BROKE LEG. LUKE NEEDED AT RANCH.

Chapter 12

The morning after she had lunch with Mr. Barlow, Sarah watched with a heavy heart as Luke rode away on Golden Boy. He stopped at the edge of her property, turned back, and lifted his hat, waving it at her. He'd told her that he hated to leave with so many things up in the air, especially since he hadn't been able to secure the lot he'd wanted, but he owed Gabe. She lifted her hand in the air then dropped it back to her side. Part of her wanted to go with him. What if Lara needed her help with Gabe hurt and in bed?

She sighed. Leaving now was out of the question. Still, she hated seeing Luke go when things between them were unsettled, but she didn't know what to do about it.

The breakfast dishes were done, and turkey soup was simmering for their lunch. Zelma sat in a rocker under the shade of an elm tree, humming and doing her mending. Feeling out of sorts and not wanting to talk, Sarah grabbed a bucket and headed to the cornfield to see if any more ears were ready to be picked. She searched for Cody, hoping he might tag along, but he stood beside his father, proudly hammering nails into a plank of wood.

She stared at her house. The completed frame rose high above her, and the men were adding the clapboard on one side. Though they had made good headway, in her anxiousness to get settled, she wished they could work faster. She'd read in the newspaper recently that one day soon, a person would be able to order a kit house—a house that came with all the pieces, a list of instructions, and all a person had to do would be to assemble it. She shook her head as she angled down the path toward the river. "Imagine that. A house in a box—or maybe a railcar." She chuckled as she crossed the rocks in the shallow river to the cornfield.

Though still morning, the sun was shining in full force. She ducked her head, tugging the brim of her straw hat down to keep the blinding sunlight from her eyes. Today would be another scorcher. She longed for a nice, cooling rain, but with them often came the threat of lightning or even a tornado—something she definitely didn't want.

As she meandered through the cornfield, she prayed for Gabe—that God would heal his leg and help him through the pain and having to stay in bed. That was always a hard thing for him to do, though he'd rarely had to in the years she'd lived with the Coulter family. She missed them all so much and had been negligent at writing them. She would tend to that task this afternoon.

She reached for a plump ear with a brown tassel. A screech rang out from behind her. She pivoted so fast that she dropped the corn. She slapped her hand against her apron pocket, realizing she'd forgotten to grab her pistol. What could have made such an eerie sound?

Standing perfectly still, she listened for the noise over the stampeding of her heartbeat. It sounded like a cat of some kind. So far, no one she heard of had run across a bobcat or cougar, but she knew a wounded one could be dangerous. She wanted to yell for Jack, but it might alert the animal to where she was—if it didn't already know.

The frightening noise rang out again, raising the hairs on the back of her neck. She'd heard the cry of a bobcat and cougar before and the creepy howling of a pair of barn cats squaring off with their bone-chilling growls, but this sounded different. Afraid to move, she peered through the stalks, searching for the source of the noise. She longed for a big stick, but at least she had a heavy wooden bucket to lob at a creature. Maybe she should make some racket in hopes of scaring it away. That would be preferable to it coming after her.

She heard some strange breathing that sounded more like a person than an animal, but she couldn't let down her guard. Fortifying herself, she sucked in a loud breath. "Jack!" she hollered, at the same time bashing the bucket back and forth through the cornstalks. After a moment, she quieted, listening. The pounding of her heart echoed in her ears.

She hadn't heard anything run away, but all was quiet. And then a squeal rang out that sounded like a baby.

"Sarah!" Pounding footsteps came from the direction of the river, but she didn't turn or shout out. She kept her eyes aimed toward the creature hidden nearby. She heard splashing and then—bless him—Jack appeared in the corner of her eye, rifle in hand. Behind him, the twins drew to a halt. "What's wrong?"

"There's some kind of critter on the far side of the cornfield. Listen."

As they quieted, the cries continued.

"You stay here." Jack gave her a look that told her not to argue. "We'll check it out."

Sarah's frantic heartbeat slowed, but she stayed on guard. If the men spooked the cat—or whatever it was—it might charge her. If it did, it would have an encounter with a wild woman with a bucket.

She heard the men creeping through the brush, and then all was quiet.

"What in the—?" one of the twins said.

The caterwauling increased. Emboldened by the men's presence, she hurried between rows of corn and stepped out to where she could see them hunched over near the banks of the river.

Jack looked over his shoulder with a concerned expression and waved her to come to him. She jogged forward, stopping behind the twins. Whatever it was must be dying or not very dangerous, because they didn't seem afraid. The twins parted, allowing her to step up beside Jack, and she glanced down.

Her heart jolted once again, beating as fast as the wheels of a runaway wagon spun. She blinked, unable to believe what she was seeing.

Sarah squatted a few feet away from the filthy child—a little girl no older than two. The whimpering girl's dark blue eyes were wide with fear. Sarah longed to hold her—to comfort her—but she had to take things slowly. "Shh. . .you're all right."

Behind her, she motioned for the men to back away. She glanced at Jack. "See if you can find her mother. Maybe she's nearby but injured."

He nodded, and he and the Peterson twins moved away, mumbled for a moment, and then split up, each going a different direction. The girl watched them leave then turned her gaze back to Sarah.

"My name is Sarah, and that tall man was Jack. The other men are Zeke and Zach Peterson. They're helping to build my house." She felt a bit dim-witted yammering about such stuff to a young child, but the calmness of her voice seemed to soothe the girl. The poor thing was covered in dirt, and her garment, which looked more like a nightgown than a day dress, was ripped and grass-stained. She had scratches and mosquito bites on her arms and legs, and her face was splotchy from crying. Though she had blue eyes, one thing was obvious by her straight black hair and skin tone—she was part Indian.

The girl rubbed her eyes and yawned.

Sarah dared to take a step closer. "Are you sleepy, sweetheart? I bet you're hungry. Would you like something to eat?"

The girl stared at her, but Sarah couldn't tell if she understood anything she was saying. They had to get her help. Sarah was going to have to pick her up sooner or later.

Remembering how Lara comforted her children when they had been injured or were frightened, Sarah started humming the song "Rock of Ages." The girl watched her but no longer cried out. Would she let her hold her?

Still humming, she moved a few inches closer. She could easily touch the child, but she didn't. If only she'd brought some food with her, but she'd recently eaten and hadn't planned to be here long.

Moving slowly, she tugged her handkerchief from her pocket and wiped her own face. Then, ever so slowly, she reached out and wiped the tears from the girl's filthy cheek. She blinked several times but didn't pull away. Sarah swiped the fabric down the other cheek and smiled. "That's a little better. What we really need is a tub of water."

But even if the girl had a bath, they had no clothing to put on her. Her eyes had a glassy look, but Sarah didn't know if that was from crying, being scared, or being overly hungry as she most likely was. She'd felt warm, but then who knew how long she'd been out in the sun?

When the wind blew in her face, Sarah got a whiff of an odor so rancid, she nearly gagged. A dirty diaper, no doubt. She'd changed quite a few while helping Lara with her babies, but she sure didn't look forward to tending to this one.

This was getting them nowhere. *Lord, please help this child understand that I'm only trying to help her.*

She softly clapped her hands together and then held out her hands. "C'mon, sweetie, let's go get you cleaned up and find something for you to eat."

The girl studied her for a long moment then suddenly lurched to her feet and toddled to her. Sarah grabbed her before she could fall and lifted her as she stood, holding her away from her dress. The sagging diaper rested around the girl's knee. "First thing, let's get this nasty thing off of you. I think Zelma has an old tea towel that would better serve the purpose." She carried her toward the creek then stooped down and slid the diaper the rest of the way off.

She crossed to the other side to get away from the smell, and then she squatted beside the bank and smiled. "How about a bath?"

The girl glanced down at the water and kicked her feet as if she understood. Sarah dipped the child's legs in all the way up to her bottom. The girl mumbled something unintelligible then kicked one leg. Sarah made quick work of cleaning her backside; then she moved upstream and washed her hands and face. Her hair was matted and dirty, but she wasn't quite brave enough to tackle that for fear she'd upset the child.

With the worst of the grime gone, she cuddled the girl and carried her back to camp. Wouldn't Zelma be surprised? How could the poor thing have ended up alone and so far from anywhere? Where were her parents? Worst of all, had someone dumped her?

Sarah held her close, knowing how it felt to be torn away from one's mother. She felt a kinship with the toddler, not just because of their Indian heritage and because they'd both lost their mothers when they were young, but also because she was alone. Sarah had family and friends now, but she'd never forget those lonely, frightening nights when she'd lived at her father's bordello, locked alone in her room while drunken men raised a ruckus in another part of the big house.

As she approached their camp, she spied Zelma still in her rocker, but her head was hanging. The poor woman worked too hard caring for all her men. Cody sat about ten feet away, still playing with the hammer and nails. He looked up and waved then must have noticed the girl, because he hopped up and started for her.

Sarah glanced down and saw that the girl had fallen asleep. How long had she been out in the brush alone?

"Where'd you get that kid?" Cody stared up at her.

Zelma must have heard him, because she raised her head. Her eyes, which still were half-mast from sleep, suddenly shot open. She bounced up from her chair, dropping her mending on the ground. "Where in the world did you find that urchin?"

"Down near the cornfield. I thought she was a wildcat at first. She scared me half to death. It's a good thing I forgot my gun, or I might've shot her."

"Lord have mercy!" Zelma touched her hand to her chest. "Don't say such a thing." She hurried to her wagon, pulled out a worn quilt, and placed it on the ground beneath the tree and near her rocker.

Sarah laid the toddler down, but she awakened, her eyes wide. She squealed and clutched Sarah's dress so hard that Sarah had no choice but to draw her back against her chest. "It's all right, sweetie. I'm not leaving you."

Turning away, Zelma hurried to her cook wagon. She rustled around then pulled out a can of milk and opened it. She poured some in a tin mug and brought it to Sarah. "See if she'll drink some of this."

Sarah took the cup and held it up to the girl's mouth. She leaned forward and gulped a drink.

After a few more gulps, Zelma pulled Sarah's hand back. "Don't let her have too much. You don't want her gettin' all wamble-cropped and spewing it up. Who knows how long it's been since the child ate."

The girl fussed and reached for the cup. Zelma spun away then returned with a small piece of biscuit. "Would you like this, precious?"

She snatched it and shoved it in her mouth.

"The poor thing is starving." Zelma ran her hand down the girl's face, then her gaze shot to Sarah's. "Why, she's burnin' up. I'm surprised she has an appetite at all."

"What're you gonna do with her?" Cody rose on his tiptoes to see the girl better. "What's her name?"

"We don't know." Sarah gently pressed on his shoulder, pushing him back. "Don't get too close until we find out what's wrong with her."

Zelma tapped her lips with her forefinger. "I think you'd best take her to town. Fred said there's a couple of doctors that've hung out their shingles."

"Pa!" Cody charged toward Jack and the twins, who strode from the direction of the cornfield. "Sarah found a kid!"

She picked up the girl and walked out to meet them. "Did you find anything?"

Jack's pinched lips told her they did. He nodded, confirming her thought. "There is a camp a few hundred yards from where we found the youngster."

"And?" Sarah braced herself for bad news.

Zeke tugged off his hat. "The mother's gone."

Zach shook his head. "She was thin and looked like maybe she'd been sick. Sad thing, to die alone like that, worryin' about what will happen to your young'un."

"Are you sure she was alone? Were there any signs she might

have had a husband? And what if there were other children?"

Jack pressed Cody's head against his leg, as if needing the comfort. "There were no signs that a man had been there. We scoured the area and didn't see any footprints other than the little girl's. As far as we can tell, she's an orphan now."

Zeke ambled past Sarah toward the wagon. "We came back to fetch some shovels so we can bury the girl's mama."

Sarah walked over to Jack but stayed back so as not to get close to Cody. She didn't want him catching whatever the toddler had. "The girl's hot. Zelma thinks she's sick and that we need to take her to the doctor in town."

Jack nodded. "I'll hitch up the wagon." He looked sideways at Zach. "Can you take care of the woman's body?"

"Yep. We'll get Pa and Amos to help if we need them, but we prob'ly won't." He moseyed off toward his brother.

"Can I go to town with ya, Pa?"

Jack glanced at Sarah, and she shook her head. He knelt in front of his son. "We don't know what's wrong with the little girl, so it's best you stay here, if Mrs. Peterson doesn't mind."

"I don't," Zelma said.

"Aw. . . Yes, sir."

"How's the hammerin' going?" Jack stood and took hold of Cody's hand. "Show me what you've done before I have to go."

Zelma shuffled over to Sarah. "What are you gonna do about her?"

"I don't know." Sarah gazed down at the girl whose eyes had closed again.

"I know you have a big heart, but you don't want to get attached. You prob'ly shouldn't be thinkin' on keepin' her, if that's what you're doing."

Sarah nodded, her heart already entwining with the little one's. "I know, but right now, I'm all she has."

⌒

Carson stared out the window at the ever-growing town. At times the almost constant hammering grated on his nerves, but that was mainly due to the lack of business. Which in truth was a good thing. He needed patients in order to stay in business, but he couldn't wish ill on anyone.

He rose and walked to the door, opened it, and leaned against the jamb, watching a group of carpenters erecting the building across the street from his. So far, he'd stitched up a half dozen cuts, set two broken bones, and treated a couple of people with stomach ailments. His father would have been proud of him.

He missed sharing his successes with the man who'd taught him most of what he knew about medicine. If only that irate Indian hadn't stabbed his father after he'd failed to save the Indian's wife. He shook his head at the senseless loss. Thankfully, *he'd* had no encounters with any Indians. He wasn't sure how he would react. Hanging his head, he blew out a loud sigh. He didn't like feeling prejudice against Indians. His father could just as likely have been killed by a white man, but he hadn't been.

If not for that heinous event, Carson might still be working at his father's side in Tahlequah in the Indian Territory instead of living in Oklahoma Territory. He'd heard talk in the café he frequented of joining the two territories into a new state, but he doubted that would ever happen. There was too much animosity between Indians and the white settlers whom the government had allowed to move in on lands that had been promised to the Indians forever. Forever sure ended up being a short time. Until his father had been killed, Carson had been sympathetic to the Indian's plight.

His gaze was drawn to a wagon moving faster than most. It headed straight for his office then slowed and stopped in front of him. He turned and went to his wash station to clean his hands then dried them and rolled down his sleeves. A man and his wife rushed in. She carried a child he'd guess to be around two—a rather grubby-looking child. His lips tightened. He despised parents who didn't take steps to clean their children properly. Didn't they know that filth led to disease?

He glanced at the mother and was instantly struck with two thoughts—she was definitely part Indian, and she was quite lovely. She looked clean, so why was her child in such a state? He glanced at the father, who looked to be much older than his wife. The man nodded.

"My name's Jack Jensen, and this is Sarah. We think the little girl is sick."

"I'm Dr. Carson Worth. Follow me. We'll go into my exam room." He spun around quickly, struggling with his emotions. This woman might be Indian—or more likely *part* Indian—but she was not the person who murdered his father. So why did his hands shake? He'd like to think it had to do with the sad state of the child, but he knew that wasn't the whole of it.

"Set the child on the table, please, so I can examine her."

"I'll try, but she hasn't wanted me to put her down," Mrs. Jensen said. She turned the girl around, but when she tried to set her on the table, the girl lifted her legs and screeched, clinging to her mother. The woman looked at him with an apologetic expression.

"That's fine. You hold her, and I'll check her that way." He grabbed his stethoscope off his instrument tray and came around the table. His lips pursed at the child's matted hair. Pieces of grass had knotted in it, and although the girl's face and legs looked fairly clean in spite of the numerous insect bites on them, she wore a necklace of dirt and grime. The girl's dress was one of the filthiest he'd encountered as a doctor, although both parents were decently dressed. He clenched his jaw, resisting the urge to scold them. While a man could still be hung for stealing a horse, there were no laws to protect children from their unfit parents. Thankfully, the girl had a strong heartbeat, although one touch to her skin told him she was running a fever. Her glassy eyes were nearly the same color as her father's, but she got her dark skin tone from her mother.

"Has she been eating?"

"She ate a little this morning, and she was quite thirsty. The truth is—"

"That's all I needed to know." Carson didn't want to hear her excuses for neglecting her child—he'd heard them all before. He lifted up the girl's dress. "At least she doesn't have a rash. That's good. Can you get her to open her mouth?"

The woman glanced at her husband then shrugged. "I don't know." She gently tickled the girl's lower lip. The child intensely watched her mother. As soon as she opened her mouth a little, he stuck in a tongue depressor and took a quick look. The surprised girl didn't move for a moment, which gave him the time needed to check her, and then she gave a cough and pulled back.

"I see no spots in her throat. I believe this is merely a mild fever that should pass in a few days. Make sure to give her all she wants to drink—fresh water more so than milk. I'll give you a powder to give to her to help with the fever, and you can give her some weak willow bark tea." He turned away so they wouldn't see the irritation in his eyes, but he had trouble keeping it from his voice. He poured some phenacetin powder in a small container and sealed it, and then he removed a bottle of camphor from his cabinet. "I suggest giving the child a bath and then applying this camphor to help reduce itching from her numerous insect bites. It's possible your daughter got this fever from the bites or being allowed to crawl around in the dirt."

The woman gasped. Anger poured from her black eyes. "Now see here—"

His office door banged open. "Doc! Doc!"

"Excuse me for a moment." Dr. Worth slid a glance toward the couple then hurried from the room.

The stranger in the waiting room grabbed his coat sleeve. "Doc, you gotta hurry. The saw slipped, and my brother cut his leg. It's bleedin' bad."

"Let me get my bag." He dashed back to the exam room. "Sorry, but I must go." He handed Mr. Jensen the container with the powder and grabbed his medical bag. "If the child's fever isn't better in two days, bring her back. And if you have other children, keep them away from her until she's over the fever. Depending on what it is, it could spread quite easily."

Mr. Jensen nodded. "Thank you, Dr. Worth. How much do I owe you?"

"A dollar."

Mr. Jensen paid him, and then Carson rushed the couple out the door and locked it. He knew he hadn't been very polite, but someone had to watch out for the interests of the child. It suddenly dawned on him that the parents had never even said the girl's name. He'd have to write it down as Toddler Girl Jensen in his record books. Putting it from his mind, he picked up his pace to catch up with the man he was following.

Chapter 13

Sarah kept her mouth clamped shut until Jack had helped her into the wagon. "Of all the nerve. Dr. Worth, my foot. His name ought to be *Dr. Worthless*. Did you see how he looked at us?"

Jack ambled around the front of the wagon, checking the horses and their riggings, then climbed up beside her. "Don't be so rough on the man. I believe he thought we were unfit parents or something."

"Well, it's his own fault. I tried to explain that we'd just found her, but he cut me off."

"I'm sure the man has seen much mistreatment of children. He was only concerned for the girl. And I was about to explain what happened when that man rushed in and interrupted us."

"Obviously Dr. Worth had no concern for *our* feelings. I don't ever want to see that rude man again."

"We may have to if the medicine he gave us doesn't help her. I'm sure once he knows we found her, he'll treat us differently." He released the brake and clucked to the horses. "I reckon we should stop at one of the stores and pick up some things for her." He flicked a glance her way. "What do you want to do about her?"

"Since the town doesn't have a lawman, I suppose we should talk to someone in the army and let them know about the girl. Her family might be looking for her and her mother." Sarah laid her cheek against the top of the child's head. Poor thing. To lose her mother and be taken in by strangers, and to be sick on top of all that. She was a good girl, all things considered.

"Are you going to turn her over to the army?"

Sarah's mouth fell open. "Are you crazy?"

Jack chuckled. "Could be. I overheard a few church ladies murmuring about just that thing once."

"That's awful. Was it recently?"

He shook his head. "When I first started preachin'." He reached over and held out his index finger near the girl's hand, and she wrapped her tiny fingers around it. His smile took on a faraway look, as if he were remembering Cody doing the same thing when he was small. "Maybe you oughta think up something to call her. Kind of awkward always referring to her as 'the girl' all the time."

"That's true. I've actually been thinking about calling her Claire."

"That's a nice name."

"Then Claire it is—unless we learn differently." Sarah smiled and looked down at the girl, who stared at the horses. It almost felt as if they were a family, just the three of them. She thought of Luke and wondered if he'd made it back to the ranch yet. What would he say about Claire? He could surely make her laugh. He had that way about him.

"Did you find anything at the mother's campsite to indicate who she was?"

Jack shook his head. "She didn't have much. No papers with a name on them. Just a raggedy satchel with a few things for Claire and some personal items."

"It must have been dreadful for Claire's mother, knowing she was dying with no one to care for her child." Why hadn't she come to town for help? Or even crossed the river and come to Sarah's? Hadn't she been concerned for her daughter?

She gazed down at Claire. Her long lashes dipped as she studied the piece of biscuit Sarah had given her. How was she going to keep from getting attached to Claire? The girl was so quiet and sweet. Sarah gently worked her fingers through another of the tangles in Claire's hair and tossed aside a piece of grass. The doctor was correct that she needed a bath, but Sarah hadn't had time to give her a complete one and was afraid to after realizing she had a fever. She sure didn't want her to take a chill.

Jack stopped in front of a big tent. They climbed from the wagon and walked inside the tent store. All manner of scents—pickles, leather, spices, coffee—assailed Sarah's senses. There were more colors in here than in a field of wildflowers in springtime. She searched for the clothing section and made her way there. She would need yards of flannel for diapers, but it would take time to stitch hems in them, so she decided to also purchase several ready-made hand towels to use right away.

"Do you think she'd let me hold her so you can shop easier?"

"I don't know, but my arms sure are getting tired."

Jack shook a multicolored cloth ball he found that made a jingling sound. Claire watched with interest. "You want it?" He clapped his hands together then shook the ball again. "Come and get it."

Claire reached for the ball, and Jack deftly picked her up. He shook it, and she actually smiled, revealing her tiny teeth. Sarah blew out a relieved breath then rubbed her upper arms. On a table in front of her was a stack of baby gowns. She held up several and picked out two to purchase.

The clerk walked up to them. "Can I help you find anything?"

Sarah nodded. "We need a case of canned milk, if you have it."

"Do you know where we can purchase a milk cow?" Jack asked, shaking the ball again. Claire grabbed it and lifted it to her mouth.

The man rubbed his chin, looking up at the ceiling. "I have the milk, but I don't know about a cow. You might try one of the other stores."

"Do you have any dresses small enough to fit Claire?"

The man studied the girl for a moment. "I have a box of nice used clothing a woman brought in to trade earlier this week, but I haven't had time to look through it. You're welcome to do so, if you want to."

"That's sounds great. Thank you."

He disappeared for a moment then returned with a crate. "Help yourself."

"Thank you. While I look around, could you please cut me ten yards of white flannel?"

He nodded. "I'm happy to do so, but if you're planning to make diapers, I actually have some ready-made ones in stock."

"You do?" Sarah hadn't heard of such a thing, but then she rarely shopped for baby items. Instead, she usually helped Lara make things for her babies.

He nodded and walked past the fabric section. He pulled

a stack of cloth diapers from a shelf and set them on top of a table filled with men's pants. "I wasn't too sure of them at first, but several women who tried them were thrilled with how they worked. You still have to pin them on, but you won't need to stitch anything."

Sarah studied the padded piece of cloth. They looked to be more absorbent than mere flannel. She checked the price. They cost more than the flannel but less than the towels she'd planned to get. "I'd like a dozen and a half of these, please."

"Make it two, and I'll contribute the extra money. It's my little way of helping, and it will save you from having to wash as often." Jack rattled the toy ball, receiving a sleepy smile from Claire. "And add this to my tab."

"I like the idea of washing less often." Sarah fingered some pink cotton fabric. It would make a cute dress for Claire, but before she purchased fabric, she probably should look through the crate of used clothes. She couldn't afford to spend a lot of money on the child, especially not until she knew if she'd get to keep her. She'd buy what she needed for now, and if the girl's family didn't come for her, she could get more later.

She thumbed through the crate of mostly boys' and men's clothing, all of which held a strange odor. Wrinkling her nose, she shoved them back and walked over to the clerk. "I'd like to order two yards each of the pink cotton fabric and the green."

"I'll see to that right away."

While the clerk tended to the task, she chose some trim and buttons for the dresses. She could alternate the colors to make collars and cuffs.

Claire started to fuss. "I think she has a problem." Jack held

Claire away from him, jiggling her. She spied Sarah and held out her arms to her.

"Guess these diapers will come in handy." She grabbed one and took Claire to a corner and laid her down on the floor.

When she rose, holding the girl, Jack lifted the handle of a white enamelware pot with a lid and held it in front of her. "You might want to buy one of these to keep those smelly things in."

"That's a wonderful idea." She flashed him a wide grin. "You can grab that wet diaper on the floor and put it in there."

He pursed his lips to one side. "I walked right into that one, didn't I?"

She chuckled and ambled toward the front. They needed to finish up and get Claire home and in bed. But Sarah didn't have a bed for the child. How could she keep Claire from walking out of the tent while Sarah was sleeping? She shook her head, unable to think of a way to prevent that problem. Only one of many problems that was sure to arise with a young child to care for.

They finished paying for their supplies, and then Jack stopped at one of the army tents and left word about finding Claire and where she'd be in case someone came looking for her.

As they rode home, Sarah watched Claire fall asleep in her lap. Giving her up if her family came calling would be difficult, but so would keeping her. She knew well the challenges of raising children, and it was even harder for a woman who wasn't married. She'd seen the things Jo had struggled with when her son Jamie was little—before she married Baron.

Though it would make her life more difficult, she was more than willing to keep Claire, but was that the best thing for the girl? This was not a decision she could make without consulting

God. Sarah lifted her gaze to the sky.

Thy will, Lord, not my will.

Luke and two cowpokes rode in from a day of moving the main herd to a new section of grazing land. It had been a long, hot day, but for him, the day wasn't over. Lara had invited him to join them for supper, and then Gabe wanted to talk to him.

While he was happy to help out his old friend, he longed to be back with Sarah. Over two weeks had passed since he left Anadarko. By now, the sides of her house were surely finished, and the windows installed. Had she started moving in yet? He had hoped to be there to witness her dream come true, but he feared he would miss it.

Shorty, the cook for the cowboys, waddled out of the bunkhouse, carrying a bucket. He waved at them. "You eatin' with us tonight, Luke?"

He shook his head as he dismounted. "Nah. Gabe wants to talk to me."

"Lucky you." Shorty set the bucket below the pump. "I wish the boss wanted to gab with me so's I could eat some of Miss Lara's cookin'."

Luke chuckled. "That doesn't say much about the supper you're fixin', what with you being the cook and all."

Shorty shrugged. "I only know so many things to fix."

Tom and Slim dismounted.

"Yeah, like beans, stew, and pancakes." Tom led his horse to the trough.

Shorty glared at him. "I realize that a man likes to dine on somethin' different now and then, but I do the best I can."

"Yes, you do." Luke smiled at the riled cook then led Golden Boy to the trough and allowed him to drink. "Why don't you ask Lara for some ideas?"

Shorty looked as if he'd told him they'd run out of beans. "I cain't do that."

"Why not?"

"Well, she's a woman, fer one."

Luke chuckled and shook his head as he led his horse into the barn. "That she is—and she's a mighty good cook."

Shorty grumbled something he couldn't hear then started pumping water into his bucket.

Luke groomed his palomino and made quick order of cleaning up. He donned a fresh shirt then headed to the house. It seemed wrong that Sarah wouldn't be there to greet him. She'd lived there for nearly as long as he'd been at the ranch. He still remembered the day she arrived here with Jo. She'd quietly watched everyone with those dark eyes and disappeared upstairs the first chance she got.

It was her attraction to horses that drew them together. He'd made sure no one bothered her whenever she came to the barn, and they'd gradually become friends.

He strode up the kitchen porch steps and knocked on the door. A delicious aroma wafted out. Before he'd left for Anadarko, he would have walked on in, but it didn't seem right now for some reason.

Beth walked to the screen, her brown eyes lighting up. She pushed on the door. "Luke! Why are you knocking? Get on in here."

He stepped inside, removed his hat and hung it on a peg near the door, and then smiled at Beth, Gabe and Lara's eight-year-old daughter. "I declare, you've grown an inch since last time I saw you."

She laughed. "That was just yesterday."

He grinned and gently tugged her braid. "I know, squirt."

"Howdy, Luke." Drew, with a small wooden horse in his hand, waved at him from where he sat on the floor, stacking blocks with Missy.

Lara looked over from where she stirred something at the stove. "Dinner's almost done." Behind her on the far wall was the large table where he'd shared many meals with the family. For a long time, this had been his home, at least in his heart. "Gabe's in the parlor. Would you mind letting him know it's time to eat?"

He gave her a brief bow. "It'd be my pleasure, ma'am."

She tossed a tea towel at him. He caught it and laid it on the table as he passed by. He figured she'd probably need it for one of the young'uns during the meal. He reached the parlor and found Gabe staring out the large front window, holding a closed book in his lap. "You're lookin' bored. Must have been deep in thought, 'cause you didn't even hear me."

Gabe's gaze shot toward him. "I was thinking."

Luke walked in and dropped onto a side chair near his friend. Gabe's leg, stiff from the plaster cast, stuck out straight in front of him, his crutches leaning against the side of the settee.

"You missin' the work?"

"Of course, but it has been nice to be home more and to be able to enjoy my children. They're growing up so fast."

"It's about time for another one, isn't it?"

Gabe snorted a laugh. "Don't say that. Isn't four kids enough?"

"I'm not the person to ask. I'm halfway to becoming a geezer, and I'm not even married."

Gabe's expression sobered, his dark eyes staring. "About that. Anything new with Sarah?"

He pressed his lips together and shook his head. "Nope. The only thing she's focused on is her house."

Gabe reached into his pocket and drew out a paper that looked much like the telegram Luke had received a few weeks ago. "Not anymore. It seems she's taken in a foundling."

"What?!" Luke snatched the paper out of Gabe's hand and scoured the brief message.

ADOPTED ORPHAN GIRL. AGE 2. NEED CLOTHING. BEDDING.

Gabe stuck a back scratcher into the upper part of his cast and tugged it back and forth on his thigh. "Ah. . .that's better. This leg is about to itch me to death. Sarah wants Lara to send her some clothes. The ones Missy recently outgrew oughta fit the girl she took in."

"What girl? Where did Sarah find it? And why is she keeping it?"

"You know Sarah. She loves children."

Luke fell back into the chair, stunned. "How will she provide for it?"

Gabe's mouth twitched as if he was fighting a grin. "It's not an *it*, it's a *her*, in case you didn't catch that."

"So? How in the world will Sarah be able to support a kid?" She didn't even have a job, and he was sure that she'd used up most of the money her father had sent over the years to pay for her house and furnishings.

Gabe leaned back. "Have you considered that this might make your quest to marry her easier?"

Luke stared at his friend, not understanding his train of thought. "How do you figure?"

Gabe rubbed his chin. "Having a child will make it harder for Sarah to find work, like she had planned. She'll have to find someone who will let her bring the girl to work with her, find some sort of work she can do at home, or she'll have to hire someone to keep the child while she works. Seems to me the best solution to her problem is marriage."

Luke let that thought churn in his mind for a moment, and then he grinned. "You know, you might be right."

Now he was even more eager to get back to Anadarko before one of the Peterson men or some other yahoo stole Sarah's heart.

A week later, Sarah handed a seed to Claire. "Put it in the crevice like you did the other ones."

She bent over and dropped the pea seed in the indentation Sarah had made in the dirt. Claire looked up in expectation.

"Very good!" Sarah smiled and handed her another seed. Claire seemed to like things in order, which was good when it came to planting.

She studied her garden. Though it was late to be planting, she prayed that they'd have enough warm days so that she could harvest a few quick-growing crops. The onions, lettuce, chard, and beets were already planted. She only had the radish seeds and then the rhubarb and asparagus crowns to plant. If only there were more time, but for this winter, she'd have to lay in a good supply of smoked meat and canned goods to see her through. Next winter would be a different story, she hoped.

Claire tugged on Sarah's skirt, and she looked down to see her hand outstretched. She handed her another seed. "You're such a good helper."

So far Claire hadn't uttered a word. Sarah didn't know if she couldn't talk, or if the girl didn't understand English, or if the trauma of losing her mother and being alone for so long had taken away her ability to talk.

She brushed a hand across Claire's head. She was growing attached to the quiet child. How could she give up Claire if her father or other relatives ever showed up? They hadn't heard a peep from the army, but it took time for someone to realize a person was missing and then to track down where they were last. It could be weeks, even months, before anyone located Claire and learned about her mother's death.

Jack, with Cody's help, drove the wagon back from the river where they'd gone to fetch water for the garden. Two barrels sat in the rear of the wagon, water sloshing over the rim whenever the wheel dipped into a rut. "We got water." Cody waved and grinned. "I'm all wet."

She glanced down to see Claire's hand raised in greeting, the tiniest of smiles lifting her lips. The girl loved to tag along with Cody—the only person nearby who was close to her size.

"Let's cover the seeds with dirt so the fellows can water them." She bent down and brushed a layer of dirt over the tiny seeds. Claire patted the soil, not yet having gotten down the art of covering the seeds. Sarah smiled. In a way, Claire reminded her of herself. Sarah had worked hard to take care of her mother, and then later she'd worked at her father's bordello, where she did most of the cleaning and assisted the cook. She'd been quiet, knowing that it helped her to go unnoticed, which in turn meant less trouble.

At least she was doing the opposite of her father. Pete Worley had used women for his own purpose and to line his pockets. Sarah longed to help others. Maybe that was why God allowed her to win land so close to town, and perhaps that was why He brought Claire to her. Most people would have sent the young Indian girl to a foundlings' home, where she'd have been just one of many lonely children. Sarah could love her and give her a home—once it was complete.

Sarah stretched her back again and gazed heavenward. But what was God's purpose for bringing *her* here—to this particular piece of property? She'd seen His hand in giving her this land and providing the money she needed for her house, but what was she to do next?

Jack stood in the back of the buckboard, dipped a bucket in a barrel, and then handed it down to his son. Cody lugged the two inches of water toward her, sloshing liquid onto his boots. "Where do you want it?"

"How about I pour and you fetch?" She could imagine him smashing down the dirt and packing it so hard the seeds couldn't burst through.

"All right." He set the bucket down at the side of the garden then spun around to get more water. Claire toddled after him.

As Sarah poured the water along the row she'd just planted, she listened to the satisfying hammering coming from her house. Soon she and Claire would be able to move in. Behind her, along the river's edge, birds and locusts sang carefree tunes. The sun warmed her shoulders, filling her with peace. She emptied the bucket, checked to see that Claire was safe, and then blew out a sigh. "Why am I here, Lord? You allowed me to win this speck of land, but what am I to do with it? Reveal to me Your purpose for my life."

"Someone's coming." Jack set down a bucket he'd filled, hopped off the wagon, and lifted Claire into his arms. "Stay close to me, Cody, until we see who they are."

The boy was halfway to the garden, but he set down the bucket and trotted back to his pa. Jack handed Claire to his son then turned toward the men, keeping one hand on his gun. He might be a pastor—a peace-loving man—but he well knew the dangers that sometimes came with strangers.

Sarah pushed up the brim of her bonnet, staring at the two riders approaching. One was a soldier and the other a man in a suit. She sucked in a breath as her hands tightened on the bucket handle. Did they have news of Claire's relatives? Or was the man her father? Had he come to take her away?

Chapter 14

Sarah dusted off her hands then stopped at the bucket of water Cody had set down and dipped her dirty hands into it. As she walked over to Jack, she dried her hands on her apron. She tried not to show her nervousness, but she feared if the nicely dressed man laid claim on Claire, she might burst into tears. In the two weeks the child had lived with her, she'd already come to love her.

Claire spied her and emitted a squeal, reaching out her hands. In spite of the girl's small frame, Cody struggled to hang on to her. Sarah quickened her pace to his side and took her, desperately hoping this wouldn't be the last day they were together.

As she held her, Claire quieted and patted Sarah's back. She kissed the little girl's cheek, but her gaze was on the strangers.

The soldier nodded at Jack. "Is this the Worley homestead?"

"It is." Jack nodded but didn't look at Sarah. She knew he was protecting her and would want to know the men's business before revealing who she was.

The soldier turned his horse so that he was facing the well-dressed man. "Since it's not far to town, can you find your way back?"

"Yes. Thank you for the escort."

Tapping his heels to his horse's side, the soldier reined it back toward Anadarko.

The other man removed his hat and focused his gaze on her. "I'm Richard P. Morgan, and I write for the *Daily Oklahoman*, a newspaper out of Oklahoma City. As you are one of the few women whose names were drawn in the lottery, I'd like to interview you for our paper—that is, if in fact you are Miss Sarah Worley."

Her gaze shot to Jack's. He shrugged one shoulder and looked at her as if asking what to do. He would chase off the man if that's what she wanted, but she couldn't see what harm an interview would cause. "I am Miss Worley. Why don't you step down, Mr. Morgan, and let's find some shade to sit in."

He dismounted, and Jack walked over to him. "I'm Jack Jensen. Would you like me to see to your horse?"

Mr. Morgan gave him an odd look but nodded and handed Jack the reins. He walked toward Sarah.

Jack glanced over his shoulder. "Cody, come and help me, son."

She led her guest away from the clatter at the house and walked past the garden to the copse of trees lining the river. "There are no chairs here, but it will be quieter."

The man looked back at her house. "Nice place you're building here." He turned back, placing his hat on again, his lips twisted and a perplexed expression engulfed his face. "I have to admit that I'm confused."

"Oh? How so?" Sarah patted Claire's back. She was falling asleep, tired from their work in the garden. She caught a glimpse at the dirt under her fingernails and grimaced. Maybe

Mr. Morgan wouldn't notice.

"You're not married?"

"No, sir. I've never been married."

"Might I inquire who Mr. Jensen is and how he's related to you?"

She thought his question a bit rude but decided to answer. "He's my brother. His family took me in when I was twelve."

Mr. Morgan relaxed his stiff posture and smiled. "Ah, I see. I was hoping you weren't going to say he was your husband."

"And why would that matter?"

"In order to legally enter the lottery, a woman had to be unmarried—or at least no longer married." He pulled a pad of paper and a pencil from his pocket. "So the children are his?"

She started to answer but hesitated. If she told him about Claire's mother and how Sarah came to care for her, would he write about it? She gritted her teeth, knowing that if he did, Claire's family would be more likely to find her. But was it fair of her to hold on to the child if she had a father or grandparents searching for her? She knew the answer. She had to be honest and trust God. "Cody, the boy, is Jack's child, but not Claire."

Mr. Morgan's eyebrows shot up to his hat line.

Sarah held up one hand, palm out. "Hold on. She's not mine either. The truth is, I found her."

"*Found* her?" The man's pencil hovered over his paper.

She explained about hearing the strange noise near the cornfield, finding Claire, and then how the men had found her deceased mother.

"That's some story."

"It's not a story. It's the truth. We reported the incident to the army."

The man scribbled half a page of notes before looking up. "What do you plan on doing with the girl?"

"Keep her, of course, unless her family comes for her."

He stared at her, but she couldn't read his expression. "That's quite a noble endeavor for an unmarried woman, don't you think?"

She narrowed her eyes. "I fail to see how that's any of your business. Did you want to interview me or simply discover if I'm married or not? Because if that's your purpose, then I believe you got what you came for."

He ducked his head and scratched behind one ear. "I apologize, Miss Worley. It's the nature of a reporter to be curious."

Nosy was more like it. Cody trotted toward her with Jack following. "Pa wants to know if you want us to take Claire so you can talk."

"That would be nice. She's fallen asleep." And her arms were starting to ache. She handed the little girl to Jack. Claire wiggled a moment but relaxed against his chest. "You doin' all right here?"

Sarah glanced at Mr. Morgan. "Yes, I believe we are."

"Then I'll take her to Zelma and be right back."

Though Sarah was sure he said that for Mr. Morgan's benefit, knowing he was so conscientious about her well-being warmed her heart. "So, Miss Worley, could you tell me how you came to sign up for the lottery? I know that some women did, but there weren't all that many when compared to the number of men who did."

"It was simple, really. I'd lived on a ranch near Guthrie with Jack's sister, Lara Coulter, and her husband, Gabe, for eight years.

I recently began to feel it was time for a change, so I spent a lot of time in prayer and came to believe that it was God's will for me to register."

"I see. And did you register at Lawton or El Reno?"

"El Reno."

"Did you travel there alone?"

Again, she wondered what business that was of his but felt compelled to answer. "Jack escorted me. We took the train to El Reno, stayed several days at a hotel, registered, and then returned home."

"What do you plan to do with your land? One hundred sixty acres is a lot for one woman to manage, especially now that you have a child."

"You may have noticed that I have already planted a garden. Next year's will be much larger. More than likely, I will rent out some of the land, but I haven't decided for sure." Maybe Jack would decide to stay and raise horses. She hadn't minded being alone—at least she tried not to think about it—but things were different now that she had Claire. She wouldn't be as free to come and go with a little one in tow. And how would she get a job? She thought of Mr. Barlow's offer.

Mr. Morgan tapped his pad with his pencil, staring off in the distance. "Could you tell me a little about how you came to live with the Coulters?"

Her heart bucked. Her mind raced. What could she tell him? Certainly not what kind of business her father had been in when she'd lived with him.

"I. . .um. . .well, my mother died when I was young. I lived with my father for a short while, but that didn't work out, so I went to live with the Coulters. And it's the best thing that could have happened to me." He didn't need to know that she'd run away from her father, and she certainly didn't want that put into the paper.

After a bit of encouragement from Mr. Morgan, she agreed to pose for a photograph. She stood quietly while the camera captured her image. A sudden thought made her heart jolt, and she worked hard to maintain her neutral expression. Her father lived outside of Oklahoma City. What if Mr. Morgan tracked him down and found out he used to own a bordello?

Carson retied the gauze on Mr. Gibbons's burnt forearm. "That should hold you for a few more days. Remember, no cooking, and don't get the bandage wet."

The man nodded as he slid off the exam table. "Kind of hard for a cook not to work over a stove."

Carson wadded up the old bandage and dropped it in his waste bucket. "You can do some of the preparation if your arm doesn't hurt too much, but I'd prefer that you rest it so that it will heal. If you twist and turn it, breaking open the scabs, it will only take longer to heal over."

"I been takin' it easy, Doc. My daughter arrived from Tulsa and is helping Mrs. Gibbons in the café. I been catchin' up on my readin' and nappin'." He chuckled. He pulled a folded paper from the rear pocket of his trousers. "Nellie brought me this copy of the *Daily Oklahoman*. Have ya read it?"

Carson dried his hands on a clean towel. "Can't say as I have."

Mr. Gibbons held it out. "Take it. I've done read through it twice. I think I'll head over to one of the stores and see if they got some new books. I need me some new reading material."

He took the paper and nodded. "Thank you. Come back in three days unless you have problems."

"Will do." Mr. Gibbons waved with his good arm and headed out the open door. Suddenly he paused and turned back. "Oh hey, there's a story on page 4 about a woman from here that won a claim. You might like readin' that."

Carson set the newspaper on his desk and finished cleaning his examination area. He swept off the back porch then closed and locked the door. His stomach gurgled as he walked down the hall to the front of the office, reminding him that he should close up shop and find something to eat. At least he had something new to read.

He looked around, making sure everything was put away and the medical cabinets were locked, and then he snatched the paper off the desk and locked the office door. He headed over to the Gibbons Café. He liked both Frank and his wife Evelyn, but he'd yet to meet their daughter. As he crossed the street, he slowed and nodded to the Wheaten family. "How's little Abe's ankle?"

Mr. Wheaten shifted the four-year-old to his other arm. "Good. I'm havin' a right hard time keepin' him off of it."

"It's been—what—four days?"

Abigail Wheaten nodded. "Yes, sir."

"If it doesn't seem to hurt him, go ahead and let him walk, but no running or jumping until next week, all right?" He directed his question to Abe.

The boy smiled. "I can walk?"

"Yes, but no running."

"Or jumpin'. I heard." He wiggled and pushed against his father's chest. "Put me down, Pa."

"Wait until we get out of the middle of the road. Good to see you again, Dr. Worth."

"You, too." He continued the several blocks to the café, nodding or smiling whenever he encountered someone he'd met. It dawned on him that he was beginning to feel comfortable in this ever-changing town. He studied the landscape filled with tents, new buildings in various stages of creation, horses, wagons, and hundreds of people. Just a few weeks ago, all these people were somewhere else, but now they'd come together to create a new community—and he felt a part of it.

This place was home now. He still missed his father, but he had the satisfaction of knowing his father would be proud of what he'd accomplished and that he had his own medical practice. He might be disappointed that it wasn't in Indian Territory, but Carson couldn't go back there.

He turned into the café, sat down at an empty table, and stared out the window. His father had helped a woman with a difficult birth, but both she and the baby died. If the cord hadn't been wrapped around the baby's neck, perhaps Carson's father would still be alive. But he wasn't, because the distraught husband had killed him.

A woman he suspected was several years younger than him stopped beside the table. "What can I get for you, sir?"

He glanced at the menu written on a slate in chalk. "I'll have the stewed chicken and noodles and coffee."

She glanced at him with pretty hazel eyes. Her auburn hair was wrapped in a bun, with curly wisps framing her face. She looked more like her mother than Frank. "Would you like pie with that? All we have left is pecan."

"Pecan is fine."

He watched her bustle past the curtain separating the kitchen from the café and leaned back in his chair. He recognized the people at two of the five tables that were filled. Each day he met someone new. Maybe one day he'd make friends with someone his age who wasn't married and they could share a meal now and then. He got tired of eating alone.

Sighing, he opened the newspaper and scanned the front page. Most of the information referred to things happening in Oklahoma City—the murder of a cobbler, a fire that burned down half a block of businesses, an article about an opera singer coming to town, and two advertisements for baking powder and one for horse liniment. He flipped the pages until his gaze landed on the article near the bottom of page 4 that Frank had told him about. He started reading about a woman named Sarah Worley and how she was one of the few women to win a claim in the lottery. Then it told about how Miss Worley had found a young girl and taken her in. Her brother and the men helping to build her house had searched for the child's mother and found her dead. There was nothing to indicate the child's name or to whom she belonged. Miss Worley told the reporter she intended to keep the toddler girl she named Claire.

Carson pursed his lips as he flipped the page. Children weren't like stray animals. Not everyone had the patience to raise a child. He thought of the woman who'd brought in the dirty little girl last week—and then he was looking at her face on page 5. He blinked. The skin on his face tightened. Miss Worley was the woman with the dirty girl?

The waitress set down a plate of steaming chicken and noodles with peas and carrots in it. He realized at some point she'd brought his coffee and a basket of biscuits, too. "Um. . .thank you."

He reread the article. The man that had been with Miss Worley must have been her brother, but they didn't look a thing alike, other than they both had dark hair. Their last names weren't the same, either, but that was easy to explain if Mr. Jensen's father had died and his mother remarried.

Carson sat back, not really feeling hungry. He'd been rather rude to the couple, but in his own defense, he thought they'd been the girl's parents. Why hadn't they told him that they'd just found her? No wonder the child had so many insect bites. How many days had she wandered around on her own? It was a miracle that she was still alive and doing as well as she was.

He nibbled at a piece of chicken. Had he been less than fair because Miss Worley looked part Indian?

And who could fault him for thinking the dark-skinned child was hers? What were the odds of her finding a half-breed child? He supposed the girl could have been of some other ethnicity like Gypsy or Italian, but she had the look of an Indian child, except for her blue eyes.

He stirred the noodles then took another bite. The food tasted delicious, but he felt bad for the assumptions he'd made and the way he'd treated Miss Worley and her brother. A doctor was supposed to remain impartial. He'd sorely misjudged them and owed them an apology.

Sarah shook the diaper she'd just rinsed out and hung it on the line. Sweat dampened her bodice and back, making her clothes stick to her. "I think someone should designate summer as no-laundry season."

"My men would get rather ripe if that was the case." Zelma chuckled as she stirred the remaining diapers in the washtub. She grabbed a knife and the bar of soap from a basket of supplies and scraped some more shavings into the steaming water. "That's a good idea, except that little gal of yours would run clear out of diapers and clothes. You should let her run around diaperless in a gown like my boys did when they were young. It's easier to clean up the mess than washing diapers so often."

Sarah knew that was what women in the past did, but she found the idea repulsive and didn't want her new wooden floors soiled.

" 'Course, if we didn't wash all month, my men wouldn't be able to change clothes every week like they do now. Although, I reckon they could all jump in the river and wash themselves and their clothes at the same time." She chuckled. "Sure would save me lots of work."

"I wouldn't mind a soak in the river." She fished another diaper out of the rinse pot, twisted it, and hung it on the line Jack had strung between two trees. She covered her eyes and looked back toward the house. "You think I should check on Claire?"

"Stop your fussin' and let's get done. Jack said he'd let you know if 'n she woke up. Besides, we're nearly done."

"Right about now, I'm wishing I had another two dozen diapers. It would mean washing a lot less often."

"That's true." Zelma lifted a diaper from the soapy water and dropped it into the rinse pot. "But just think how long it would take to wash 'em all."

"That's a good point."

"If'n you don't wanna wash diapers, you'll hafta set out a chamber pot that little gal can use. Johnny's the only one of mine that wore diapers, and after he wet 'em, I just hung 'em up and let them dry out several times before I washed them."

Sarah cringed at that thought. And with this heat, the smell… she shuddered. Next time she went to town she'd buy a small chamber pot.

Beth had been out of diapers by the time she was two, but she hadn't been through everything that Claire had. And Sarah had no idea as to the girl's actual age. She had to be near or past two, because her second set of molars were nearly all in. She tossed the final diaper over the sagging line.

Sarah didn't have much when she was young, but she had a loving mother. At least she did until she was ten. Poor Claire would never even know her mother. Or her real name, her birthdate, or her parents' names. The thought made Sarah's heart ache for the little waif.

"Someone's coming." Zelma waved her hand toward the house then tossed a final shovelful of dirt onto the fire until a black plume of smoke was all that remained. She lifted her basket of supplies and the pot the soiled diapers had been in. I'm heading back to start supper. You think you could get one of the men to empty these wash pots? Don't do it yourself."

"Sure." She gazed toward the lone rider heading for the house. "I wonder who that is."

She reached for Zelma's basket. "Let me carry that."

"I probably should argue with you, but I'm so worn out that I don't have the strength." She handed Sarah the basket.

"If you'd like to rest, I can start the meal."

Zelma smiled. Her eyes looked tired, and she turned her head as she started to yawn. "You're gonna spoil me. Are you sure you don't wanna marry one of my boys? I'd sure like to keep you around."

As much as she liked Zelma, her stomach clenched at the thought of being stuck for life with one of the Peterson men. They'd all been nice to her, but if they didn't change their ways, they might never attract a woman. Imagine only changing clothes once a week, especially with the hot, dirty work they did. No wonder such a strong odor clung to them. At least Luke usually cleaned up before coming to eat and changed his clothing daily. Zach, Zeke, and Johnny weren't bad looking, and they worked hard, but they most certainly weren't the cleanest men she'd met. The whiff of them at supper, after a long day's work, nearly stole her appetite a few times. Did they notice that she always tried to sit upwind of them? As grateful as she was to them for building her house, she'd be glad to see the Peterson men leave, but she'd dearly miss Zelma. "I don't see that happening, but I do wish we were neighbors."

"Me, too." She covered her mouth as she yawned again. "I may have to take a short rest. It seems the older I get, the more I need 'em."

"Go ahead. You work hard and deserve a break. Just tell me what needs doing to start the meal."

"Lookie. That stranger's heading our way."

She gazed across the field to see the man had turned his horse away from the house and plodded toward them. Jack stood on the porch, arms crossed over his chest, watching.

As the rider neared, she tensed. "That's Dr. Worth. He's the rude man who treated Claire. What is *he* doing here?"

"Maybe he wanted to check on the girl and see how she's doin'."

More than likely, he'd come to make sure she hadn't mistreated her. She hadn't been mistaken about the harshness in his voice and the way he'd looked at her and Jack with scorn.

"Best you see what he wants and get it over with. I think I will lie down, but don't let me sleep too long."

Sarah nodded then glanced down at her damp clothing. She wasn't in a proper state to receive guests. The doctor had dismounted and walked toward her, his expression softer than she'd expected. Still, she lifted her chin. She wouldn't allow him to talk down to her again.

"Good day, ma'am." He removed his hat and nodded at Zelma as she passed. He turned his gaze on Sarah. "Afternoon, Miss Worley."

How was it he knew her name? He certainly hadn't asked that day they were in his office. "Claire is sleeping."

He smiled. "How is she doing?"

"Better. Her fever is gone, and her appetite is good."

"I'm glad to hear that." He curled the brim of his hat, lifting his gaze to hers, looking away, and then back. "I. . .uh. . .owe you an apology. I was quite rude to you and your brother the other day. I've already apologized to Mr. Jensen."

Sarah breathed in a sharp breath. If he'd said the sky was green, she wouldn't have been more surprised.

"Have you had any luck finding Claire's family?"

"How do you know about them?"

"I read the article about you in the *Daily Oklahoman* yesterday. There was a section that mentioned how you found the girl. I thought—" He looked away.

"I know what you thought."

He sighed. "I see all manner of situations, Miss Worley. I've had parents bring in sick children who look like they've barely had any care. Three-month-old babies who've never had a bath. Children with animal bites or burns. I've even seen people come into my office with dogs that were healthier than their children."

She couldn't imagine such a thing. "That's dreadful."

He nodded. "Yes, it is. I'm sorry that I thought ill of your parenting skills. I didn't realize you'd just found the girl. I should have applauded you for bringing her in to get checked instead of thinking ill of you and your brother."

Such a humbling apology was the last thing she'd expected from him. Perhaps she'd misjudged him as he had her. "I forgive you, Dr. Worth. I'm sorry for the bad things I thought of you, too."

He smiled. "Shall we start over?"

She shifted Zelma's basket to her other arm and returned his smile. "That sounds like a good idea."

"Would you allow me to carry that for you?" He returned his hat to his head and reached out his hand.

She passed him the basket and started walking toward their camp. "Thank you."

He fell in beside her, leading his horse. "Can I ask what you plan to do with Claire? The newspaper indicated you thought you might keep her."

"Yes, that's exactly what I plan to do."

"That's a big commitment for a woman who isn't married. Are you aware there's an orphanage in Oklahoma City? I can contact them on your behalf and see if they have room for the child."

Sarah stiffened. She couldn't believe the gall of the man. First he completely misjudged her, and now he was bordering on meddling. She'd just forgiven him, and already he was trying her patience. He certainly was mistaken if he thought he could talk her into giving up Claire. She paused to face him. "I just told you that I am keeping Claire—unless, of course, her family comes for her."

He pursed his lips. "Is your brother planning to live with you?"

"I hardly think that's any of your business."

He stopped and turned toward her. "I'm only thinking of you and the girl. Raising a child alone won't be easy, especially for a woman."

She lifted her eyebrows. "You think a man would have it easier?"

He shifted his feet and looked past her for a long moment. "Not necessarily. But it is easier for a man to find work and provide a living than it is for a woman."

She crossed her arms. "What makes you think I'm not wealthy?"

He shrugged, his blue-gray eyes capturing hers. "I doubt a wealthy woman would enter the lottery in hopes of winning a claim on virgin land. More than likely, she would buy a house in an established town or land that already had a house on it."

She lifted her chin. "Or maybe she wanted a brand-new house so she could make it exactly what she wanted it to be." She glanced at her house. The outside was complete, and the windows were in. The men were finishing the inside, and then the Petersons would leave, and she would move in.

Dr. Worth blew out a loud sigh. "Look, Miss Worley. I didn't come to argue with you. But you need to understand that orphaned children are not the same as stray animals. You can't just find one and decide to keep it."

"There are no laws against it that I've ever heard. Claire is better off with me than in some cold, dark orphanage where she'd be lonesome and scared and maybe mistreated. I take good care of her, and she's happy here. With God's help, we'll get by." She remembered her awful life at the bordello and how she'd learned at such a young age that men could abuse women. And there were some despicable men who even preyed on young children. At least Claire would be safe with her.

"I see your mind is made up. I honestly came here to apologize for the way I treated you that day in my office. I had no plans to talk about the girl. It's just that as a doctor, I've had parents bring in children in such a sad state that I didn't want to return the child. Some people are better off not being a parent."

Sarah stiffened. Was he referring to her or one of the parents he was talking about? "I thank you for your concern, but I can assure you, Dr. Worth, that Claire is in good hands. Jack had only found her a few hours before we brought her to you. I had no clothes to change her into and thought it was best to get her checked out by a doctor before I went shopping."

They neared the camp, and he handed back the basket. "I'm sorry for upsetting you. It certainly wasn't my intention." He tipped his hat and mounted his horse. "Good afternoon, Miss Worley."

She nodded a tight-lipped good-bye. She couldn't figure out the man.

Jack walked toward her, his gaze curious. "How did your visit with the doctor go?"

"He doesn't think I should keep Claire."

Jack didn't say anything. He just watched the doctor ride away. "He apologized to me and asked permission to talk to you." Jack flicked a humorous glance her way.

"You should have sent him packing."

Jack's lips twitched. "He must have really irritated you."

She punched him in the arm. "Stop laughing. It's not funny. He doesn't think I'd make a good mother."

"Did he say that?" Jack sobered, turning to face her.

"Not exactly in those words."

"He's probably just concerned for both you and Claire, as I am. It won't be easy raising her alone. At some point, you'll need to get a job or find a way to make an income. I know your father sends you money each month, but one day he won't be around to do so, and you need to plan ahead."

"Don't you think I've been stewing on that very thing?"

He nodded. "Yes. Knowing you, I'm sure you have. What options have you come up with?"

She nibbled on her lower lip. Would Mr. Barlow allow her to watch Phillip if she had to bring Claire? "I haven't settled on anything yet, but I have been tossing around ideas."

"That's good. I met your neighbors to the north. It's a young couple, Polly and George Endicott. They have a son who looks about three. Maybe she'd be willing to watch Claire if you do manage to find work."

"That's good to know. I should ride over and meet them soon." Sarah watched a pair of vultures circling in the direction the doctor rode. At least Dr. Worth was in good company.

Jack cleared his throat, drawing her gaze back to his. "I have to tell you that I don't like the idea of heading back to Gabe's ranch and leaving you here."

"Luke should be back before long."

Jack stared at her for a long moment. "True, but how long do you expect him to stick around unless you're willing to marry him? You need to put the poor man out of his misery. He loves you, Sarah."

"But I don't know if I love him—not in the way a woman should love the man she marries."

"You need to figure that out before it's too late and you lose him. He'd make a good father for Claire."

She swatted at a fly buzzing her face. "I know that. But you're aware of my past. I'd never seen a loving family until I came to Gabe and Lara's house. I just don't know if I trust my own heart. Marriage is for a lifetime, and now I have Claire to be concerned with."

He gave her a hug around the shoulders. "I guess it's time you do some praying, little sister."

She nodded. She didn't tell him that she had started praying about that very thing but still had no answer. She cared about Luke, but she also cared for Jack—in different ways.

Claire's cry alerted her that the girl was awake. She headed into camp and found her sitting on a blanket with Cody next to her, playing with his wooden animals. When Claire saw her, she smiled and lifted her arms. Sarah picked her up and cuddled her, relishing the way the little girl wrapped her arms around her neck and hugged her. Sarah's heart warmed. Now, this was love.

Chapter 15

Carson watched the buzzards circling in the clear blue sky off to his left as he rode back to town. He slapped the dangling reins against his leg, pulling back gently when his mount started to trot. He'd completely botched his apology to Miss Worley. He shouldn't have mentioned sending the child to the orphanage, but he was just trying to help. Too bad the stubborn woman wouldn't listen. He sighed.

In truth, Claire might be better off with her. He'd judged her parenting skills based on the condition Claire had been in the day they found her. Of course the girl would have been in a terrible state if she'd been wandering alone, as the paper had said. Thank the Lord she hadn't fallen into the river or encountered a wild creature.

Yes, he was concerned about Claire, but his real problem was that he was attracted to Miss Worley, and that was very disconcerting. She was part Indian, after all, and ever since his father's death, he'd had trouble not judging every Indian he saw. His father would have been sorely disappointed in his behavior. Carson never understood his father's love for the red-skinned people, although he'd been happy to work at his father's side, helping to care for them—at least until that fateful day.

God was surely disappointed in him, too. As a Christian, he knew God loved all men—and women—no matter their race. Miss Worley was no more responsible for his father's death than Claire or Jack. He gazed up at the sky. "Help me, Lord, not to judge all people of Indian blood because of one man's heinous mistake. I realize how irrational that is, but I can't seem to stop. I'm angry at my father's senseless murder. I don't know how to let go of my anger."

Could it be that coming to Anadarko was part of God's plan for him? He never would have made the move if not for his father's death. A pastor he'd heard once said that all our days are numbered, and only God knows that number. He said that no one could take your life before God's time for you to go. If that was true, then his father's death had been God's will.

He squeezed his eyes closed, trying to grasp the concept. A warm breeze caressed his face, almost as if God had blown a breath in his direction. He felt a freedom—a peace—that he hadn't felt in a long while. All this time he'd been angry and upset, trying to move on with his life on his own instead of turning to God.

As he rode down the streets of Anadarko, several people nodded while others lifted a hand, waving at him. He smiled back. He had a home here, and he was making friends. It was time he let go of the past and faced his future.

Instantly, his thoughts shot straight to Miss Worley. She certainly was pretty, with those black eyes glinting when she was upset. It still surprised him that he was drawn to her. He admired her desire to help the girl. He just hoped it wouldn't fade as she realized how much work was involved in raising a child. Too many people took in children like those on the orphan train or ones from an orphanage to make them personal slaves. He doubted that was Miss Worley's reason for taking in the young girl. Claire was too little to be of any help. In fact, she would add to Miss Worley's workload.

As he reached his small barn, he reined his horse to a stop and dismounted. He unfastened the cinch and tugged off the saddle. Perhaps there was something he could do to help out Miss Worley. Sometimes people paid him with food supplies he wasn't partial to, like turnips or beets. Chickens and sometimes a cow came his way, but he preferred to eat his chicken and beef prepared by the hands of someone else. Though he could do surgery on a person, he couldn't stand participating in slaughtering animals.

He dropped the saddle onto the wooden block, remembering something that happened years ago, way back before his mother died. At his mother's request, when he was just a child, he'd tried wringing a chicken's neck, but in the end he'd turned the bird loose and told her it had gotten away. That was one of the few times he'd lied to either of his parents. He smiled at the memory. After looking that poor ugly hen in the face, he just couldn't kill her. Even then he'd had a merciful heart. He preferred fixing injured animals and people.

He hadn't seen a milk cow at Miss Worley's place. He'd never taken one in trade, or that would be something he could pass on to her since he had no need for one. He'd recently accepted several smoked hams, but he could never eat that much pork. Maybe he could do some swapping for a goat. But then he'd have the issue of getting Miss Worley to accept it from him. He smiled. Where there was a will, there was a way.

☙

After a day of hard work at Sarah's house and enjoying a good supper that she and Mrs. Peterson had cooked, Jack rode into Anadarko. He'd put Cody to bed in Sarah's tent with Claire and gone for a ride. He couldn't explain his restlessness to Sarah when she'd asked where he was going so late in the day. Maybe she hadn't realized that it was eight months ago today that Cora had died.

He missed his wife and still didn't understand why God had taken her from him. It was probably just as well that he wasn't preaching at his church in Guthrie now. Those first sermons after her death had been difficult, and he feared his anger and confusion might have come through, even though he'd tried to hide it.

He rode down the quiet street, noting the changes. A week had passed since he'd been to town, and there were more completed buildings. Most were still raw wood, but a few had been painted. Plenty of tents remained, where people either lived or ran their business. There was something exciting about witnessing the birth of a town. Everyone was filled with hope.

He'd be lying if he said he was. In truth, he'd been disappointed at not winning land, and a time or two he'd been jealous of Sarah. He'd been hoping for a fresh start in a new place with not so many memories of Cora.

Jack nodded at a man who closed the door of his barbershop and started down the street. A hound dog that had been lying down in front of the building rose and stretched then followed the barber. The man had a slight resemblance to Gabe. His friend had encouraged him to take time away from the pulpit after Cora's death, but Jack hadn't wanted to create more havoc for his congregation.

Gabe told him he needed time to grieve Cora's death, but he'd told himself that he had to be strong for Cody. The boy hardly ever asked about his ma anymore. Did Cody remember how Cora had hummed as she worked around the house? Or that she never let him and Cody leave without kissing them both good-bye? Surely his son wouldn't forget the special cake and big to-do his mama had made for his birthday each year.

Jack's heart clenched. Would Cody remember any of that after a few years had gone by? He couldn't begrudge his son the fact that kids were more adaptable than adults.

A ruckus down the alley on his right made him slow his horse. A woman screamed, and a man who looked to be attacking her stumbled into Jack's view. He reined his horse, kicked him into a trot down the alley, and headed straight for the man.

The stranger looked up and let go of the woman, stepping back just as Jack's horse plowed into him. He fell onto his backside in a pile of debris, looking surprised. Jack jumped off and grabbed him by the collar. "A man's got no business roughing up a lady."

The man made a noise in the back of throat then spat to the side. "She ain't no lady."

Jack pulled the smelly drunk to his feet. "She's a woman, and as such, should be treated with respect."

"L'me go. You can have the trollop. She ain't worth fightin' over." The man pushed at Jack's chest, and he turned him loose. He waited until the man had gone inside what he just realized was a saloon. He'd been so deep in thought he hadn't noticed the tinny piano music or the raucous laughter.

He backed up his horse and looked at the woman for the first time. She wore the typical low-cut show dress of a saloon gal, revealing her—. He jerked up his gaze, trying to focus on her pretty but painted face and not anything lower. She swiped her hand across the corner of her mouth, where blood trickled down.

"Thank you for helpin' me, mister, but you shouldn't have gone to the trouble. I don't deserve to have a good man like you standin' up for the likes of me."

"Everyone deserves to be treated kindly, ma'am. Can I ask your name?"

"My real name is Charlotte VanBuren, but I ain't used it in a long while. Folks here call me Sadie."

"I'm Jack Jensen. If you want to leave this place, Miss VanBuren, I can help you."

She stared at him, blinking her eyes as if she wasn't sure he was real. Then she snorted. "There ain't nowhere else for a woman like me to go."

"Yes, there is. You don't have to live this life. I'll help you if you want to leave."

For a moment, her eyes lit with hope before they glassed over again. "I cain't leave. My little sister's in school, and I need my pay to keep her there." She ducked her head and then fluffed her overly short purple skirt. "I gotta keep her in school so she don't end up like me."

"There are other ways for a woman to make a living."

She huffed a crude laugh. "Not for one who cain't neither sew nor cook."

"You could learn."

She eyed him. "What are you? A preacher man?"

A grin tugged at his lips. "Sometimes."

"I ain't never heard of a *sometimes* preacher."

"I have a church back in the Guthrie area, but I'm here to help a family member get settled on their land."

She moved closer then ran her finger down the buttons of his shirt. She cocked her head. "You a drinkin' kind of preacher?"

Jack shook his head and stepped back. "No, ma'am. I'm not. If you're not interested in my help, I'd best be on my way." He tipped his hat. "Remember, God loves you as much as He does me or any other person in town. I'll be at this same spot this time next week. If you decide you want to leave this place, be here ready to go."

"She ain't goin' nowhere." A bald man with a bushy mustache stormed off the porch with another larger man following. The drunk he accosted shuffled out the door behind them with a smirk on his face.

"Get inside, Sadie," the first man said. "I don't pay you to stand out here and gab with strangers."

"You don't hardly pay me nuthin'."

He slapped the back of his hand against her cheek. Sadie gasped and pressed her palm to her face. She flashed Jack an apologetic glance then rushed up the steps and into the saloon. The man rounded on him. Too late, Jack realized the bigger man had crept around behind him. The giant grabbed Jack's arms, pulling them back. He struggled against the man's hold, but he couldn't break free.

"You ain't welcome here. I don't cotton to strangers comin' here and tryin' to steal my girls." He balled his fist and slugged Jack in the belly, forcing the breath from his lungs. Two more punches to his gut bent him over. The mustache man slugged him in the face, three times. Blood filled Jack's mouth and pain flooded his body. He hauled back and belted his fist against Jack's temple. His head was flung sideways, and the big man released his hold, allowing Jack to fall to the ground. He fought to keep conscious.

The drunk stumbled over and gave him a benign kick in the side, spilling some of his whisky onto Jack's shirt. He murmured a curse then headed back inside.

Nasty scents assaulted him as he lay in the filth of the street. Men often vomited or relieved themselves outside a saloon. Jack didn't want to think what he was lying in, but he couldn't move. Pain stabbed his belly and face. It looked like he had two horses waiting on him, but he knew that wasn't the case. He needed to get home. Sarah would be worried, as would Cody if he woke up and couldn't find him.

Another man exited the back door of the saloon, and Jack braced himself for more pain. The man bent down. "You think you can get up, mister? Sadie asked me to help you. Said you was just tryin' to help her, so I'm obliged for that. I'm rather partial to that gal."

Jack nodded and struggled to sit up. His gut screamed at him. He worked his jaw, glad it wasn't broken. The man helped him to his feet. Jack wobbled but managed to keep standing. He pressed his arm against his stomach to hold back the burning pain.

"You wanna walk to the doctor or ride?"

He shook his head. He needed to get back to Sarah's. "No doctor."

The man lifted one eyebrow. "I got orders to get you to a doctor. Sadie knows how Hamlin and his ogre can beat up a man."

"Fine. Take me to Dr. Worth then." Jack managed to climb onto his horse and hang on as the man led the gelding down the street. Things sure hadn't turned out well tonight. What would Sarah say when she saw him?

The crickets outside created a peaceful atmosphere as Sarah sat on her cot in her tent, praying for Jack to return soon to get Cody and take him to their tent. It wasn't until she'd finished her evening Bible reading that she realized what day this was—the day Cora had died eight months ago. No wonder Jack had been moping and restless much of the day. Most days troubles ran off him like water on oiled canvas, but not today.

As she ran her brush through her long hair, she wondered what it would be like to lose a spouse you loved so much. She'd never been in love. Hadn't ever known anyone who was until she met Gabe and Lara, whose love was still strong after twelve years of marriage. Then Jack had married Cora and brought her to live at the ranch. Sarah had watched their fresh, new love grow into something more mature and endless. But it had ended—when Cora died.

A much as she wanted her independence, a part of her longed to be loved as Gabe and Jack loved their wives. She thought about Luke, and an odd feeling stirred in the pit of her stomach. He asked her to marry him, but did he truly love her? They'd been friends for so long that it was hard to think of him as her husband, but on the other hand, it made her sad to think of not having him in her life at all.

Maybe after she moved into her house and realized that dream, she could think about marriage, especially if Claire's family never came for her. But she couldn't dwell on that right now. She was worried about Jack.

She set the brush on the crate she used for a table, walked to the tent's opening, and stared out. She yawned, longing to shed her clothing and don her nightgown, but she'd decided to wait until Jack had returned.

Behind her, Cody slept on a quilt next to Claire's pallet. Their soft breathing comforted her, making her feel not so alone. At least she'd have Claire to keep her company—she hoped—after Jack and Cody returned home. No one had come to claim the girl yet, but she knew that news traveled slowly, and it could take months before the child's family discovered her whereabouts. Sarah nibbled her lip. She didn't want to give up Claire. She'd already come to love her.

A noise drew her gaze outside again. She spun around and tugged the gun Luke had given her from her satchel. She could hear the jingle of harnesses drawing closer, which meant whoever had ridden onto her property wasn't Jack. But who could be out at this hour? She rushed back and turned down the lantern, hoping the stranger hadn't already crested the hill and seen it.

Her heart thudded as she listened to the vehicle draw nearer and nearer. She breathed in a ragged breath. A deep voice called, "Whoa."

Sarah tightened her grip on the pistol. She tried to call out, "Who's there?" but her voice wouldn't work.

"Miss Worley? It's Dr. Worth."

What was *he* doing here at this hour? In spite of the odd timing of his visit, she was relieved it wasn't a stranger who'd come calling.

"Your brother got into a fight and was injured. I've brought him home."

Sarah gasped. She wasn't sure what concerned her more—that Jack had been fighting or that he was injured. She shoved her gun back into the satchel, kicked the bag under her cot, and then grabbed the lantern. She flipped her hair over her shoulder, turned up the lantern, and rushed out of the tent.

Dr. Worth had climbed down from his buggy and was helping Jack descend on the passenger's side. He moved slowly as if in pain and grunted loudly when his feet hit the ground. What could have happened? She'd never known Jack to get in a brawl. Yes, his life had been rough before he became a Christian, but not since then. Not in all the years she'd known him had she ever seen him lose his temper. She hurried to his side and held up the lantern, unable to hold back her gasp at his swollen and cut face. And he reeked of whiskey. "Have you been drinking?"

"Of course not." He grunted out the words as if they cost him to utter them.

"He needs to lie down," Dr. Worth said. "Where is his tent?"

"About ten yards behind mine." She held up the lantern to light the way as the doctor assisted Jack.

She hurried inside the tent and lit Jack's lantern, setting hers on the crate beside it. The doctor helped Jack inside and lowered him to his cot.

He sat there, head hanging. "I feel as if I've been run down by a herd of stampeding cattle."

"What happened? Were you robbed? Can I get you anything?" Her heart ached at seeing him so battered.

The doctor touched her arm. "He could use some water. I have some powder I want him to take that will ensure he gets a good night's rest. The questions that I'm sure are running around in that pretty head of yours can wait until tomorrow."

She wanted to ask him how she was supposed to sleep when she had so many questions, but she didn't. "I'll get him a drink."

She grabbed her lantern and returned to her tent, where she kept a bucket of water in case she or Claire got thirsty overnight. As she filled her tin cup, the questions flooded her again. Was Jack so upset over this being the eight-month anniversary of Cora's death that he'd gone drinking? It seemed so inconceivable that she couldn't believe it was possible.

In Jack's tent, she handed Dr. Worth the cup. The doctor mixed in the powder then passed the cup to Jack. He grimaced as he slurped the water. His eye would surely blacken, and something was obviously wrong with his stomach, because he kept his hand pressed against it. He gave the cup back then slowly reclined, moaning as he did. He turned onto his side and curled up. The doctor tugged off Jack's boots. Sarah laid a light blanket over him then turned down the lantern.

She flipped her hair over her shoulder, grabbed her lantern, and walked the doctor back to his buggy. "What happened?"

"I don't know exactly. Jack didn't say much, I'm guessing because his mouth hurts." He inhaled a loud breath. "The man who helped him to my office said he'd been in a fight at one of the saloons. When I talked to him the other day, I didn't get the impression he was the kind of man who frequented those places."

"He's not." Sarah hated the way her voice rose in her defense of Jack. "He's a pastor and a good man."

Dr. Worth eyed her, as if he wasn't convinced.

"Look, Doctor, you don't know Jack, and I do. If he was at a saloon, he had a reason for being there."

"You and the children shouldn't be alone. Jack won't be any help should you have trouble. And a tent isn't exactly safe if a wild beast or someone bent on trouble came around."

"Are you trying to frighten me?" Sarah lifted her chin.

"No. I'm concerned for your safety."

She relaxed her spine. "I have a gun, and I know how to use it." She offered a teasing smile. "In fact, I had it pointed at you not too long ago."

His eyebrows lifted. "Is that a fact?"

"It is. Would you care for a cup of coffee before you ride back to town? It's probably not too warm, but we always keep a pot on the coals."

"No, thank you, but I would like a cup of water, if you don't mind. I've lived in both the Oklahoma and Indian Territories, and you'd think I'd be used to the heat by now."

"Early September is almost always hot, even this time of night, but give it another month, and things will start to cool down." She placed the lantern on a tree stump. "Excuse me while I get your water." She hurried into her tent, checked on the children, and dipped out another cup of water.

Outside, the light from the lantern created a warm glow, illuminating the doctor. Insects buzzed, and crickets and tree frogs serenaded them from the darkness outside the ring of light. Sarah handed the doctor the tin cup. "Thank you for bringing

Jack home. I was worried about him. It's not like him to ride out at twilight, but I'm sure he had his reasons." His mind had been on Cora, she was certain of it, but it wasn't her place to tell the doctor that bit of personal information.

He downed the water and handed the cup back. "If you'll show me where to put your brother's horse, I'll tend to him."

"I can do it. I'm sure you need to be on your way."

"I don't mind." He walked around to the back of the wagon and untied Jack's gelding. "Where does he go?"

"We just hobble them in a grassy patch since we don't have a corral built yet." They walked a short ways from the tent, and Dottie nickered to her. "This is fine. I can move him in the morning." She set the lantern down and found the leather ties in Jack's saddlebags. While the doctor removed the saddle and bridle, she hobbled the gelding. She patted his neck then picked up the bridle and lantern while Dr. Worth lugged the saddle and pad to Jack's tent.

"A smart man would have removed the saddle before taking the horse out to pasture."

Sarah smiled. "I suspect you're a smart man or you wouldn't be a doctor. I should have thought to take off the saddle, but this hasn't exactly been an ordinary evening."

"No, it hasn't. But I sure don't mind the company."

Sarah shot a quick glance at Dr. Worth. She certainly had misjudged him. "I can't tell you how much I appreciate that you brought Jack home instead of doing the easy thing and keeping him overnight at your office. I doubt I'd have slept a wink, not knowing where he was. And what would I have told Cody in the morning?"

"Cody?"

"He's Jack's son."

"Oh, that must have been the young boy I saw last time I was here."

"Yes." Sarah held back the tent flap so the doctor could deposit the tack in the tent.

"Thank you, again." She cleared her throat. "How much do I owe you for Jack's care?"

"Your brother already took care of that. I'll come back by tomorrow to see how he's faring."

"Can you tell me why he kept holding his stomach?"

"It's badly bruised, most likely as result of someone's fist pummeling him over and over."

Sarah gasped. "Poor Jack."

"You might want to reserve your sympathy, Miss Worley, until you learn the full truth of what happened."

Once again, Sarah stiffened. "No need for that. I know Jack. He's not a fighter."

Dr. Worth offered a sad smile in the flickering light of the lantern. "I hope, for your sake, you're right. Good evening." He tipped his hat and stepped up into his buggy.

She watched him go, both grateful to him and annoyed with him. But then, he didn't know Jack as she did. She smiled in the dark. He'd probably be coming out in the near future to apologize again.

Chapter 16

Carson guided his buggy toward town—at least he hoped he was headed in the right direction. He glanced at the rising moon on his left, making sure it stayed on the same side of the buggy. Thankfully, Sarah lived close to Anadarko. He should see some lights from town any minute.

As the buggy jostled across the barren land, his thoughts turned back to Sarah. His strong attraction to her surprised him, especially after their initial meeting. He'd been wrong that day and had let his prejudice overrule his normal compassion, but then he did think that she and Jack were not caring for Claire as they should be.

He smiled, remembering the stubborn tilt of Sarah's chin when she was angered and how her dark eyes sparked, even in just the light of the lantern. And the sight of her hair down, flowing clear to her waist like a dark velvet cape, had made his mouth go dry. He still thought she had no business living on the prairie, especially if her brother was going to leave her at night and get into fights. But Sarah was stubborn and determined.

He realized that his grip on the reins had tightened, and he forced himself to relax. That stubbornness he first despised would probably be the very thing that would help her make a home on her land. That was, if some unsavory man didn't take advantage of her one night while Jack was off gallivanting. The day Carson apologized for how he had misjudged Jack and his sister at their initial meeting, Jack had seemed understanding and forgiving. Was he doing the same thing again—misjudging Jack when he didn't know the whole story?

As he drove into town, he thought about Sarah and the children out there alone in nothing but a tent. He didn't like how unprotected they were with Jack passed out thanks to the laudanum Carson had given him for the pain. When he'd visited Sarah's previously, the family working on the barn had made camp near the river, but he hadn't seen or heard them tonight. Had they finished the house and left? It had been too dark to tell. But if the house was completed, why was Sarah still sleeping in the tent?

He slowed the horse as he pulled up in front of his office. Instead of driving around to the barn, he stopped. Tapping the seat, he thought over the plan that had taken root in his mind. He didn't like the idea of going into his house and sleeping in his bed when he was so edgy. There was only one thing he knew to do, so he set the brake, hopped down, and unlocked his office. He quickly penned a note concerning his whereabouts, tacked it to the front door, and locked it. He hurried upstairs, grabbed his quilt and pillow, and drove back to Sarah's.

After tending to his horse, he tossed his quilt down a proper distance from the tents and sat down, leaning against a tree. His rifle rested in his lap. No one would bother Sarah—or the children—now. He yawned. All was quiet except for the normal nighttime sounds. Before long, his eyelids felt as if they had weights on them. His mind blurred, and he caught himself dozing. Sitting up straighter, he concentrated his thoughts on the pretty woman who slept not far from him—surely that would keep him awake.

$\backsim$

Sarah's bed shook as if she were experiencing an earthquake.

"Wake up! Sarah! Didn't you hear me say there's a man sleeping outside?" On his knees, Cody bounced beside her on the bed. "C'mon, Sarah. Wake up."

A man? Outside? She bolted upright. Had Jack awakened and stumbled out of his tent and fallen?

Cody tugged on her hand. "Come and see."

Sarah glanced at Claire's pallet. The girl was sitting up, gnawing on a bread crust. She held it out, grinning, and rattled off a string of jabber. "Where did Claire get that bread?"

"I got it from Miss Zelma. You weren't awake yet, so I took care of Claire."

Sarah smiled and mussed his hair. "Could you watch her a bit longer while I check on the stranger?"

Cody nodded and dropped down in front of Claire.

Sarah glanced down at the dress she'd slept in, in case she needed to tend Jack, and now it was hopelessly wrinkled. She couldn't change with Cody there, so she peered out the tent flap. Claire whimpered. She wanted to pick her up, but she needed to see who was out there first. Sure enough, she could see the man Cody was talking about, near a tree. He looked as if he'd been sitting there, possibly leaning against the tree, but he was slumped over now. Past the man, an empty buggy sat.

She grabbed her satchel, carried it outside, and then removed her gun. She didn't want Cody to know where she kept it. Claire started fussing, and she could hear Cody sweet-talking her. She glanced down the hill to see where the Peterson men were, but none were in view.

Sarah crept over to the man. As she drew near, her heart beat faster. Suddenly she stopped as recognition dawned. Dr. Worth? What was *he* doing here? She stopped beside him and couldn't help staring for a moment. Since she'd been grown, she'd never seen a man sleeping before, except for Jack when he'd curled up in his bed last night. Dr. Worth's nut-brown hair was mussed, and his dark lashes fanned his tanned cheeks. His jaw was shadowed with whiskers. With his wire-framed glasses off and his body so relaxed, he looked less intimidating. She swallowed hard as she realized the inappropriateness of what she was doing. She bent down and shook his shoulder. "Wake up, Doctor."

He mumbled something she couldn't understand then rolled over onto his right side. Then he suddenly lurched to his feet and spun around, his hand forking his hair away from his eyes. Sarah jumped back and instinctively lifted the gun. As if unsure of what he was seeing, Dr. Worth bent down and grabbed his jacket then fished his glasses from a pocket and put them on. His gaze dropped to the gun, and then a charming grin lifted his lips. "Do you plan to shoot me, Miss Worley?"

"What? Um. . .no." She lowered her arm. "Why are you here?"

"To protect you and the children, of course." He grimaced and bent his body to one side as if stretching his muscles.

"You fell asleep on the job."

"Sarah! You all right?" She glanced over her shoulder and saw Zelma and the twins hurrying toward her.

"I'm fine."

Dr. Worth cleared his throat. "Are those the people who are building your house?"

"Yes. I told you I wasn't alone."

"But I thought. . . Well, I didn't see them last night, so I figured they'd left."

Zelma breathed heavily as she drew to a stop next to Sarah. "Cody said—a stranger was—sleepin' up here."

"He's not a stranger. Jack got roughed up last night when he went into town, and the doctor was kind enough to bring him home."

"And he stayed?" Zeke eyed the doctor like a man would a rabid coyote, his twin brother doing the same.

Sarah searched her mind for a reasonable reply. "Um. . . well, Jack was in pretty bad shape. What if he needed the doctor and he wasn't here?"

Zach scratched his whiskery face. "That does make sense. Sarah would've had to leave them young'uns and ride to town in the dark if Jack had needed the doctor."

"Or she could've come and got Ma. She knows as much as a doctor." Zeke eyed his brother.

Zelma looped an arm through each of her sons. "C'mon, you two. Things are fine here, and I've got breakfast halfway done. I need to get back to it. Sarah, bring the doctor over to eat. It's the least we can do for 'im."

Zelma almost forcibly tugged her sons toward her camp. They didn't look as willing to go as she did. Sarah was grateful for their concern but glad they had gone. She glanced down at her toes sticking out from beneath the hem of her skirt. She must look a fright. She hadn't fixed her hair or put on stockings and shoes. Feeling self-conscious, she looked at the doctor. "Thank you for watching over us, Dr. Worth. You're welcome to stay for breakfast if you like, but I need to return to my tent for a few minutes."

"I'll check on Mr. Jensen and then be on my way. I do appreciate the offer, though."

Sarah spun around, eager to get away from the confusing man. Why had he felt the need to protect them? Because he'd given Jack medicine that would make him sleep all night? It was a kind thing to do, although unnecessary. Still, his sacrifice of a decent night's sleep disarmed her. Would he do that for any of his patient's families? She doubted it, so why do it for her? Was it penitence because of how he'd treated her the first time they met?

Cody stepped out of the tent, lugging Claire. The girl grinned and waved, jumping so hard he almost dropped her. Sarah took Claire and gave her a hug then patted Cody on the head. "Come back in my tent. I need to tell you something."

He looked up at her and nodded.

Sarah sat on her cot and placed Claire next to her. She motioned Cody to come to her then took his hands. His thin eyebrows dipped together in concern. "I need to tell you that your pa got hurt last night."

His blue eyes, so much like his father's, widened. "How bad is he hurt?"

"I suspect it will look worse than it actually is." At least she hoped that was the truth. "He'll probably be sore for several days and move slower than normal. The best thing we can do is let him rest."

"And pray for him."

She smiled. "Yes. That's true."

"Can we do it now?"

Sarah nodded, took hold of Cody's hand, and closed her eyes. "Father, we ask you to heal Jack's wounds and help him feel better quickly." *And help him tell me the truth about what happened. Don't let him get drawn back into the life he once had.*

"Amen!" Cody said. "Can I see Pa now?"

"The doctor is with him right now. I need to finish dressing, and then we'll go see if he feels like eating some breakfast."

"Can I help get it?"

She tugged the sweet boy into her arms. "Of course, you can. That would make your father happy."

Cody hugged her back. "I love you, Sarah."

Her insides warmed like hot syrup. She'd missed the hugs she frequently received from Lara's children. "I love you, too." She placed a kiss on his cheek then set him back. "Now, run outside for a bit."

"You want me to take Claire?"

The girl bounced at the mention of her name.

"Thank you, but I think she'll be fine here."

"Pa likes pancakes—and coffee. I think I'll go see what Miss Zelma's making for breakfast."

"That's a good idea."

The eager boy rushed from the tent, and she could hear him running. She hoped seeing his pa so beat up wouldn't upset him too much. As she changed Claire's diaper and gown, she wondered again at Dr. Worth's actions. Why would he feel the need to come back and protect her? Did he think she was incapable of protecting the children and herself? Or was there more to the situation than she was seeing?

As Luke waited for the railroad attendant to open the stock car so that he could retrieve Golden Boy, he studied the town. Much had changed in the three weeks that he'd been gone. The depot had been finished, and buildings in all stages of construction filled his view. Tents still dotted the area, but it was looking more and more like a town. He patted the pocket that held the telegram informing him that the lot he wanted was for sale.

Golden Boy whinnied, and Luke started forward as the attendant led the gelding down the ramp. The horse spied him and nickered, trotting forward. Luke handed over his claim ticket.

The porter, a brawny man about Luke's age, nodded and pocketed the ticket. "What do you want to do with that big trunk you had shipped, Mr. McNeil?"

"I'll need a wagon to haul it. Can you store it in the depot until I make arrangements?"

"Yes, sir. Just hang on to your other claim ticket."

"I appreciate that." Luke checked the cinch on his saddle and mounted. He headed for Third Street to find Mr. Brownlee's store and pay him for the lot. His gut tingled. Before long, he'd be in business.

He tipped his hat at a couple of women walking past. His herd of horses had fared well at Gabe's, and the several he'd broken in during his three-week stay would only need a bit more work before he could sell them as green-broke mounts.

He reined his horse to a halt at Brownlee's, slapped his reins over the hitching post, and then strode inside the new shoe store. The familiar scent of leather greeted him. Boots lined the whole wall to his left, with some fancier dress shoes on racks in the back. A man assisting a seated gentleman in a suit looked his way and smiled. "I'll be right with you, sir."

"No rush. I'll just have a look at your boots. Never know when a man might need a new pair." Like for a wedding. All he needed was a wife. He picked up a dark brown boot, admiring the fancy stitching on the shaft. He looked at several more before the customer left without making a purchase. The clerk walked up to him.

He glanced down at Luke's worn Justins. "I'd say you're about a size eleven. I like a man who cares for his boots." He held out his hand. "Herbert Brownlee at your service."

Luke shook the man's hand. "Luke McNeil. Seems to me you'd prefer men who didn't take good care of their Justins. That way you'd have more business."

"I suppose that's one way to look at it. Your name sounds familiar." Mr. Brownlee rubbed his clean-shaven jaw, and then his eyes brightened. "Say, aren't you the fellow buying the lot next door?"

Luke smiled. "That I am. Got the money in my pocket. You got the deed?"

"Yes, sir. It was a shame my brother decided not to stay. That's a nice corner lot he had. If the workers hadn't already started on my building, I would have traded him. Clyde couldn't handle the Oklahoma heat. Went back to Wisconsin, he did." Mr. Brownlee walked around the shiny wooden counter and pulled an official-looking paper out from under it. "Just pay me the money and sign on this line, and you're in business, Mr. McNeil."

It took less than a minute to conduct their business. Luke grinned the whole time. He had achieved one of his longtime dreams. He was a landowner. Albeit, it wasn't the ranch he'd thought he'd own, but he would still be working with horses—and running a livery would leave him more time to pursue the woman he loved. Not to mention, the town lot cost much less than what he'd sold his homestead for, so he'd made a nice profit.

He left the store whistling a jaunty tune and more than a little glad Mr. Brownlee hadn't asked him what kind of business he planned to start. The man might not like being so close to a livery, especially during the heat of summer.

Luke walked across his land, thinking about where to raise his building and corral. There wasn't room for many horses, so maybe he could rent some of Sarah's land to keep them on. They would be close if needed.

He spent the next hour walking around town, trying to find a crew to work on his building, but all of them were booked with other obligations for a long while. Maybe the family building Sarah's house would be interested. From the work he'd seen before he left for Gabe's, they'd done a good job.

As he rode out of town, he relished the fact that although there was a blacksmith in town, no one he'd talked to knew of another livery. That would be good for his business. He mentally made a list of things he needed to buy—ropes, curry combs, and other grooming tools, farrier tools, a buggy, buckboard, not to mention whatever he would need for his private quarters. At least he was used to getting by without much. There hadn't been room in the bunkhouse for things of comfort. Besides, what did a man need with those? He wouldn't mind a big bed with a thick mattress, and maybe a chair and table, but he didn't require much else.

He tallied up the cost of the things he still had to buy. Good thing Gabe was giving him some of his older tack, saddles, and a spring wagon that he planned to replace soon. That would help, although he'd probably have to spend quite a bit more time in repairs than if he could afford to buy new gear. Hopefully, the day would come when he could. First, he must find someone to construct his building and a place to live, and then he'd see how much money he had left from what he'd saved all these years.

His thoughts shifted to Sarah, and his gut tightened. He'd missed her. There'd been few times since she'd come to live with Gabe that they'd been parted for so long. Dare he hope she'd missed him too?

As he crested the next hill, he reined Golden Boy to a stop and stared at Sarah's brand-new house. It rose up from the prairie as bold as an oak. The two-story house wasn't nearly as large as Gabe's and Lara's, but it would suit Sarah well. She'd finally achieved her dream. Would there be room for him in her heart now that she had?

⌒

Sarah's footsteps echoed as she walked through the upstairs rooms of her vacant house. The scent of fresh wood greeted her in each room. Claire squealed, her voice echoing, as she chased Cody around the empty space that would be Sarah's spare bedroom. The swish of shovels plunging into the dirt outside her kitchen drew her to the back of the house.

She peered down and saw Jack toss some dirt into the growing pile. Though she had nothing to put in it yet, she would soon have a root cellar. Hopefully, her vegetables would thrive enough that she and Claire could enjoy them this winter. Jack set his shovel down and dipped a cup in the bucket of water that sat under a small persimmon tree. He swigged down the water then winced as he stretched. Several days had passed since Dr. Worth had brought him home. Although Jack hadn't wanted to talk about the incident, he had insisted more than once that he hadn't been drinking.

All she could do was pray for him. He wouldn't allow her to tend his wound, instead preferring to ride into town to Dr. Worth's office. A man had his pride, and she sure didn't want to step on his, so she'd kept quiet, although she couldn't help wondering what had happened.

Turning away from the window, she realized the children had left the room. As she walked down the short hall to her own bedroom, her excitement increased. She could hardly wait to get her bed set up and to sleep inside. She still hadn't decided whether to put a bed for Claire in the same room or in the other bedroom. At least Jack had built gates at the top and bottom of the stairs so she wouldn't have to worry about the girl falling down them if she woke up at night and left her bed, or if she tried to sneak up them during the day.

Cody pulled Claire back from the open window.

Sarah brushed her hand across his head. "Thank you for keeping a good watch on Claire."

The boy flashed a smile. "I don't mind. She reminds me of

Missy, but she don't talk as much."

Sarah smiled at the mention of Lara's youngest daughter. Though Claire wasn't tall enough to do more than touch the windowsill with her fingertips, it wouldn't be long before Sarah would have to worry about her climbing out of them. How had Lara survived the anxieties of raising four children?

She had help. Gabe, for one. And Sarah had assisted, too.

Missing her friends, she walked to the window and stared out. From up here, she could see clear to Anadarko. Thankfully, the sounds of the town didn't carry this far.

Claire shrieked and grabbed Sarah's skirts at the same time a rider on a palomino caught her attention. The man had been staring at her house, and now he trotted toward it. She sucked in a gasp and leaned out the window to get a closer view. "Luke!"

Cody squeezed in beside her. "Luke's back?" The boy waved. "Hey, Luke!"

Sarah could barely speak for the joy racing through her. "Go tell your pa." She picked up Claire and hurried toward the stairs. What would Luke think of her ward? Surely Gabe or Lara would have told him about Claire. Had he brought the clothing and things she'd asked Lara if she could borrow?

She slowed her steps as she made her way down the stairs and looked around her parlor. She could hardly believe this was her home, and she couldn't wait to show it to Luke. He'd been the one she'd confided in first when she decided it was time to leave the Coulters' home. She rushed out onto the porch and waved.

Luke kicked his horse into a lope and quickly closed the gap between them. He jumped off before the horse completely stopped, jogged up the steps, and stood in front of her, grinning.

She smiled, so glad to see him again. Except for Jo, she'd never had a friend as dear as Luke. "Welcome to my home."

"It's beautiful. I stopped on the hill and was admiring it when I saw you in the window. You did it, Sarah."

"I did." She beamed at him.

He lifted his hand and jiggled Claire's. "So this must be Miss Claire." He tipped his hat. "A pleasure to meet you. I'm Luke."

Instead of leaning her head on Sarah's shoulder as she often did when meeting a stranger, Claire stared at Luke with wide eyes. He shook her hand, and a smile broke loose on the girl's face.

"Still the charmer, I see."

He straightened and strutted around on her porch like a proud rooster. "What's not to like?"

Sarah chuckled at his goofy antics.

Quick footsteps sounded at the side of the house, and Cody and Jack appeared.

"Luke!" Cody raced up the stairs and flung himself at Luke. Good thing Luke noticed and caught the eager boy, spinning him around.

Jack, covered in dirt, stayed at the bottom of the stairs.

Luke carried Cody and trotted down then slapped his friend on the shoulder. "You're a smart man staying off Sarah's spankin' new steps with all that dirt on you."

Jack nodded and glanced down at his filthy pants and boots. "I'm not about to be the one who dirties them first. I don't want a broom to my backside."

Sarah laughed. "I don't even have my broom yet, but I do thank you for your thoughtfulness."

Luke set Cody down and shook Jack's shoulder. "You digging

a well or something?"

"A root cellar." He slanted a teasing look at Luke. "We could use another pair of hands."

Luke leaned against the stair railing. "I don't mind helping, but I have a few things to do first." He flicked a glance at Sarah. "I got a trunk full of stuff that Lara sent for you and that little gal."

Sarah gasped. "A whole trunk?"

"Yep. I need a wagon to haul it out here." He straightened, and a proud expression made his handsome face even more comely. "And I've got news of my own. I bought a lot in town. Gonna open a livery."

Sarah moved down the steps and set Claire on the ground then gave Luke a hug from the side. "That's wonderful." And she meant it. Although she'd been upset when he first showed up in El Reno because she thought he'd followed her, she realized now that she wanted to have at least someone she knew living near her. She dearly missed the Coulters and their children, and having Luke close meant she didn't have to say good-bye again. She'd been surprised at how much she'd missed him.

He hugged her back, holding on longer than was proper, gazing down at her with an expression that made her mouth go dry. When Jack cleared his throat, Luke stepped away. Sarah searched for something to say to rid the moment of its awkwardness. "How is Gabe doing?"

"Good. He's walking around on crutches now and scowling because he can't tend to all the things he thinks he needs to. I don't know why he's so worried about the ranch. He's got a good, responsible crew. While I was there, I worked more with my own horses than Gabe's."

"I'm surprised you didn't stay longer." Jack dropped down to sit on one of the steps, and Cody joined him. Claire backed up to the lowest step but missed, landing on the ground, eliciting quiet chuckles from the adults.

Sarah gazed at the people she loved—each one in a different way. They made this house a home. And the place would be lonely when they left, but she couldn't dwell on that. It would steal the joy of finally having her own place. "I'll ask Mr. Peterson if we can borrow his buckboard. Some of the things I ordered for the house are at the depot. I've been waiting to get them until the men were done with the inside."

"If he says yes, I'll drive you." Luke glanced behind him. "Do you have a corral built yet?"

"No. We've been concentrating on the house. With the weather dry, I thought we'd best get a root cellar dug so Sarah would have a place to store her vegetables. Next we're building a small barn and corral. Mr. Peterson and Amos have been hauling wood for the barn from the depot while me and the twins dig the cellar. It's almost done, although we'll need to shore it up some."

Luke flicked a finger toward his eyebrow. "What happened to you?"

Jack shrugged. "Nothin' much."

Luke stared at him for a moment then turned his gaze on Sarah. "You have a real nice place here."

"Thank you." His opinion meant a lot.

Luke rubbed his hand across his jaw. "Do you know if the Petersons have plans to work somewhere else when they're done here?"

Sarah nodded. "I believe they do."

Luke sighed and looked down.

"What's wrong?" Jack asked.

"I can't find anyone who isn't already committed for months to build my livery."

"You and me can do it." Jack waved a dirty hand in the air. "After I finish here."

Luke's expression brightened. "I thought you were heading back home to Gabe's soon."

"Eventually, but if I have a friend who needs my help, how can I turn my back on him?"

Luke grinned and slapped Jack's shoulder, creating a cloud of dust. "Thanks. I appreciate it. I think I'll talk with Mr. Peterson and see if he can help me figure out how much lumber I need to purchase."

"Good idea. I'd best get back to work." Jack rose. "Cody, you want to help dig for a bit?"

The boy jumped up. "Sure, Pa."

Claire struggled to stand and looked up at Jack and jabbered something. Sarah lifted her up and tickled her tummy. "Oh no. You're not going with them. You're helping me. One dirty child is enough."

When Jack and Cody left, Luke gazed at Sarah. "Have you had any luck finding Claire's family?"

"No, but I can't say that I'm sorry. This little gal has sneaked in and wound herself around my heart." She tickled Claire again and then looked at Luke. The longing expression on his face made her heart lurch, before he blinked and his ever-present smile returned.

"I don't doubt it. She's a pretty little gal. In spite of her blue eyes, she looks part Indian. Don't you think?"

"I do, and maybe that's one of the reasons I've become so attached to her. Who else could love a part-Indian orphan more than me?"

Luke stared at her so long, she felt the need to squirm, but she held still. "Lots of folks could. I could."

His meaning went deep, all the way to her heart. He had no qualms about raising a half-breed child, but she knew that most men wouldn't feel the same. Too many white people resented the Indians for their fight to hang on to the land the government had promised would be theirs for eternity. Maybe now that most of the Indian lands had been opened to settlement, those prejudices might change.

Suddenly Sarah felt a warm, wet sensation on her hip. "Oh!" She set Claire away from her. "Someone needs a dry diaper."

Luke chuckled. "I'll leave that task to you and go talk to Peterson about borrowing his wagon."

She watched him stride away, tall and confident. Luke McNeil was a good man, and there was no denying that she was happy he was back.

Chapter 17

Sarah straightened, pushing her fist into her lower back to relieve the ache she'd gotten from bending too long. While Claire napped, she wanted to weed and water the garden. Claire enjoyed helping her, but the little girl tended to pull up the vegetable seedlings along with the weeds.

Sarah pushed back her straw hat and gazed up at the gray sky. The clouds blocked a bit of the sun's heat, but due to the humid promise of rain hanging heavy in the air, the bodice of her dress was damp with sweat. Cooler weather couldn't come fast enough.

Scratching at a trickle, she bent down and finished weeding the row of turnips. Next she needed to water. Though she'd had the foresight to plant her garden between the house and the river, today she wished it was closer to the water. By the time she finished her chores, she'd be ready for a nap but Claire would be awake.

Cody trotted toward her covered in grime. He must have rubbed his nose with his dirty hands, because the end of it was black. "Johnny came back to help with the cellar. Pa said it was too crowded and for me to see if you needed help. Can I weed the garden with you?"

"You look like you already have." She chuckled. He'd need several dips in the river to wash off all that dirt.

He glanced down at his pants. "I digged a lot. I put the dirt that came out of the cellar into buckets so it can be moved to some other place. Pa's cuttin' wood so he can shore it up."

She wiped her hands on her apron. "Tell you what. Let's clean you off, then could you go into the house, quiet as a mouse, and see if Claire is still napping?"

A big smile brightened his features, and his head bobbed. "I can pretend to be an In'jun and sneak up on her."

Her smile dipped. Where had he learned about Indians sneaking up on people? Probably from Drew. Lara's younger son was quite a handful and loved playing make-believe. With the edge of her apron, she wiped the smudge off his nose and cleaned his hands as best as she could without water. "Why don't you just be Cody and see if you can tiptoe up the stairs without waking Claire?"

"Aww. . .that's not as much fun."

She ruffled his hair. "Go on. Then when you get back, you can help me water the garden."

"All right." He spun and raced for the house.

"Make sure you close the gate at the top of the stairs so Claire doesn't fall if she wakes up and goes wandering." Thankfully, there was precious little in the house that she could get into at the moment.

He waved a hand but didn't slow down.

She grabbed the bucket and hurried toward the river. She had a feeling that if Claire wasn't yet awake, she would be soon. At the river's edge, she filled her bucket three-fourths of the way then lugged it back to her garden. She'd just emptied it on her row of chard when Cody ran out of the house and hopped down the stairs.

"She's still sleeping, Sarah," he yelled as he ran.

Oh, what Sarah wouldn't give for some of his energy. As he reached her side, a buggy crested the hill and drove toward the house. Who could that be?

She glanced down at her dirty apron. At least it hid her sweaty bodice, but it was filthy from her kneeling in the dirt and attempting to clean up Cody. Ah well, there wasn't much she could do about it.

The driver must have seen her, because he turned the horse toward her. From the Petersons' camp, she could hear their dog barking at the approaching buggy. She was glad the dog stayed at their camp and didn't charge her visitor.

"Who's that?" Cody reached up and took her hand.

"I'm not—" Her heart lurched. Stephen Barlow? She'd almost forgotten about him in the chaos that followed finding Claire and finishing the house. She pasted on a smile as she realized she'd never gotten back to him about the employment he'd offered. Now that she had Claire, she doubted the offer would still stand. She wasn't sure how that made her feel. She liked Phillip and would be happy to try to help the lonely boy, but she could never replace his mother—and she sincerely hoped his father knew that.

"Good afternoon, Miss Worley." Mr. Barlow pulled the buggy to a halt. He stepped down then lifted Phillip to the ground. The boy grinned and waved, and Sarah waved back.

Cody gazed up at her with an expression of awe. "He's got a boy like me. Can I play with him?"

"We'll have to ask Mr. Barlow."

Stephen eyed Cody as if unsure he wanted his son socializing with such a dirty urchin.

"Cody has been helping with the root cellar today, so I hope you'll excuse the state of his clothing." *And mine.* Mr. Barlow probably thought she looked as grimy as the boy.

"What's a root cellar? Can I see it, Papa?"

Mr. Barlow twisted his lips to one side. "You may look at it, but do not go inside. Aunt Esther will pitch a conniption fit if you return home all dirty."

"Yes, sir." Phillip walked toward Cody with eyes filled with anticipation.

"Cody, this is Phillip. Why don't you show him the cellar, but remember what his father and yours said. Don't go inside, especially if the men aren't there."

"Yes'm." Cody walked over to Phillip. "I'm Cody. C'mon, and I'll show it to you. It's a big hole in the ground."

Phillip nodded and looked back at his father and smiled. The boys walked away; then Cody broke into a jog with Phillip following close behind.

Mr. Barlow watched with an unreadable expression on his face. "It's good for my son to play with another boy his age."

Sarah walked closer to him. "Are there none in town?"

He harrumphed. "None that Aunt Esther thinks are good enough. I'm sure if she saw Cody, she'd—" He removed his hat. "I don't care to talk about her. I see your house is finished."

"All except for the painting on the outside, but there is still much to do inside. I've only received one of my shipments of furniture so far. It arrived yesterday. Most of my things are still in the railcar at the depot, waiting until I have time to unpack it." At least her bed had been in the shipment that she and Luke had sorted through. Once it was set up, she was able to give her cot to Claire until she could either order a bed for her or the men could find time to build one. With Claire still wetting her diapers, Sarah wasn't willing to share her bed.

"Yes. I remember all that was involved when my wife and I moved to a new home. It's quite a lot of work." He stared off as if lost in thought for a moment then pinned her with his gaze. Unexpected apprehension flickered in his eyes for a moment. "Have you decided whether you can spend time with Phillip or not?"

Sarah nibbled her lower lip. "I have thought about it, but there's been a complication."

He lifted his eyebrows. "And what is the nature of this complication?"

"A little girl."

"What?"

Sarah scratched some dried dirt off her finger as she wrestled with how to explain Claire. "I found—or rather—my brother found a little girl, wandering all alone. She looks to be around two. She was filthy and covered in scratches and insect bites."

"That's dreadful. Did you locate her family?"

She nodded. "We did, but her mother was dead. There was nothing in their meager supplies to indicate who they were."

"So, why is this a problem? Surely you turned the child over to the authorities."

She looked down. He had the same attitude Dr. Worth initially had. For some reason, with Stephen being a father, she'd hoped he'd feel differently. "No, I didn't. She was scared and alone. I'm keeping her unless her family comes to claim her."

Stephen's eyes widened. "You can't just keep any child that comes along, especially with you not being married. You should be concerned about your reputation."

Her reputation was none of his business. People already looked down on her because she was a half-breed. At least she could help one child. "What would you have done? She's a little girl, confused and frightened. She misses her mother. I can't send Claire off to some lonely orphanage where she'll be one of many unwanted children. *I* want her."

"But she isn't yours to keep."

"She is unless her father or another relative comes for her."

He lowered his head and shook it, as if sorely disappointed in her actions. The disappointment was hers. She'd expected better of the man, but then she barely knew him.

"And what of Phillip?" he asked.

"That's partly up to you."

"Me?" He looked up.

"Are you willing to let me spend time with Phillip if I have to bring Claire with me?"

"I dread to think what Aunt Esther will have to say about this unexpected occurrence." He turned away and bent over with his gloved hands on one of the wagon wheels. "It was my hope that you could give my son your undivided attention."

"I understand, but that's no longer possible. Besides, it might be good for him to play with another child, even one younger than him. You saw how eager he was to join Cody. In fact, he merely waved at me then left with little hesitation."

"I've explained to him that you are not his mother."

Sarah walked over and stood beside him. "Good. He needs to understand that. How did he take it?"

"He was disappointed, of course. But I think he knew all along that was the case. I think he was simply flabbergasted at seeing someone who resembled his mother so closely that he overreacted."

"Does that bother you?"

He turned. "Not at all. Although you have similarities to Rosalia, there are differences, too. You're taller, for one. Your hair is a lighter shade, and your eyes are darker."

Sarah swallowed at his intense stare. Was he looking for a replacement for his wife? Or merely someone to spend time with his son to give Aunt Esther a rest? She thought of all she had to do to get her house in order. Caring for Phillip would certainly cut into her time, but it would also give her some extra money. Still, she wasn't ready to give him an answer.

"Who is that?"

Sarah glanced across the yard to see Luke standing at the corner of the house, his hand on his hips. "That's a friend of mine, Luke McNeil. He's helping with the cellar."

Mr. Barlow turned toward her. "Is he married?"

"No, why do you ask?"

"It's inappropriate for you to have an unmarried man here working for you. You must be fastidiously careful of your reputation, Miss Worley."

"And exactly what does that mean?" She crossed her arms.

"How do you expect me to get my house built without the help of men, not all of whom are married?"

"I didn't mean to cause a disagreement. I'm only stating what others will say if you're not careful."

Luke started toward them. Cody and Phillip raced past him and ran toward the buggy. She had never seen Phillip so excited.

"I saw it, Papa. A cellar is a big hole. Does our house have one?"

"Come, Phillip. It's time to go."

"But I want to—"

Stephen glared at his son, and the boy quieted. Head hanging, Phillip walked toward his father then allowed him to lift him into the buggy.

Sarah's heart ached for the lonely boy. Still, in light of his father's accusations, she didn't feel she could work for him. "I think, all things considered, that it's better if I decline your offer."

He stared at her a long moment then gave a curt nod. "I wholeheartedly agree. Good day, Miss Worley."

Good-*bye* was more like it. Sarah managed a smile and waved at Phillip. The poor child looked on the verge of tears. Her heart ached for him.

"But I thought we were going to get to play longer." Cody leaned against Sarah's side, and she rested her hand on his shoulder.

"Not today."

As the buggy turned, Phillip gave a limp wave.

Luke strode up to her. "Who was that?"

"It was that man I met in town who'd hoped I'd watch his son several days a week."

"What did you tell him?"

The same thing I told you, she wanted to say but didn't. Luke had done nothing to deserve her ire. "I said that it wouldn't work out. I'm much too busy now."

"Good. I don't like the looks of that dandy."

⌒

Jack saddled his horse at twilight. A week had passed since his attempt to lure Sadie away from the saloon where she worked had failed. Part of him wished he'd never promised to return, but how could he not at least try one more time to help the young woman?

He glanced across the field to his tent, illuminated from the lantern light in Luke's tent. Cody was already asleep, tired from all the digging and other things he'd done today. How could one little boy run and climb and do so much without falling down exhausted?

"Where are you goin'?"

Jack startled at Luke's voice. "Uh. . .got some business to tend to in town."

"At this hour?"

"Yeah."

Luke stared at him over the horse's back. "Would it have anything to do with that shiner you got?"

Jack didn't want to talk about it, but he could see that Luke wasn't going away. "Could be."

Luke rested his arms on the saddle. "If you need help, all you have to do is ask."

"I know." What he didn't know was if Sadie would even show, but if she did, he might need backup in getting her away safely. He still hadn't figured out where he was going to take her. Guthrie would probably be as good as any place, but he couldn't travel alone with an unmarried woman he didn't know, especially one dressed in a frilly saloon gal's outfit. He really hadn't thought things through. He simply knew he had to keep his promise and show up a week from when he last saw her.

Luke had been a good friend and wouldn't fault him for trying to help Sadie. With a sigh of resignation, he told his friend what had happened last time he'd gone to Anadarko.

In the waning light, Luke's eyes widened. "You want to help rescue a shady lady?" He chuckled and shook his head. "I should have known you got beat up being a good Samaritan. Sarah was afraid you'd fallen into your old ways and had gone back to drinkin'. I reassured her you hadn't."

Sarah thought he'd told her a falsehood? That disappointed him more than he could express. "After those bruisers beat me up for trying to help Sadie, one of them poured whiskey on me. That's why Sarah doesn't believe me."

"I never said she doesn't believe you. She's concerned that your grief over Cora's death will push you to do something you wouldn't normally do."

That eased his conscience some where Sarah was concerned. She cared about him, and it was natural for her to worry. "I'll never drink or do anything that could hurt Cody. He's my main concern now."

"And yet, here you are, ready to ride to town alone to help a gal who probably wants your help less than she wants the coins in your pocket."

"I made a promise."

"To a lady of the night."

"Don't forget about Jo. If she can escape that kind of life, other women can, too. You don't know Sadie's circumstances or how she ended up being where she is."

"You're right." As if ashamed of his comment, Luke hung his head for a long moment. "If you're dead set on going, let me ride with you and make sure you get out of there without a beating this time."

Jack smacked the end of the reins against his hand. "With you here, I won't worry about Cody. If he wakes up and doesn't find me, he'll go straight to your tent."

"So? Take him to Sarah. She won't mind keeping him. And she'll probably tell you to bring Sadie back here. Sarah wouldn't have the life she does now if Jo hadn't taken her along when she escaped that bordello."

Jack clenched his jaw. He'd hoped not to have to involve her this time. "I reckon you're right. It would be good to have someone along in case of trouble. My ribs are still sore from last week's walloping, so I won't argue if you want to ride along, but I don't know that it's a good idea to bring Sadie here."

"Then what did you plan to do with the gal if you did manage to get her to leave the saloon?"

"I hadn't gotten that far."

"Don't cheat Sarah out of the chance to help someone in need."

"You're right."

Luke straightened. "I like hearing that."

"Don't get used to it." He tossed his reins to Luke. "I'll get Cody. You might want to saddle your horse."

"I already did."

"I'm not surprised." His heart warmed at his friend's dedication.

"You were coming along whether I wanted you or not."

"Yep. Friends watch their friends' backs."

Jack chuckled as he walked toward his tent. The Lord sure had blessed him with good friends and family.

Thirty minutes later, Jack waited behind a tree out back of the saloon where Sadie worked. He had no idea when she'd come outside—or *if* she would. Did she even remember that this was the night he'd promised to meet her?

A door creaked, and he slipped behind the tree. As dark as it was at the back of the lot, he doubted anyone could see him. Still, he needed to use caution. He leaned to his right and peered around the trunk. His heart bucked. There she was. But she wasn't alone.

A bearded man in overalls pawed at her as she tried to slip out the back door. "Aw, Sid. Leave me be. It's time for my smoke."

"I don't mind keepin' you comp'ny, darlin'."

"Go back inside, and I'll make it worth your time later." She pasted a smile on her face that made Jack's belly churn. No woman should have to live at the beck and call of a man's lust.

"Promise?" The old geezer licked his lips and leaned forward.

Sadie grabbed hold of his beard and turned his head, placing a kiss on his leathery cheek.

Jack thought he heard the man chuckle. Sadie slipped out the door, free and clear, while the geezer disappeared inside. She glanced around as if looking for him. She muttered a curse. "I knew better than t'trust a man. They never keep their promises."

Jack eased around the tree. "I do."

She jumped then glared at him. After a long moment, she started toward him, but footsteps came toward the door. Jack ducked behind the trunk.

"What do you want?" Sadie obviously despised whomever it was she was talking to.

"Just checking on you. How come you're out here?"

"I finished with my last bum and needed some fresh air." She barked a harsh laugh. "The cowpoke smelled as if he'd been rollin' around in cow patties. It sickened my stomach."

The man guffawed. "Hurry back in before the boss notices you're gone."

"Thanks, Gus. I appreciate that you watch out for me."

"Always have. Always will."

After a few long moments, Sadie's posture relaxed. Then suddenly she turned and ran toward Jack.

He grabbed her, pulling her behind the tree.

"We gotta go. Now!"

"All right." Jack peered toward the door and saw no one. "C'mon."

He grabbed Sadie's hand, ignoring how she wreaked of smoke and booze—a pale comparison to the flowery perfume Cora used to wear.

"Hold it right there." The man who'd thrown most of the punches at him last week stepped out the door, his gun trained in their direction.

Sadie uttered a noise like an animal caught in a trap.

"Shh. . ." Jack held tight to Sadie's hand for fear she'd run back to her prison.

"No. You hold it, mister, and drop that gun while you're at it." Luke stepped out of the shadows of the alley with a bandanna covering the lower half of his face.

"Let's go," Jack urged her. She ran toward his horse and had her foot in the stirrup before he got there. He reached behind her to boost her up, but there was no decent place for him to put his hands. Thankfully, she mounted on her own. Jack slid on behind her, reached around and grabbed the reins, and then turned his horse and gun toward the man at the door.

"Get back inside before I blow a hole in your knee." Luke played the part of a reckless henchman well.

"You'll regret this. All of you." The man backed inside the door then turned and moved out of sight.

Luke saluted Jack with his gun then backed away, disappearing in the dark alley.

"Hold on." Jack parked his heels in his horse's side, and the animal leaped forward. He turned his horse in the opposite direction of Sarah's house and raced away from the Hairy Dog Saloon, fearing the men would follow. Once out of town, he reined his horse back toward her house.

"Yeehaw!" Luke rode out of the shadows.

Sadie jumped.

Jack glared at Luke, though he doubted his friend could see his expression. "Good thing both my hands are occupied, or you'd have a bullet hole in you. 'Bout scared me half to death, you numbskull."

"Howdy, ma'am. My name's Luke McNeil."

"Sad— Um. . .Charlotte VanBuren. I can't thank you enough for helpin' your friend get me free of that horrible place."

"Happy to do so."

Jack rolled his eyes as he shook his head. Leave it to Luke to take all the glory.

Chapter 18

At the sound of riders approaching, Sarah turned down her lantern then opened the door and peeked out. In the moonlight, she recognized the light color of Luke's horse, and she could see enough to know that there were two riders on the other horse. When Jack had explained he'd been helping a saloon girl, she'd actually been relieved and chastised herself for doubting his good character.

She braced herself to host a guest. If only she had some parlor furniture or a place to sit. Hopefully, the fact that her home was a sanctuary away from that nasty saloon and horrid life where the woman lived would be enough. She rushed outside to the porch railing. "It's about time you got here. I've been so worried I nearly wore a hole in my new floors."

The horses stopped, snorting and prancing from their ride. Good thing there was a three-quarter moon tonight so they could see their way easily and safely. Luke hopped off Golden Boy and held the reins of Jack's horse while he helped the woman dismount. He escorted their guest up the stairs while Luke took the horses to the pasture. It wouldn't be good if men came looking for Sadie and found the horses still saddled and standing out front.

Sarah slipped inside and turned up the lantern just enough that they could see. She smiled, although the fresh wood scent of her home was replaced by the malodorous stench of smoke and whiskey. "Welcome to my home. I wish I had more to offer, but I've just moved in."

Sadie laughed. "I'd stay in a pigpen if it got me outta that ghastly place." She sobered and looked around the dim room. "I bet it'll be real nice here once you get furniture."

Sarah's heart softened toward the rough woman. "Thank you." She looked at Jack. "You'd best grab Cody and get to your tent in case we have any unwelcome visitors."

"Yes, ma'am." He started for the stairs then paused. "Sarah will take good care of you. I'll see you in the morning, and we'll make plans on gettin' you away from this area."

Sadie walked up to Jack and lightly touched his arm. "I wasn't real sure if you'd come back after the beatin' you took last week. Most men wouldn't have attempted to help someone like me in the first place. I don't know how to thank you."

Jack smiled. "You're welcome, and you can thank me by never going back to your old life. And that's what the saloon is—your *old* life. In the Bible, there's a verse—Second Corinthians 5:17—that says, 'Therefore if any man be in Christ, he is a new creature: old things are passed away; behold, all things are become new.' When you get away, I hope you'll find a Bible and read that for yourself. You can not only leave the saloon and start completely over, but God can wash away past indiscretions and make you new on the inside. I know, because he did that with me—and my sister Jo, who used to live in a brothel."

Sadie sucked in a loud gasp. "Is that true?"

Jack touched her shoulder. "It is. Sarah can tell you more if you want to know about her tonight, but I should get my son and hurry to my tent. I'd like to look disturbed from my sleep if any of those henchmen from the saloon happen to come this way."

"Go—and thank you."

Jack nodded then hurried up the stairs.

"I have a bucket of water in my kitchen area if you'd like to wash off. Once Jack has left, I'll give you one of my nightgowns. I'm glad you came, Sadie."

The woman stiffened for a moment then turned from watching the stairs. "My real name is Charlotte VanBuren. I'd like to go back to it now that I'm starting over. Would you mind calling me Charlotte or Lottie?"

"Of course not. Whatever you prefer. And please call me Sarah."

"Then Lottie, it is. Thank you for your kindness." She batted her eyes as if struggling not to cry.

Sarah heard Jack on the landing and lifted the lamp so that he could see to descend. Once he was down, she opened the door. "Good night, and thanks for what you did. It was a good thing."

He nodded, cast a quick glance toward Lottie, and then left. Sarah closed the door and locked it then walked through the empty parlor to her bare kitchen with Lottie following. A small dressing table had been in the load of furniture that had arrived, and she'd put it in the kitchen so she'd have a place where she could wash up. "I'll run upstairs and get some things for you to wear if you want to go ahead and wash off. I'm sorry I can't offer you a bath."

Lottie gazed down at her clothes. "I imagine I must smell something awful to you, not to mention how I look."

"Please, think nothing of it. I don't tell many people this, but I'm sure it will surprise you to learn that my father owned the bordello where Jack's sister was all but held hostage. When I was still a girl and my mother was near death, he came to get me and took me to live with him."

Lottie's eyes widened. "In a bawdy house?"

"Yes. He did keep me separate from the women for the most part, but he couldn't hide the awfulness of the place. It was so bad that I gladly left with Jo when she ran away."

"Thank you for telling me. I guess you would understand more than most."

"I admire you for taking the risk to get away from that place. I know it wasn't easy, and I'm sure you have fears for the future, but we'll help you, so please try not to worry."

Lottie's lashes fluttered. "Thank you."

"I'll leave this lantern for you and run upstairs."

"Won't you need it?"

"There's another one in my bedroom. I left it for the children."

Lottie frowned. "You mean there's more than one?"

Sarah chuckled. "Yes. I'll explain about Claire when I come back." She hurried away, glad she'd told Jack to bring Lottie to her house. She'd been hesitant at first, fearing trouble and not wanting anything to upset Claire, but the decision to bring Lottie here was the right one. Like Jo, another woman would be escaping the horrible, degrading life of a prostitute. She prayed as she climbed the stairs that Lottie would come to know God's love and the freedom and hope that came with His forgiveness.

Holding her skirt back from the open fire, Sarah leaned down and flipped the fish she was frying for supper. She straightened and turned to Zelma. "What time will you be leaving tomorrow?"

"At sunrise. We want to be sure to get an early start."

Sarah nibbled her lip and stared at her house where Lottie was watching Claire. "Do you think our plan will work?"

Zelma set a crock of butter and two jars of jam on the tailgate of her wagon. "I don't see why not. After gettin' a look at that pretty gal at our noon meal, Zach and Zeke are bickerin' between themselves over who gets to pretend to be Lottie's husband on the drive to Cottonwood Grove."

Sarah wondered how Lottie would react to the twins arguing over her. It wasn't as if one of them was actually marrying her. She hoped Lottie would feel honored rather than uncomfortable by the men's eagerness to pretend to be married to her.

"You think my boys made Lottie uncomfortable?" Zelma carried the platter of corn bread to the tailgate.

Sarah peeked at the fish. Almost done. "Why do you ask?"

"I noticed she kept her eyes down durin' most of the noon meal."

"Your men were very kind to her, but it was obvious that she was uncomfortable with so many males present. I should have made it clear to Lottie that no one told them about her former vocation. Only you and your husband are aware of it, because I couldn't ask for your help unless you knew the whole truth."

"Prob'ly a wise idea not to tell them. I'm not sure how my boys would'a reacted to learnin' that. It's better they don't know so they can treat her like a young woman deserves."

"I'm so glad you feel that way. After all you've done for me, I didn't like the idea of deceiving you. I'm glad Jack and Lottie agreed we should explain things to you and Mr. Peterson."

Zelma shuffled over and gave Sarah a hug. "It's a kind thing you're doin' for that girl. Not too many others would've helped someone like her."

"You'll come back as soon as you get her safely to Guthrie? Are you certain I'm not asking too much of you?"

Zelma's tired eyes sparkled. "Are you kiddin'? This'll be my very first train ride. I'm as excited as the twins." She covered her mouth and chuckled. "Did you see Johnny sulking 'cause he ain't goin'? He'd rather be ridin' than workin', but his pa needs 'im."

"Oh, before I forget." Sarah shoved her hand into her pocket and pulled out two double eagle coins. "This should be plenty to get you to Guthrie and back and pay for your meals. If you have more than you need, why don't you pick up some supplies we're running low on? Maybe some things that are hard to find around here."

"Happy to. Is your lady friend doin' all right? She seemed mighty cramped in that dress you gave her."

"I think so. Although the dress was a bit tight, I suspect it was the men making her antsy." She pulled several paper dollars from her pocket. "Here's some additional money for fabric and things I need. Would you please pick up four yards of pink, light green, yellow, and lavender fabric so I can make a quilt for Claire, as well as thread for it? I hate to ask you to go to so much trouble, but the supplies in town are a bit limited still. Lara sent me plenty of clothes, but there was no quilt, and Claire will need one come winter."

"Think nothin' of it. That will be more fun than I've had in ages. I never have gotten to shop for little girl belongin's, what with all my young'uns being boys. How about you? Anything you need? Didn't you give Lottie some of your clothes?"

Sarah nodded. "I could use another nightgown since I gave her my extra one." She leaned closer to her friend, lowering her voice. "And some unmentionables. Lara can help with that since she's familiar with my size and what I like. I'll write a note for you to give her, explaining what I want."

Zelma nodded. "Your friend and I'll take care of all that, so don't worry."

Bending down, Sarah ladled the fish onto the platter, handed it to Zelma, and then removed the pan from the fire. "Lara is more a sister than a friend. Jack is actually *her* brother by birth. We all claim one another as siblings, but I'm not a blood relative."

"You think that matters? I know it doesn't to Jack." Zelma rang the loud triangle.

"No, it doesn't, and I'm so grateful. They're really the only family I have."

Zelma crossed her arms over her ample bosom and lifted her brows. "What about Luke? That handsome feller cain't keep his eyes off you—and don't think I haven't seen you gawkin' at him."

Sarah stiffened. "I don't gawk at Luke."

Zelma wagged a finger. "I know better. Maybe you don't realize how much you watch him when he's around, and when he isn't, half the time you're starin' off, lost in thought. Prob'ly pinin' for him." Her expression relaxed as she gazed past Sarah. "The men are comin'."

"I'll run back to the house and let Lottie know it's time to eat.

She may not have heard the bell. And I don't pine over Luke."

"Uh-huh. It's best you consider your feelin's for 'im. Even my boys know what's what. Luke's a good man, and some other gal's liable to nab 'im away from you."

She hurried toward her house before Zelma shouted something about Luke that the men could hear. Was it possible he truly loved her? If only she knew more about the love between a man and woman.

She fingered the necklace he gave her as she walked to the house. His generous gift had touched her heart and had drawn her thoughts to him each day when she put it on. The necklace was too special to leave behind in her tent—or the house—where someone could sneak in and steal it. She usually wore it under her dress so people wouldn't ask questions. It would be hard to explain that a man she wasn't related to had given it to her.

The front door opened as she approached the house, and Lottie stepped out carrying Claire. The little girl squealed and reached out her hands. Sarah hurried up the stairs and took her, setting Claire on her hip. "How was she?"

"A little confused, but she let me dress her. I just kept talking and smiling. She's a real sweetie. It's kind of you to take her in, like you did me."

Sarah smiled. "It's the Christian thing to do, and I like helping others."

Lottie belted out a harsh laugh. "I've spent plenty of time with 'good Christian men' upstairs at the saloon. None of them were kind like you or Jack."

Sarah nuzzled Claire's cheek, hoping Lottie didn't notice her blush at the mention of her time above the saloon. Gathering her composure once again, she straightened. "Those men were not true Christians. They were depraved men who took advantage of you and lusted for women they weren't married to. A godly man would never treat you the way you've been treated. I hope your experience won't close you off to one day finding a decent, God-fearing man to marry."

"No one would ever want a gal like me."

Sarah tugged a tress of her hair out of Claire's grasp and tucked it behind her ear. "I told you Jo's story. You should take heart from that. She found a good husband, and you can too if you change how you've been living. Lara will help you. She took me in and helped me become the woman I am now. She will help you, too."

Lottie's gaze turned toward the Peterson camp. "Where's Jack's wife?"

"She's dead. We lost her when she was birthing their second child."

Lottie sucked in a breath. "Did he lose the baby, too?"

Sarah nodded. "It was a terribly sad time. We'd better go if you want to get some supper. The men won't wait long after they've been working so hard all day."

She nibbled her lip. "Do I have to go down there? Couldn't you bring me a plate? Seems like it would be safer, just in case someone comes lookin' for me."

Looping her arm through Lottie's, she gave the woman a gentle tug. "You might as well get used to being around people. You won't be able to hide out at Gabe's and Lara's for long. She'll have you going to church and helping neighbors in need. Besides, it's important for you to get to know the Petersons so you'll feel comfortable around them."

They strolled toward the Petersons' camp, arm in arm, as if they'd been friends for decades instead of days. Birds and tree frogs serenaded them from the direction of the river. "Zelma said she wanted to leave at sunrise."

"It doesn't seem right for me to hide out in their wagon."

"You need to keep out of sight in case those men come looking for you. Pretending to be a woman about to give birth is the perfect reason for being on your back in the wagon."

Lottie snorted. "Being in that position's what got me in trouble in the first place."

Sarah's cheeks heated again. "But this time it will be your escape."

"Thank you for all you've done."

Sarah released her new friend's arm and hugged her shoulders. "You're very welcome. We are all so happy to help you start a new life."

Lottie flashed an ornery grin. "Don't think I haven't noticed the way you and that handsome Luke cast looks at each other. He's your beau, isn't he?"

Sarah wanted to crawl under a rock. Why did people keep saying that? "Luke is a very good friend of mine. That's all."

"I don't believe that for a moment. I'd be willin' to bet you all the coins in my money belt that he's in love with you."

She nearly groaned. Maybe it would be best if they both grabbed a plate and ate at the house. Claire shrieked, and Sarah noticed Cody running toward them.

"We finished the cellar—all except for the door. Pa's gonna let me help him build it tomorrow."

She walked down the porch steps, ruffled his hair, and handed

Claire to him. The girl leaned in and gave him a slobbery kiss. Cody's eyes widened; then he scrunched up his face. Lottie laughed along with Sarah. She pulled out her handkerchief and wiped off his cheek.

"That's yucky, Claire." He turned and carried the girl to camp.

Lottie playfully bumped Sarah's hip, drawing her gaze.

"Looks like Luke isn't the only one in love."

Sarah gasped and covered Lottie's mouth. "You hush before someone hears you."

Lottie chuckled as Sarah removed her hand. "You think those Peterson men don't already know? You must think they're dumber than sheep."

"What do you mean?"

"Why do you reckon none of them have tried to catch your eye? They know who you belong to." With a proud smirk, she hustled toward the food.

Sarah stood there thunderstruck. Had Luke said something to the Petersons? He had no right to do that, not that she was interested in any of Zelma's sons. But if he had, he and she were going to have a powwow. She hurried to catch up with her new friend. "So what did Luke tell them?"

Lottie swatted her hand in the air. "He didn't have to say nuthin'. It's obvious to anyone with a lick of sense that there's something between you and that handsome cowboy."

What was obvious? If only she knew what it was that she and Luke were doing to attract attention. Did she stare at him? It wouldn't be odd if she did since they were such good friends. But she didn't think she did. Still, she would sure try not to do so in the future.

With a heavy heart, Sarah waved good-bye to Lottie. Fred and Zelma drove their covered wagon with the twins riding their horses behind them. All of the men were armed in case of trouble. No one had come looking for Lottie, so maybe they wouldn't encounter trouble. At least she prayed that would be the case. Lottie peeked out the back of the wagon and waved.

Sarah did the same. Though she'd eaten Zelma's pancakes, an ache had taken residence in her stomach. She hadn't known Lottie long, but she'd enjoyed having her as a guest—once she'd shed her aromatic saloon garb and had washed the smoke and garish perfume from her skin.

Claire's belly laugh drew Sarah's gaze to the old quilt she sat on. Cody had been tasked with keeping her occupied while Sarah washed the breakfast dishes, and from the looks of it, he was doing a fine job—although she wasn't sure how long he could keep up his fervent activity. He ran around the quilt, and then when he managed to get behind Claire, he leaped close to her and said, "Boo!"

Each time Claire jumped and then giggled. Sarah smiled at the sweet scene. Claire had certainly become more comfortable with them, but she still didn't talk. It was hard to know what to expect when she wasn't certain of her age.

She returned to her task. The water would be cold if she didn't get busy. As she washed each plate, dipped it in the rinse bucket, and then dried it, she listened to the rhythmic echoes of the hammer and saw. With the exception of Jack, who was working on the door to her cellar, everyone was building her barn. Amos, Johnny, and Luke had made good progress getting the frame up.

The barn would be small, with just three stalls and a tack room with enough space for a bed, in case Jack or Luke visited her down the road, and a loft for storing hay. They also planned to construct a corral so that Dottie and the cow Sarah planned to buy could graze and enjoy the warm Oklahoma days without Sarah worrying about them running off.

With the dishes dried, she returned them to the Petersons' cook wagon and cleaned the mixing bowl and skillet then dried and put them away. She missed Zelma even more than Lottie. The woman had become like an adopted mother, and she dreaded the quickly coming day when the Petersons would leave permanently.

And Jack was leaving—as soon as the barn was completed. She couldn't help wondering if his desire to return home had something to do with Lottie. Her new friend hadn't shared her age, but she had related with great pride that she had a sister, ten years younger than she, who attended the Sam Houston Normal Institute. Lottie hoped to be at Amelia's graduation next spring in Huntsville to celebrate her sister becoming a teacher.

"Lord, make it possible. Please help Lottie change her ways for herself and her sister."

"Who ya. . .talkin' to?" Cody lugged Claire over to her. In spite of the cool morning temperatures, his hair was damp with sweat from his energetic effort to entertain the little girl.

Sarah picked her up and cuddled her. "I was praying."

"Oh, you talk out loud to God like Pa does."

"Sometimes, but I mostly pray in my head."

Cody frowned. "Pa said I can do that, but I can't figure out how."

Ready for a break, Sarah walked to the quilt and sat. She patted the fabric, and Claire bent down copying her. Cody shuffled over and flopped down.

"It's not hard at all. You simply think your prayer. I was praying for God to help Lottie, but instead of thinking my prayer, I said the words out loud." She tapped her lips, thinking for a better way to explain things to the six-year-old who stared at her with serious blue eyes. "Say you want to pray for your pa. You might think: *Heavenly Father, please keep my pa safe when he works. Protect him from harm.*"

Cody nodded. "I've done that before. Is that all there is to prayin'?"

"Your father knows far more about it than I do, but I believe it's that simple. Just think your request or your thoughts of praise. Sometimes we're in public places, like on a train or shopping, when we feel the need to pray." Claire toddled toward the edge of the quilt. Sarah rose on her knees and tugged her into her lap, kissing her head. "More than likely, we wouldn't want to pray out loud and have someone nearby overhear us, so that's the perfect time to talk to God in your head."

Slowly, he nodded. "I get it. Prayer is just like me talkin' to God like I'm talkin' to you. Only sometimes you don't use words."

Sarah fought back a smile. She thought about telling him that you always use words, but sometimes you don't vocalize them, but she didn't. He understood in his own childish way, and that was all that mattered.

His sober expression brightened. "Can I go help Pa now that the dishes are done?"

"Yes, you may. Thank you for doing such a wonderful job of keeping Claire entertained. She loves playing with you."

"Aw. . .she's not so bad—for a girl." He hopped up and broke into a run toward the barn.

Sarah shook her head and chuckled, so glad God had seen fit to send her an orphaned girl instead of a constantly moving boy. She glanced down and caught Claire gnawing on the corner of her apron. Was she getting another tooth? Surely she couldn't be hungry already.

One thing was for certain, she'd better change her diaper if she didn't want a wet dress. She understood why so many people chose to let their toddlers go without a diaper until they could use the chamber pot, but she'd learned from Lara, and her friend diapered her children for sanitary reasons.

"Come along, sweet pea. Let's go up to the house and change you."

Claire jabbered as they slowly walked together toward Sarah's house. She studied her new home, loving the look of it. She still hadn't decided what color to paint it. "What do you think, Claire? Light green, yellow or white?"

"Aw-wo-lol." Claire looked up as if answering her.

Sarah laughed. "I've never heard of that color, although I suppose it was closer to yellow than white." She gazed at the house again. "Maybe we could use both colors. Yellow for the outer walls and white for the trim." She closed her eyes, trying to envision it, but saw the house in a soft green instead. Last time she'd considered colors, she'd contemplated green. The more she thought about it, the more she liked it.

At the door, she set Claire down and reached for the knob, but the jingle of a harness drew her around. A buggy headed her way. "I wonder if Dr. Worth is coming for another visit."

As the carriage crested the hill, she realized it was a fancy surrey with a fringed top drawn by a fine pair of matching gray horses. A nicely dressed man and a woman sat on the seat—neither of whom she'd met. A thrill of excitement rushed through her. Had some of her neighbors decided to come and visit?

She walked down the stairs, holding Claire's hand as she toddled alongside her. The couple looked to be in their early to midfifties. The woman's dark hair had tinges of silver, and it was pulled up in a tidy bun on the crown of her head. She had a sweet smile on her face and waved as the man drew the wagon to a stop. He hopped down then strode around the buggy and helped his wife to the ground.

They walked toward her. Sarah smiled, wondering what had brought them here today. The woman's gaze latched onto Claire and held. Sarah lifted her into her arms and hugged her.

Luke and Jack jogged around the side of the house, both carrying rifles. The couple paused and stared at them. The woman's eyes widened. Suddenly the man grabbed his stomach. He flashed his wife an apologetic glance and jogged toward the men. He leaned toward Jack and whispered something. Jack pointed toward the back of the house, and the man ran around the corner.

"Oh dear. I'm so embarrassed." The woman covered her mouth with her fingers and glanced at Sarah. "Please forgive my Henry. He ate something that evidently disagreed with him."

"Don't think a thing of it. I'm Sarah Worley." She waved for the men to come closer. "This is Luke McNeil and Jack Jensen." Luke stopped on her left, and Jack crossed in front of her to flank her right side. Could the couple have come searching for Lottie?

She hadn't been expecting a respectable-looking man and woman but rather a gang of rough henchmen.

"My name's Carolyn Powell, and Henry is my husband, like I mentioned."

Luke moved closer to Sarah as she offered a smile. "It's a pleasure to meet you, Mrs. Powell."

The woman lifted her eyes toward the house. Her smile dimmed for a moment before returning. "You sure have a lovely home. Did it take you long to build it?"

"Over a month, with a six-man crew—most of the time. We're still workin' on the barn," Jack said.

Luke leaned close to Sarah's ear, making her breath hitch at his nearness. "Don't like her," he whispered. "She's got a mustache."

Sarah elbowed him.

"It reminds me of the first place that Henry and I lived in before we had our two daughters. Is it true you won this land in the lottery?"

"Yes, it is." Sarah shifted Claire to her other arm. Why was this stranger questioning her? Was she merely making conversation while her husband used the necessary? Maybe that was the only reason they'd stopped. No matter, she wanted to treat them kindly. "I'd invite you in, but my parlor furniture hasn't arrived, so there's no place to sit. I can offer you coffee if you'd care to walk down the hill to our cook site."

Mrs. Powell looked that way then shook her head. "It's nice of you to offer, but with Henry not feeling well, it's best we don't dawdle."

"Do you live in the area?" Sarah asked

The woman shook her head. "No."

Mr. Powell hurried back, coming around the far side of the house, moving quicker than when he'd left. "Did you tell them yet?"

"Tell us what?" Luke asked, his gaze suspicious.

Mrs. Powell approached Sarah and smiled. She reached a hand toward Claire and caressed her head. "We can't thank you enough for what you did. And if not for that newspaper article telling how you found and rescued the girl, we'd never have known what happened."

Sarah frowned and glanced up at Luke, but she could tell by his shrug that he had no idea what the lady was talking about. Jack gave a brief shake of his head when she looked at him. "What do you mean?"

"You're the folks that found our daughter, Ellen—God rest her soul." She touched the handkerchief to her eyes. "This sweet child is our granddaughter, and we've come to take her home."

Chapter 19

No! Luke stiffened as he watched Sarah's pretty skin go pale. She gasped a throaty sound like an animal caught in a trap as her grip on Claire tightened. His heart broke for her. She loved that little gal so much that there'd been a time or two that he'd been jealous.

"What proof do you have that you're related to *this* child?" Jack shifted, raising his rifle so that it pointed toward the Powells instead of the ground.

Mr. Powell lifted his hands. "There's no reason to get riled. We have papers. I'm reaching in my vest to get them, so don't get trigger happy." He cautiously put his hand inside his jacket and pulled out a folded document and handed it to Jack.

Shaking it open, Jack held it so that Sarah and he could read it.

"What is it?" Luke stepped behind her and looked over her shoulder. Sarah leaned back slightly, pressing against his chest.

"It's a declaration of birth," Jack said. "An Ellen Powell Wolf had a baby girl almost two years ago."

Luke moved around to Sarah's side again, standing close to

her. "That doesn't prove *this* little girl is related to you."

"What more proof do you need? Isn't it enough that we came for her?" Mr. Powell shot a nervous glance toward the side of the house.

Luke wondered if the man was about to head back to the privy.

"Anyone could come claiming the girl was theirs." Luke wrapped his arm around Sarah, who was trying hard not to cry.

Mr. Powell frowned. "Why would they if they weren't related? Caring for a child that young is a lot of work."

Luke lifted his chin. "I can think of several reasons."

"Our Ellen has—" Mrs. Powell clutched her throat and looked as if she were going to cry. She raised her lacy handkerchief, touched it to the corner of her eyes again. "She had—red hair and green eyes like the woman you found. Her daughter had dark hair like this girl." Mrs. Powell's lip quivered. "We didn't approve of the man Ellen married, I'm afraid. She got upset with us and left." She dabbed her eyes." The next time we saw Ellen, she was about to birth her child. She had her baby and stayed with us for a while, but then she left after we had another disagreement and took our sweet grandbaby." Her gaze caressed Claire, causing the knot in Luke's belly to tighten. "We haven't seen them in over a year and a half. I can't believe how much the baby has grown."

"A man's word should be enough. Besides, we talked with a Dr. Worth in town, and he told us how to get here." Mr. Powell bent and clutched his belly. "We need to be going, Carolyn." He didn't look to be a grieving father. Maybe his present condition was all he could deal with at the moment.

"What was your granddaughter's name?" Sarah asked softly.

Mrs. Powell smiled. "It's Elizabeth. Please, may I hold her?"

The same name as Gabe's oldest daughter. Luke's heart felt

as if a wild mustang had stomped it to pieces. He could feel Sarah shaking against his arm, and he tightened his grip on her shoulders, pulling her against his side. Claire, oblivious to the disturbing goings on, picked at one of the buttons on Sarah's dress. The girl sure didn't look anything like Mrs. Powell—if the woman was even telling the truth.

"I'm not feeling so good." Mr. Powell bent over, his hands on his knees. "I think I should head back to that doctor's office."

"I'm sorry, but we really should go. I can't thank you enough for caring for Elizabeth. You probably saved her life." She held out her arms. "Please, let me have my granddaughter. You can see that I need to get my husband back to town."

Sarah bent her head against Claire's, hugging her. She sucked back a sob and bravely handed the woman her granddaughter. Claire gazed up at Mrs. Powell then back at Sarah, but she didn't cry. Was it possible she recognized her grandmother?

Luke clenched his teeth together. He wanted to shoot something. Punch a tree trunk. How could Sarah be so brave? He wanted to yell how unfair this was. How could God allow this to happen?

To see Sarah struggling not to cry twisted Luke's gut. As long as he'd known her, she'd never cried but had taken on each new thing with quiet acceptance. But this was too much. His fist curled.

Jack walked to Sarah's side and rested a hand on her shoulder. "We all knew this day might come."

"I know." Her voice quavered. "But I didn't want it to."

"Say your good-byes." Jack stared at the ground as if those words were the hardest ones he had to utter. Was he thinking of the day he'd said farewell to his dying wife?

Sarah reached out and took hold of Claire's hand. "Never forget I love you, sweetie." She reached down and grabbed hold of Luke's hand. "Please, tell me where you live, so I can visit her. I can't bear"—she sucked back a sob—"to never see her again."

"We're from Carthage, Missouri." Mr. Powell helped his wife into the buggy then hurried around to his side and climbed in. He tipped his hat then slapped the reins against the horses' backs. As the surrey pulled forward, Claire's wails filled the air.

A pitiful moan oozed out as Sarah fell against Luke's chest, holding him as she never had before. He held her close, resting his cheek against her head as he glared at the Powells' surrey.

The horses trotted away, disappearing over the hill. Luke stared at the sky as Claire's wails eased, softened by distance.

Sarah's whimpers cut him clear to his soul. He wanted to rail at the heavens, but it would do no good. What was done was done. Claire was gone, and with her, part of Sarah's heart had been ripped out.

"Cody didn't get to say good-bye." Jack shot Luke a pain-filled glance then strode around the far side of the house, his head hanging.

Luke stood there, helpless to comfort Sarah. All he could do was hold her. This was so unfair. Sarah was a good woman and didn't deserve the horrible pain she was suffering. He kissed the top of her head and cuddled her as tight as he dared. What would this do to Sarah? How would she get over the loss of Claire? She loved that little girl—and so did he.

Jack ran back to the front of the house. "Fire!"

Sarah pushed away from the comforting cocoon of Luke's arms. "Fire?" She followed Luke and Jack around the side of the house and found flames crawling up the side of her parlor wall and creeping through the open window. "No! No!"

"Get buckets. Blankets." Jack raced around the back of the house. Sarah heard him order Cody to stay at the barn and to yell if the fire started in that direction.

The two Peterson men who'd been working on the barn, rushed toward them then turned and followed Jack toward their camp.

"Stay back. I'm going upstairs to get blankets." Luke pinned her with his sapphire gaze. "Don't come in. I can't lose you."

He jogged to the front of the house, and she followed. "I can help."

"No! Stay there." He rushed inside.

Sarah gazed in the open door at the flames licking her window. "Oh, God. Please don't let my house burn. I've already lost Claire. Protect Luke." Her thoughts turned to Claire, and for just this moment, she was grateful the girl wasn't here. What if she'd been inside napping? Her heart felt split in two, but she'd rather the Powells have Claire than for her to have perished in a fire.

Luke raced out the door and tossed the blankets at her. "I'm going to saddle Golden Boy so we can get water faster." He jumped over the porch railing to the ground and raced toward the pasture where the horses had been staked.

Sarah jogged down the stairs, carrying her new wool blankets to the side of the house. She dropped one and started swatting the fire, but her efforts only seemed to fuel the blaze. Heat seared her face. Tears coursed down her cheeks.

Amos and Johnny returned, one carrying her soapy dishwater and the rinse pot. Jack raced past the back of the house, holding four buckets, and headed for the river.

Amos tugged the blanket from her, dropped it in the rinse pot, and then pulled it out and slapped it against the siding, over and over. The stubborn flames refused to yield and continued spreading out of reach at an alarming rate.

Johnny tossed the soapy water onto the fire, grabbed the empty rinse pot, and charged toward the river. Sarah lifted the other blanket, so heavy with water that she had to drag it over to the grass nearest the house, and dropped it onto the smoldering sod. The fire charged up the side of her house in almost a straight and narrow line.

Jack returned from the river, carrying two buckets. He set one down and splashed the other on the fire then grabbed the other bucket and repeated the action, his mouth pressed together in a tight line. "This fire was no accident."

"What do you mean?" Sarah held her hands to her mouth, watching the flames lick higher.

Jack waved his hand at several empty bottles on the charred grass. "Powell must have done this."

"It's true." Breathing hard, Amos tossed aside the smoky blanket and grabbed the one she'd put on the grass. "This fire was set on purpose. No other way it could've started."

Sarah sucked in a breath then started coughing. "Why would Mr. Powell do this? We gave Claire to them." She couldn't bring herself to call her Elizabeth.

"I don't know. " Jack shook his head, snatched up the other

empty bucket, and ran for more water.

She stepped back, not liking where her thoughts were taking her. Luke rode up to her on his horse and leading Jack's mount. Hungry for answers, Sarah touched Luke's leg. "Jack thinks Mr. Powell set the fire. I don't understand. Why would he do such a heinous thing?"

His normally happy gaze grew hard. "Because they aren't Claire's grandparents. He probably set the fire, thinking we might realize they were frauds. The fire would keep us busy while they made their escape."

Sarah covered her mouth as she gasped. She squelched the instant speck of hope that tried to blossom. "What makes you say that?"

"I remember Jack said Claire had blue eyes the same as her mother, not green ones like Mrs. Powell said. A real mother wouldn't forget something that important."

"No, a mother wouldn't." Tears stung Sarah's eyes. She should have caught Mrs. Powell's mistake herself, but she'd been too distraught at the possibility of losing Claire. She pressed her fingers to her aching eyes. "Oh, Luke, I let them take her. I just gave away the little girl I love."

The horses pranced and stared at the fire, the whites of their eyes showing. Pain filled Luke's eyes as he gazed at her. "What should I do? If I go after Claire, I can't help fight the fire. You could lose the house."

"Go! Forget the house." She could build another one—live in a tent—but there was only one little girl who'd stolen her heart.

He tossed the reins of Jack's horse to her. "Get him to Jack." He stared hard at her. "I'll get our Claire back."

He wheeled Golden Boy around Jack's horse, sent her a stare that said so much she could hardly breathe, and then he slapped the reins on the palomino's flanks. The gelding bolted forward into a gallop.

"Here." Amos held out his cupped hands, his face blackened from sweat and soot. He boosted her onto the horse, and she turned him toward the river. "Help us, Lord. Please help Luke to find Claire and get her back."

As she drew near the river, Jack jogged toward her, lugging two buckets. She pulled the horse to a stop and slid off. Amos ran up behind her and grabbed the buckets, and headed back to the house.

"Where'd Luke go?" Jack leaped onto his horse.

"He just realized the Powells aren't Claire's grandparents."

His eyes widened. "I had a gut feelin' something wasn't right. I shouldn't have forced you to give her up."

She shook her head. "It wasn't your fault."

Amos ran up to him and handed Jack the empty buckets. He trotted the horse down the hill, passing Johnny, who carried the other buckets.

Sarah didn't know what to do.

She stared at her house, knowing in her gut it was a lost cause. Too little water and manpower, and too much fire. She gasped. "My clothes!" She hurried toward the front of her home. If only they'd had rain recently, but everything was dry as old dead bones from the summer heat. At least she could save a few of her things. She hiked up her skirts and charged into the house. Surely she had time to save her clothes and the trunk of things Lara had loaned her.

The buggy wheel tracks made an easy trail to follow as they cut through the dry grass toward town. Luke scanned the area ahead between him and Anadarko, but he didn't see the couple. They'd be harder to find in town. He'd check Dr. Worth's office first, since Mr. Powell mentioned it, but he didn't expect to find them there. What if they merely drove through town then headed away from Anadarko on the other side? He'd never find their tracks.

Several men on horseback galloped toward him. He hoped they weren't looking for Lottie, because he didn't have time to deal with that now. As he drew nearer, he recognized Dr. Worth. He rode up to Luke, looking concerned. "Some men in town said they saw smoke coming from this way."

"It's Sarah's house."

The man's brown eyes widened. "Is she all right?"

"She's fine. Can you help?"

The four other men nodded in unison and rode off toward Sarah's at a fast pace. The doctor struggled to hold back his horse.

"Did y'all pass a fancy surrey with a well-dressed couple in it?"

The doctor shook his head. Luke didn't like the look on the man's face as he gazed in the direction of the smoke rising from the house. Was he concerned about Sarah because he was a doctor, or was it something more?

No time to worry about that. He nudged Golden Boy forward then slowed as they entered town. He glanced at every buggy he saw, hoping—praying—he'd see the Powells' gray horses. He continued on First Street, peering down the side streets each way. When he reached the end of First, he rode across to Second and went through town again. People ambled along both sides of the streets, and several buggies were parked along them. He searched each one.

"Help me, Lord. Don't let those lying kidnappers get away." He wished there was a marshal in town, because he doubted the soldiers would be willing to help him. He reached the end of the street, trotted his horse over to Third, and started down it. He *had* to find Claire. He couldn't return to Sarah without her.

He'd almost passed Hampton's General Store when he recognized Mr. Powell coming out, carrying several cans of milk and a thick package. The man had removed his jacket and tie and showed no signs of having a bellyache. Luke's eyes narrowed. He faced forward and kept riding, but as he passed the next alley, he flicked his gaze sideways. His heart bucked. A buggy was parked up next to a building. Mrs. Powell stood beside it, bent over. Claire's frantic cries gutted him. Mrs. Powell yanked off the wet diaper and tossed it behind her. She stood Claire on her feet and shook her. "Hush, I said. All that racket is making my head ache."

Luke clenched his jaw. He tapped Golden Boy's sides, making the horse trot. Once he came to the end of the block, he reined the horse to the left, and then left again on the next street. He dismounted and tied the gelding to a hitching post in front of a lawyer's office. The Powells were sure going to need a lawyer once he was done with them. He quickly walked to the alley where he'd seen the buggy and peered around the corner. Mr. Powell sauntered toward it.

"Hurry up, Henry. You want them to come after us? You know they will soon as they get that fire out."

Mr. Powell belched. "They ain't getting it out anytime soon. I made sure of that." He set the cans of milk in the back of the buggy.

"Hurry up and open that package. I need a diaper."

Mr. Powell did as ordered and handed her one. Mrs. Powell laid Claire on the floor of the buggy and put the fresh diaper on her. "C'mon! We need to get out of town. Fast!"

Mr. Powell spun around. As he rounded the buggy, his boot clipped the wheel and he fell flat on his face.

Luke licked his lips, tasting success. This was the best chance he'd get. He glanced around, relieved that no one else was near, then pulled his gun and stepped into the alley. Mr. Powell lay on the ground, his face to the wall. Luke tiptoed toward the wife, whose back was to him.

"Get up, you fool. We gotta get going." She bent down and yanked on her husband's shirt.

"Hush, woman. I hit my head when I fell." Mr. Powell reached a hand to his forehead.

Claire's wails slowed as she spied him. She sniffled, reaching out her hands and stealing a huge chunk of his heart. Luke reached the buggy and snatched Claire. She clutched him so hard she pinched a hunk of skin. She sobbed against his shirt, much as Sarah had done. The woman rose and glanced at the buggy then froze as she realized she wasn't alone. Luke prayed they'd go peacefully to the army office.

Mrs. Powell snarled like a guard dog. She spun around, and faster than he could believe, drew a pistol from her waistband. She fired.

Claire wailed. Hot pain pierced Luke's shoulder, but he held onto his precious cargo and his gun. He gritted past the pain and glared at the woman. "Drop that gun. Now!"

Her face turned several shades of red before she complied. She shook her head, finally looking as if she'd given up. "Why couldn't you just let us go? You'll break our daughter's heart."

Luke wasn't sure what she was talking about or how he was going to handle the pair now that he was shot. Blood oozed from his wound. "I don't know what game you're playin', but we both know you aren't related to this girl."

She dabbed at her eyes. "Our Ellen has lost three babies. She's pining away for the want of a child. I thought that little gal would make her happy. I never counted on the lady that had her wanting to keep her so much."

Several men rounded the corner then paused to take in the scene.

Mrs. Powell pivoted toward them. "Help us! He's trying to steal our baby."

The men glared at Luke, and one pulled out his pistol.

"She's lying. That woman shot me and stole this sweet child from a friend of mine. I aim to take her back."

"No-o-o! Don't let him take my baby." Mrs. Powell clutched her heart and fell to her knees. The woman should have been an actress.

"Maybe you oughta give the kid back," the taller cowboy said.

Luke lifted his chin and stared hard at the man. "Take us all to army headquarters, and we'll get this farce straightened out."

Mrs. Powell hopped up. She searched the ground, turning one way then the next.

Mr. Powell slowly rose, moved around to the front of the wagon, and pointed a gun at Luke. "Give my wife that girl, or I'll put a bullet in the kid."

Luke made eye contact with the man standing behind Mr. Powell and knew the man had finally realized the truth. The man flipped his pistol around, grabbing it by the barrel and knocked the butt into the back of Powell's skull. Powell dropped like a steer whose back hooves had been lassoed.

"No!" Mrs. Powell cried out at her husband's demise but turned on Luke, charging him. He back-stepped, lifting his gun and pointing it at her face. His hand shook from his wound, but he managed to hold the gun steady enough. She stopped and glared at him. "You've ruined everything."

He smiled, in spite of how he felt. "I prefer to think that I saved the day."

One of the cowboys grabbed her from behind. "Get a move on, lady."

His friend hoisted Mr. Powell to his feet again—albeit barely. The man could hardly stand.

"Let's get them to the army office; then I need to get home. These two set my friend's house on fire on top of stealing this little gal." He kissed Claire. She'd stopped wailing, but she did an odd little sniff-hiccup thing he'd seen Gabe's kids do after a big cry. Her nose was red and her skin splotchy. The poor thing felt hot. He kissed her head again, and she leaned against his shoulder in a display of trust that moved him to the core. She barely knew him, and yet she trusted him and got comfort from being in his arms—well, arm.

"We need to get you to a doctor before you collapse." One of the men who'd been in the back of the group approached. "You want me to carry her?"

Luke shook his head. "Dr. Worth headed out to help fight the fire. Is there another doc in town?"

"Yep. A block over."

"I can get myself there if you'll take care of them."

"M'name's Albert Owens." He rocked his head in a backward motion. "That's Ed Sheridan."

"Luke McNeil. I can't thank you enough from helpin' me. I'd shake your hands, but—" he glanced at his bloody shoulder. He holstered his gun, managing not to wince, and gave the man a nod of gratitude.

"Think nuthin' of it. Glad to he'p," Ed said.

"Tell the officials that I'll be down there as soon as I can to give a statement. They know where to find me if they need me before then."

Luke hoisted Claire up to get a better hold. She grabbed his shirt, whimpering, as if she thought he was getting rid of her. "Not on your life, sweetheart. Hold on a bit longer."

He tottered to the hitching post where Golden Boy waited. He loosened the reins then flipped them over his horse's neck and started shuffling to the doctor's office, knowing the horse would follow. Riding would be quicker, but he couldn't mount with Claire in one arm and a bullet hole in his shoulder.

His vision blurred as he turned onto the street Albert had indicated. His gaze latched onto the doctor's shingle, hanging two doors down. People eyed him, but no one offered to help. He stumbled as he attempted the stairs and finally fell against the door. Claire fussed at being pressed against the glass.

On the other side of the door, he saw a woman's eyes widen as she stared at him. She yelled over her shoulder for the doctor then opened the door. The woman's face blurred. Luke stumbled on the threshold but managed to step through the doorway and handed Claire to her on his way to meet the floor.

Chapter 20

Carson's heart broke for Sarah as he reined his horse to a stop in front of her burning house. The right side of it was completely engulfed in flames. He doubted anything short of a downpour could save it. What a horrible loss.

Jack rode toward them fast. Carson slid off his horse and tied him to a bush a safe distance from the inferno. He followed the other men from town as they jogged toward Jack. Ted Buckner grabbed one of the buckets and tossed it onto the flames. A loud hiss rose up along with a cloud of smoke. A man he didn't know took the other bucket from Jack and dumped it. They passed the buckets back to Jack. He quickly mounted his horse.

Two of the men grabbed charred blankets and started beating flames. Loud whacks mixed with the eerie crackle of fire and stench of smoke. One of the men Carson recognized as being a Peterson who'd help build the house jogged toward them, two more pails in tow.

Carson looked all around then at Jack. "Where's Sarah?"

He frowned. "She was out here a while ago."

Carson's heart did a somersault at his sudden thought. "You

don't suppose she went inside, do you?"

"No—" Jack's tanned complexion paled. He dropped the buckets, tossed his leg over the horse's neck, and slid down. He threw the reins toward Ted. "Keep getting water at the river."

He broke into a run, as did Carson. Surely Sarah wouldn't have gone into a burning house—unless the little girl had been inside.

The front door was open and they burst through. Jack paused and looked around the smoky, empty downstairs. Then he darted up the steps. Carson covered his nose and mouth and peeked into the smoke-filled parlor. Flames had burned up one side and were spreading across the ceiling. Thank God it was empty. Sarah might lose her house, but at least she wouldn't lose her furnishings, too.

He heard arguing upstairs and ran up to the second floor. The smoke grew thicker as he reached the landing. He yanked his handkerchief from his pocket, covered his mouth, and then bent over to avoid the worst of the smoke.

"No! Got to save Lara's trunk."

"We have to get out. Now!" Jack yelled.

Carson reached the door of a bedroom that held only a bed and a cot. The mattress was half off the frame. Where was the girl?

Jack stood in a face-off with Sarah, whose arms were filled with clothing. She noticed him step into the room, and relief softened her expression. "Carson can help with the trunk."

Jack scowled at him, as if his presence had encouraged her. "It's not worth our lives."

"It's Lara's. I have to save it."

Jack shook his head then gave Carson a hard look as he stepped around Sarah. He handed Carson a crate of diapers. "Help her downstairs. Fast."

Jack grabbed the trunk as Carson took hold of Sarah's arm and led her to the stairs. She coughed but hung on to the clothes she carried. They burst out into the fresh air, hurried down the porch steps, and out into the yard. He looked back at the house, as Jack ran out, his face blackened.

The flames had reached the front of the house and were eating their way toward the porch. Beside him, Sarah coughed. He bent over, mimicking her as he struggled to get fresh air into his lungs. Sweat poured off of him from the heat. Suddenly he realized he hadn't seen the little girl. He bolted upright. "Where's Claire?"

Sarah's sad expression crumpled even more, and she turned toward Jack, falling against him. He wrapped one arm around her. "She's gone."

"Gone where?"

"Long story. Have to wait." Jack eyed him with a look that said not to mention it.

One of the Peterson men jogged around the side of the house. He looked at Jack and shook his head. He strode over to them and stared at the house, too. "There's no savin' it now. The other men are wetting the grass in hopes of keepin' the fire from spreading to the barn or starting a prairie fire."

"Cody! Gotta check on my son." Jack turned toward Carson. "Could you stay with Sarah? It's been a hard day."

"Of course."

Jack gave Sarah's shoulders a squeeze and placed a kiss on her head then backed away. "Will you be all right?"

She nodded but didn't say anything. She just stood there with her head hanging, the piddling bit of clothing she'd salvaged in her arms. Carson hated the conflicting emotions roiling through him. Was there more between Jack and Sarah than he first realized? And what happened to the girl? "Why don't we move back? It's not good for you to breathe in smoke. And let me hold those." He held out his arms.

She shook her head, hugging the garments to her. "I should make some coffee. The men may want it"—she choked on a sob then regained her composure— "after they're. . .done."

"Cool water might actually taste better than coffee."

She glanced up, looking alarmed. "My rain barrel is at the back of the house. We should move it so we don't lose the water. It's much better for drinking than the river water."

There hadn't been much rain lately. He doubted there would be any to salvage—either the men had used it, or by now, it would have soot in it and not be drinkable. Still, she needed to do something to help. "Let's walk around the side that isn't on fire yet and check on the barrel."

She fumbled with her clothing until she held them in one arm then looped her hand through the arm he offered, and he led her around the house. He hated the way she trembled, but he had to give her credit for not crying, albeit she had every right to do so. She paused and stared wide-eyed at the rear of the house. Flames galloped across the wooden siding as if in a race to beat the blaze at the front to the far side. A window fifteen feet away exploded. He and Sarah jumped. He tugged her back, hating that this had happened to her new house.

"The barrel is gone." The accepting tone of her voice, as if she expected everything to be destroyed, made his heart feel as if someone had encased it in plaster. "Sarah, let me take your clothes and put them in that buckboard by the barn."

She finally nodded and held them out. He relieved her of that small burden, tried not to consider the fact that he carried not only two dresses but some of her unmentionables. He laid the items carefully in a relatively clean spot in the back of the buckboard then swung around and studied the rear of the house. Over half of it was already on fire.

Jack stood inside the barn, comforting his son. Carson started forward, but his gaze landed on a barrel sitting out in the open. He was grateful for one thing going right. "Sarah, isn't this the water barrel?" He lifted the lid and looked in. "It is. Someone must have moved it away from the fire."

She eased her head around and nodded. "I think so." She moved slowly—almost lethargically—toward him. Had the smoke affected her more than he realized, or was the trauma of the burning house responsible for her downheartedness? He'd read in medical journals about doctors studying how traumatic events affected people. Sarah was showing some of the symptoms, but that was certainly understandable.

She walked over to the barrel and looked in. "There's still some but not much."

He reached down and snagged the tin cup floating in the water. He filled the cup and handed it to her. She took it and stood there, staring into the cup. "Sarah, you need to drink it. Your body has had a shock."

She did as told then turned back and stared at the house. "There's no saving it. I'd hoped at first. . ."

He hated the forlorn tone to her voice. He wished he had the right to wrap his arm around her and offer comfort, but all he had to give her were words of encouragement. "It can be rebuilt."

She shook her head. "I don't have enough money for that."

His stomach tightened. Did that mean she'd leave town? He wasn't sure when he'd come to care for her, but he realized now that he did. "What will you do?'

"I don't know. The land is mine, but I have to live on it for fives years and improve it before I get the official title. If I don't, I could lose it."

"You have years to get that done. Perhaps you could start with a small house and add on later."

She shrugged, as if thinking about it was too much.

"Let me take you to town. Get you something to eat. There's a new hotel you can stay in."

She shook her head. "Thank you, but I need to stay here. I have to prepare lunch for the men."

Carson wanted to say the men could fend for themselves, but after fighting the fire, they would be exhausted.

"I need to do something. I can't just stand here."

"Where do you do your cooking?" There hadn't been a stove inside the house, so he knew she didn't cook there."

She looked down the hill to her right. "At the Petersons' camp."

"Why don't we walk down there? You can still watch what's happening, but the heat won't be so fierce." He still had his handkerchief in his hand and longed to wipe the sweat and grime off his face, but he held it out to her instead. "Why don't you wet this and clean your face?"

She looked at him and blinked. "My face is dirty?"

"Just a little soot." And sweat.

"Oh. I must look like you do."

He glanced into the barrel, hoping to catch a glimpse of his face, but the water level was too low.

"Could you get me some more water, please? I can't reach it."

"Certainly." He dipped the cup again and handed it to her.

She poured the water over the handkerchief, dropped the cup in the barrel, and then wiped her face. "That feels good." When she pulled the soiled hanky away, her dark eyes widened. "Oh my. You weren't joking."

He relaxed his tense stance, glad to hear her sounding closer to normal. At least there was a pitch to her voice instead of the monotone that had been there a moment ago.

She gazed up at him then stared off in the distance. "A couple showed up this morning, claiming to be Claire's grandparents. They knew enough information that we believed them." She swallowed hard. "I gave her to them. Just handed that poor little girl over."

"Why wouldn't you if they were her relatives?"

She looked at him again, her gaze bleak. "That's what I thought, too, even though it broke my heart to give her to them. Mr. Powell—the supposed grandfather—started the fire before he left."

Carson gripped the edge of the barrel. "Why would he do that?"

"To keep us from going after him—when we realized they'd lied. I don't believe they are related to Claire at all."

"Oh, Sarah. What are you going to do?"

"Luke figured it out and went after them."

"Who's Luke?"

A sweet smile—one he didn't at all like since it related to a man—softened her expression. "He's a very good friend of mine.

He realized the Powells had said Claire's mother had green eyes when they were actually blue, just like her daughter's. I pray he finds them and brings her back."

He ached to ask about her relationship with this Luke. Who was he to Sarah that in spite of all she'd been through this morning, she'd have almost a starry-eyed look when she talked about him?

Carson felt as if he were losing the battle to win Sarah's heart. If this Luke fellow brought the child back, he'd be a hero in Sarah's eyes.

⌒

A hammering in his head pulled Luke from the blackness. The room swirled. He closed his eyes then slowly opened them, staring up at a brand-new ceiling. As the dizziness fled, he realized the pounding was actually hammers nearby and not in his skull. His shoulder and upper arm burned as if someone had poured lantern oil on them and set them afire, exactly like that man had done to Sarah's house. Sarah!

He bolted upright, hissing and grabbing his arm.

"Hold on there, young man." A stranger pushed him down. "In case you don't remember, you've been shot. My name's Dr. Littleton. You are fortunate that the bullet passed all the way through your shoulder, but you've lost a lot of blood. You need to rest."

Luke glanced around the spotless room. "Where's Claire?"

"My wife is seeing to the girl. She was quite upset to leave you, but she settled down once Tillie gave her something to eat. She's asleep now."

The tension eased from his neck a bit. "I appreciate all you've done, but I can't stay here, Doc. When I left this morning to rescue Claire from the folks who'd pretended to be her grandparents and stole her, my dear friend's house was on fire. I have to get back there."

He shook his head. "There's nothing you can do. By now the fire is either out or it will have done its damage."

"You don't understand. I'm going back. One way or another."

Dr. Littleton crossed his arms and stared at him with a humorous expression. "I suppose you're going to hop on that fine horse of yours and hold on to that little girl and ride back to your friend's place."

Luke had to admit the plan sounded less reasonable coming from the doctor's mouth. He could ride back and leave Claire napping for the time being, but Sarah would have a fit if he didn't bring her gal home. And he'd promised.

"If that's the only way, I reckon I have no choice."

Doc shook his head and mumbled something about stubborn men. "If I must, I'll drive you home in my buggy."

Luke smiled. "I'd appreciate that—a whole lot."

An hour later, Luke stared at the charred remains of Sarah's house. Dark smoke still rose up from the ashes, but he saw no flames. There was nothing left to burn. The ache in his gut was far greater than the one in his shoulder. Sarah's pretty house—her dream—was a total loss.

Beside him on the seat of Dr. Littleton's buggy, Claire babbled something and then shoved a gummy biscuit the doctor's wife had given her into her mouth. At least Claire's return would help Sarah get over the loss of her home. Would she give up on her dream now and go back to Gabe and Lara's place? If she did, what would he do? The idea of owning a livery had grown on him, but Anadarko held little draw if Sarah wasn't here. But at the same time, what was the point of following her back home if she had no interest in marrying him? Sooner or later, he'd have to give up if she kept refusing him. A man had his pride, after all.

Behind them, from where he was tied to the buggy, Golden Boy nickered. Luke glanced toward the Peterson camp to see Jack riding their way. As he drew close, he saw the exhaustion on his friend's face. Jack stopped his horse and frowned. "What happened to you?"

"Got shot as I played the knight in shining armor. This is Dr. Littleton. He's the one who fixed up my shoulder."

"I appreciate that, Doc, and thanks for bringing this galoot home." Jack nodded; then his gaze connected with Luke's. "I'm glad you're all right. Don't know what Sarah would have done if she lost you. I'm real glad to see you got Claire. Sarah needs some good news."

Claire squealed and waved. Jack smiled and returned her wave, grinning—probably for the first time today.

"Sarah made lunch. She saved you some. There's enough for you, too, Dr. Littleton."

"Thank you, but my wife will have my meal ready when I get home."

"We're beholdin' to you. Guess I'll check again to make sure no more fires have started." Jack reined his horse toward the debris.

Luke pointed the doc where to go, and as they drew near, he noticed Sarah, one of the men he'd passed earlier, and the Peterson men sitting around the campfire. He didn't like the way the stranger sat so close to her.

Sarah lifted her gaze then shot to her feet. She threw down her plate, hiked up her skirts, and raced toward him. His heartbeat kicked into a higher gait. If only she was running to him and not Claire.

He picked her up with his good arm. "Lookie there, sweetheart. Your mama's comin'."

Doc stopped the buggy as she drew near. Her yellow dress was blackened with soot, but intriguing wisps of her hair had tugged loose from the long braid that hung down her back. Tears glistened in her black eyes. "Claire! Oh, thank You, God."

Claire bounced on his thigh and shrieked, holding out her arms. Sarah leaned against his leg and snatched her. She hugged the girl so hard, he thought she might break something. He smiled seeing how happy he'd made Sarah.

Doc leaned toward him. "Now I understand why you were in such a hurry to get back."

Luke couldn't help the sad smile he gave him. Too bad Sarah wasn't as happy to see him. He looked at her again, and her smile dimmed.

"What happened?"

"He got shot rescuing that little girl," the doctor offered.

Sarah shifted Claire to her hip. "How bad is it?"

"Nothing a few weeks of rest won't help, as long as the wound stays clean." Doc eyed him to make sure he understood. "Be sure you come back to my office so I can check it in two days."

Luke grunted. "Too much to do to rest."

Sarah narrowed her eyes. "I'll see that he follows your orders."

Luke kind of liked the sound of that, even though it probably meant he'd be in bed for days. What he didn't like was that the stranger from camp had followed her. Nor did he care for the expression on the man's face as he gazed at her. Just who was this interloper?

The man glanced at Dr. Littleton. "Nice to see you again, Clem."

"You, too, Carson."

"Doc, this is Sarah Worley. Too much squealin' goin' on to tell you sooner." Luke rose, hating the weakness in his limbs. He managed to climb down without embarrassing himself. Sarah walked up to him, leaned in, and kissed his cheek. Instant strength rushed through him, and he straightened.

"I can't thank you enough for bringing Claire back. Are you hurting badly?"

"You can talk later," Dr. Littleton said. "Mr. McNeil lost quite a bit of blood and may be weak for a few days. You'd best help him find a seat before he falls down. I wanted to keep him until tomorrow, but he was more than a little insistent that he needed to get back to you."

Luke glared at the man. He wouldn't have minded his speech if not for that Carson fellow. But a man shouldn't have his weaknesses aired in front of strangers.

Jack rode back, dismounted, and then untied Golden Boy. "C'mon, Luke. I'll help you up. It's a bit far for you to walk."

He nodded his thanks, even though Jack practically had to shove him up into the saddle. His arm blazed like a prairie fire, but he did his best not to grimace. He hated the fact that his bed sounded like a good place to be, but he wouldn't head for it until the stranger left. The man needed to know where things stood with him and Sarah. Too bad *he* didn't know.

Chapter 21

Sarah smiled as she carried Claire back to the campsite. The girl jabbered, as if retelling her adventurous story. Jack rode alongside Luke then helped him to dismount, but instead of heading to his tent, the stubborn man dropped onto Zelma's chair. Amos and Johnny smiled at Claire as they headed toward the barn.

Cody ran to her. "Hi, Claire. Are you glad you're back?"

Concerned for Luke, she handed the toddler to the boy. "Can you play with her for a few minutes?"

"Sure." He lugged her to a spot near Luke then sat her on the ground and joined her.

Carson stood two yards away. "Walk me to my horse? I probably should get back to town."

Sarah glanced behind her then nodded.

"I'm real sorry we didn't arrive in time to save your house."

"Don't be. It's not your fault. Without rain, I doubt fifty men could have stopped the blaze."

He smiled. "I know this is a terrible time to ask, but I was hoping you might join me in town for supper one evening. I'm happy to ride out and pick you up."

Sarah shot a glance at Luke and caught him scowling at them. "Thank you, but I don't know what's going to happen now."

"I hope you'll consider rebuilding."

She shook her head. "I really don't know. It's too soon to make a decision."

He pursed his lips then nodded. "I understand. Please let me know what you decide, and the dinner offer stands—anytime you're available."

"Thank you. I probably should go. Luke will sit there all day if I don't make him go to his tent."

Carson frowned. "Do you and he have an understanding that I should know about?"

Dr. Worth was interested in her? How had she not noticed? She avoided his gaze as she searched her mind. How could she explain Luke to him? "He's a very close friend."

"That's all? A friend?"

And the man who rescued Claire. "It's hard for me to put my feelings for him into words."

"I see. I should be going."

Sarah reached out and touched his arm. "Thank you again for all your help."

He nodded once more then turned and strode toward his horse. She hated the thought that she'd disappointed him. Why couldn't men simply be friends instead of wanting more? She knew how to be a friend, but it was the *wanting more* part that scared her.

She walked toward Luke. He definitely wanted more. Though thrilled at having Claire back, she had nearly dropped her when she first caught site of Luke's pale face and fresh bandage.

"Who is that man?" He asked as she drew near.

"I'm sorry for not introducing you."

"I'm not."

She almost smiled at his pouty, little boy look. "Dr. Worth is the man who checked out Claire when we first found her."

"He sure seems friendly."

Jack chuckled as he poured a cup of coffee. Luke glared when he handed him the cup. "That hole in your shoulder sure has made you crabby. Why don't you go lie down and do us all a favor?"

"It isn't the wound."

"Then what is it?" Sarah asked.

Both Jack and Luke looked at her like she'd suddenly lost all of her hair. She reached up to touch it, wincing at the silly thought.

"He's jealous of the doctor," Cody said.

Jack spewed his coffee, and Luke choked on his.

Sarah's face grew warm. Luke was jealous? "There's nothing between Dr. Worth and me."

Luke rolled his eyes. "How can you be so naive?"

She shoved her hands to her hips. "What does that mean?"

Jack picked up Claire. "Cody, c'mon. Let's tend to the horses."

"Why? I was havin' fun with Claire."

Jack shot his son a look. "She can help us."

Cody fell into step with his pa. "Aw. . .she's too little to help."

Sarah focused on Luke. His face was even paler than when he first sat down. "You need to rest."

He attempted to stand but fell back down. "I hate bein' so weak and useless."

Sarah hurried to his side. "You are *not* useless. I wouldn't have

Claire if not for you." She leaned down and reached for his good arm. "Come on. Let me help you to your tent."

Luke grimaced as he slowly forced himself up. Concern washed through Sarah. She'd never seen him like this. He was always so confident and strong. He wrapped his arm around her shoulder, and she helped support him on the walk to his tent. As they reached it, she paused, unsure whether to go in or not.

"I hate saying it, but I don't think I can move another step without your help."

"All right." She struggled to pull open the flap with one hand but managed.

They stepped inside and moved straight toward Luke's cot. She couldn't help looking around the tidy tent. For some reason, she'd expected it to be messy. She helped him onto the cot, and he sat there breathing hard. He reached down and attempted to remove his boot but failed.

Sarah knelt in front of him. "Let me help." She tugged and tugged, and finally the boot came loose and she fell onto her backside. Luke chuckled for the first time since his return. "Don't laugh or I'll leave the other boot on your foot."

He smiled at her, the emotion shining from his eyes making her mouth go dry.

Disconcerted, she rose onto her knees. "Give me your other foot."

He stuck it out, and thankfully this boot came off easier, allowing her to retain her dignity. She set them under his cot.

He smiled up at her. "I'm much obliged for your help."

She gently pushed on his good shoulder, but he didn't move a speck. "You need to lie down."

His blue gaze captured hers, sending her heartbeat fluttering. "Do you have feelings for that doctor?"

"What? No! He's only a friend." She snatched the folded blanket off the end of Luke's cot, needing something to dwell on besides his intense stare.

"Are you sure? He looked at you as if you're a big steak he wanted to devour."

"For heaven's sake, Luke. Don't exaggerate."

She tossed the blanket on the bed and turned to leave, but his hand snaked out and captured hers. "Don't go. Please."

"Then stop talking nonsense."

He looked down. His sad expression twisted her insides into a knot. What was that look for? Did he honestly think she had feelings for Carson?

"Will you please lie down?"

He shook his head and looked up. "Not until I have my say."

"Fine then. What do you want to say?"

He struggled to stand but didn't have the strength. He sighed and tugged her down beside him. He gazed into her eyes for a long moment. "I love you, Sarah. I have for years, but I'm finally accepting the fact that you don't feel the same toward me."

Her breath caught in her throat. "I do care for you. You're my best friend, next to Lara and Jo."

He snorted. "I don't want to be your friend. I want to be your husband."

Her hands shook. What did she know of love? About being a wife? "I don't know what to say. I appreciate so much that you risked your life to bring Claire back. I do care for you, but I don't know if I'm ready to marry."

Sadness filled his gaze. "I've said my piece. I've asked you to marry me, but I won't ask again. You'll have to decide what it is you want and whether I'm part of that."

She reached up, cupping his cheek, hating how her indecision had hurt him. Tears burned her eyes. "Please don't be sad. I'm confused, especially now that I've lost the house."

He nodded. Then suddenly a fire lit in his eyes. He tugged her forward, pressing his lips against hers. His passion ignited, laying claim to her as his kisses branded her with his love. A flame started deep within her, turning into a roaring blaze like she'd never before experienced. Frightened of her intense feelings, she pushed away. Luke jerked and cried out from where she'd accidentally touched his injured shoulder.

Sarah bolted to her feet. Stared at him for a moment then ran out of the tent. She looked around, glad no one was near, and raced toward the river.

What had gotten into Luke? Her heart pounded, and her lips felt swollen. She touched them and found them still moist from his kisses. She gazed at the glistening water. Was it possible she truly was in love with Luke?

⌒

The Petersons' dog barked and ran toward the nearest hill, tail wagging. Sarah rose from stirring the big kettle of beans. Her heart had barely resumed a normal rhythm since leaving Luke's tent an hour ago, and now it was pounding again. She set the spoon down and jogged up the hill, hoping for a glimpse of Zelma.

Sarah gasped. What was Lara doing here? Her dear friend

sat next to Zelma on the wagon seat. She raised her hand and waved. Mr. Peterson rode alongside the wagon with one of the twins walking behind it and the other one riding his horse. Tears burned Sarah's eyes. She'd never needed to talk to Lara as much as she did now. She knew the moment Lara noticed the charred remains of the house.

The wagon stopped, and Lara climbed down the side and stepped into Sarah's open arms.

"What are you doing here? Oh, I've missed you."

"Me, too."

Beth peeked through the wagon's opening and waved. "Howdy, Sarah!"

"You brought the girls, too!" Sarah wiped the tears from her eyes.

Beth and Zelma helped Missy climb onto the bench, and then Lara lifted her younger daughter down while Beth managed to shinny down herself. The four females enveloped each other in a big hug. Zelma beamed at them from the wagon's bench.

"I'm so glad to see y'all." Sarah kissed the girls.

"Hey!" Cody ran toward them, and the girls hugged their cousin.

"We thought we'd come to help you move in and set up house." Lara's expression dimmed. "What happened to your house?"

Sarah shook her head. "It's a long story." She looked up at Zelma, who'd been staring at the house remains with a sad expression. "It's good to have you back."

"Good to be back, but I have to admit, it's a sad thing to see that pretty house a heap of rubble. Was it lightning?"

"No. Let's get the wagon parked, and then I'll explain what

happened. Where's Lottie? Did you get her settled somewhere?"

Lara nodded. "My neighbor, Mrs. Easton is staying with her and cooking for Gabe until we get back. I think she's going to be all right." Lara smiled. "She sure asked a lot of questions about Jack."

"I'm so glad she's all right. It was a brave thing Jack did." She gazed up the hill. "I'm afraid we'll need to go to town and get a hotel room for you since I have nowhere here for you to stay."

"I think it would be a good idea for you to come, too. You could do with some pampering." Lara smiled and tucked a loose strand of hair behind Sarah's ear. "Now, where's that sweet little urchin of yours? Zelma's been telling me all about her."

"Napping, but I should check on her. It's been a rough day for all of us."

Sarah and Lara walked over to where the tents had been staked and ducked inside Sarah's tent, which Jack had set up again. Claire lay on the cot, still asleep. Staying in town was probably a good idea since she had next to nothing in the way of possessions.

Lara bent over the sleeping toddler. "She's precious. Her coloring is similar to yours."

Sarah smiled, warmed by her friend's comment. "Except she has blue eyes, like her mother's."

"And you know nothing about her?"

"No. Nothing at all." She motioned her friend outside.

Lara gazed in the direction of the barn. "Are Jack and Luke working up there?"

"Not Luke. He's recovering from a gunshot wound."

Lara's gaze zipped to hers. "How did that happen?"

"Let's have a seat, and I'll explain everything. But first let me peek in on Luke and see if there's anything he needs."

She crossed over to his tent. "Luke? Can I come in?" When he didn't answer, she lifted up the flap and peered in. He lay on his side in a way that she couldn't see his face. Her stomach fluttered as if butterflies had invaded it. There was something so romantic about watching him sleep. She hated seeing him hurting, especially when he got injured helping her. She shouldn't be here. She backed away and dropped the flap then looped her arm through Lara's. "C'mon, and I'll tell you what all's happened."

As the morning birds serenaded him, Luke wrestled with the shovel. Digging with one hand was a chore, but finally he hit the top of his money box. He didn't bother to dig it out but smashed the lid with the shovel point. He bent down, sucking in a sharp breath when hot pain seared his arm and torso. Sweat beaded on his forehead from the exertion.

He pulled out the bag that held his cash and carried it to his cot. He plopped down, breathing hard, and dumped out the cash, staring at his life's earnings. It was more than enough to build a livery and to stock it fairly well. But that dream had quickly died after yesterday's talk with Sarah. He couldn't fight her anymore. She didn't want him, so he needed to leave. It would be less painful for them both.

Footsteps shuffled his way. He tossed his blanket over the money as Jack lifted the flap.

"What's all that racket?" He glanced at the pile of dirt and lifted one eyebrow. "Why are you dressed? You're supposed to be resting."

"Can't. Got something to do. Would you saddle Golden Boy for me?"

Jack narrowed his eyes. "You got no business riding anywhere in the condition you're in."

Luke glared at him. "Either you saddle him, or I'll do it myself. I'll even ride bareback if I have to."

Jack stepped inside, but he couldn't stand up straight. "What's so all-fired important that you have to do it now?"

Luke stared at his dirty socks, cringing that Sarah had seen them. "I had a talk with Sarah last night. I've finally realized that I need to leave. I'm going back to Gabe's."

"You can't ride that far. You'll never make it."

"I can, and I will—at least as far as the train depot."

Jack smirked. "At least you still have some sense. I'll go saddle *our* horses."

"You're not going."

"I am as far as the depot. I want to make sure you make it on the train without passing out. Then I'll wire Gabe so he'll know to meet you in Guthrie."

"I don't need him to."

Jack grunted and backed out of the tent.

Luke flipped the blanket back. He pulled out fifty dollars then shoved the rest of his money into the bag. He grabbed one of his boots and stomped into it. Though he wouldn't admit it, he was glad Jack was riding with him. He just hoped they didn't encounter the women in town. He wanted to make a clean getaway.

As he struggled into his other boot, he couldn't help wondering if he was a coward to ride off without telling Sarah good-bye. But what else was there to say? She'd made her feelings clear.

By the time Jack returned, he'd managed to toss his clothes and personal items into his saddlebags and satchel. He exited the tent and gazed a final time at the ruins of Sarah's house. He'd never understand why God allowed it to be destroyed.

"You ready?" Jack tossed Golden Boy's reins over his neck. Luke handed him the saddlebags, and Jack tied them on then looped the satchel over the saddle horn. Jack boosted him up, and Luke almost fell off the other side. He clutched the horn and held on with his knees until the wave of weakness passed. Then he wiggled back into the saddle.

"Here." He handed Jack the bag with the majority of his money in it, along with the short note he'd penned to Sarah.

"What is it?"

"Just guard it well until you can give it to Sarah."

"You're not going to tell me what it is?"

"No." Luke took a final glance around the place he'd hoped might have been a new beginning for him and Sarah. Instead, it was the end. He gathered the reins and nudged his horse forward, saying good-bye to his long-held dream of a life with the only woman he'd ever loved.

Sarah had thoroughly enjoyed her time with Lara and the children at the hotel last night. Cody had joined them so he could be with his cousins. They walked out of the hotel, their stomachs full after a delicious breakfast she didn't have to cook.

Lara looked around. "This town reminds me of Guthrie in the beginning. They've made good headway, but I was surprised to find that there is a hotel already."

Sarah laughed. "You have to admit it's not much of a hotel, but at least we didn't have to sleep under the stars. Too many mosquitoes this time of year for that."

The children ran ahead. Claire wiggled to get down, so Sarah let her walk but held on to her hand. They strolled past new buildings and others still in the process of being erected. Fewer lots than on her last visit still held a tent.

"Have you made a decision about what to do?"

Sarah shrugged. "What choice do I have? Zelma informed me that the people who needed them next had wired them that they were going to have to hold off on their building project, so the Peterson men are free to rebuild my house, if I only had the money."

Lara's mouth twisted the way it did when she was thinking. The children stopped to peer in a barbershop window, and they soon caught up with them.

"It looks like there is still plenty of work in Anadarko. What if you offered to let the Petersons live on your land for free? Some of the men could work on your house while the others found jobs in town? It could benefit all of you."

"True, but I still don't have the money to rebuild. I paid Mr. Peterson last night for building the house and barn. I could tell he hated to take it, but they'd done the work and deserved the money. It wasn't their fault that awful man set fire to the house."

"Why *did* he do that?"

"To insure their getaway with Claire."

Lara shook her head. "I can't believe they wanted Claire to give to their daughter. I feel bad for the woman, but stealing a child is unconscionable."

"Yes. It's horrible."

Lara grasped her hand. "I'll talk to Gabe when we return home. I'm sure we could loan you the money you need."

Sarah shook her head. "Thank you, but I don't want to start out in debt."

They reached the town square. Sarah lifted up Claire as they crossed the street. "Why don't we sit and let the children work off some of their energy?"

"That sounds delightful." Lara smiled, but her light green eyes held concern.

While the children chased one another on the square, Sarah and Lara sat down on a bench someone had recently built.

"Have you thought any more about Luke?"

"Only all night. I don't know what to do."

Lara squeezed her hand. "Sarah, you've been in love with Luke for as long as I can remember. What's holding you back?"

She gazed at her friend. "What makes you say that? How can you know that I love him when I don't even know it?"

"Because whenever he walks into a room, your eyes go straight to him and your mouth tilts up in a special smile you reserve for him alone. Or when we're eating at the table, you cast shy glances his way. I've felt for years that God meant for you to be together."

"Then how come I don't know it?"

Claire stopped her stiff-legged run to look at Sarah, as if worried by the tone of her voice. She toddled toward her, flopping against Sarah's skirts. She picked up the girl, hugging her. "I know I've hurt Luke by not agreeing to marry him. He's such a good man. But what if I marry him and he leaves me like my father did my mother?"

Lara draped her arm around Sarah's shoulders. "Luke would never do that. You're worrying far too much. Everyone but you can see how much you two are meant for one another. The only thing I know to do is pray about it, and if it's God will for Luke to be part of your life, you simply need to surrender to it."

She had prayed. Over and over and over. Sarah watched the children gleefully playing while she felt so miserable. She'd wrestled half the night, struggling to know what to do. All she could think about was that amazing kiss that had set her body on fire and how Luke might have been killed rescuing Claire.

She couldn't stand the thought of him not being in her life. His smile brought her joy every time she saw it. She loved the teasing glint to his eyes. She loved everything about him.

And that kiss. Oh my. It was like nothing she'd ever experienced. She could spend a lifetime receiving kisses from Luke and never grow tired of them.

"Pa!" Cody ran to the edge of the lawn, waving.

Jack turned his horse and rode up to them, looking solemn. Sarah rose, sensing something else bad had happened. Jack looked at her with sad eyes and held out a dirty burlap sack. In the distance, the train whistled. "Luke asked me to give you this."

"What is it?"

Jack shrugged. "Don't know. I didn't look."

Sarah took the bag and sat down. Her stomach clenched as she was overcome with unease. She pulled the bag open and stared at what had to be hundreds of dollars and a single piece of paper. She tugged out the paper and turned it over. Her heart tightened. "It's from Luke."

"What does it say?" Lara asked.

Tears burned Sarah's eyes. "It's his savings. He wants me to use it to rebuild my house."

"But what about his livery?" Lara looked at Jack the same time Sarah did.

"He's not building it. He's at the depot now, returning to Guthrie."

"No!" Sarah jumped up. "I don't want his money."

"Then you'd better hurry if you plan on givin' it back." Jack held out his reins.

Sarah handed Claire to Lara. She snatched the reins and lifted her foot. Jack hauled her up. As she dropped into the saddle, he tossed the reins over his horse's neck. Sarah grabbed them, adjusted her grip, and then turned the horse toward the train that was already pulling into the station. "Heyah!"

The poor animal lurched forward and galloped down the street. People cast Sarah angry looks as they jogged to get out of her way. "Please, God. Let me get there in time."

She made the short distance quickly, but the people who had disembarked were already clearing the depot. Sarah slid off the horse, slapped the reins around the hitching post, and ran up the stairs. She searched the depot, but Luke wasn't there. The conductor closed the door to the first car. Sarah lifted her skirts and ran to the back of the third car, hoping to find an open door. "Please, God."

She reached for the handle, pressed it down, and pulled back. It opened! She stepped inside. People where still standing in the aisle, finding their seats—and then she looked up. Luke stood at the far end of the aisle, staring at her. He shook his head and walked toward her. She backed out the door and held it, not wanting an audience for what she needed to say.

He stepped onto the landing between the rail cars and closed the door, his gaze wary.

She held up the bag. "I don't want your money."

He snorted a laugh. "I should have known. You don't want anything to do with me."

The pain in his voice gutted her. She'd done this to him. "You're wrong. I don't want your money. I want you."

His gaze shot to hers, tentative—hopeful. "What?"

"I'm so sorry, Luke. I've been stupid. Stubborn. Scared."

"Scared of me?"

"No, scared of my past. Scared that if we married I'd spoil whatever good there was between us."

"But you don't feel that way now?"

She shook her head, smiling. "No. I've finally surrendered to God's will."

He leaned against the wall, looking less miserable. "And what is His will for you?"

"To be your wife. It took me a while to realize it, but I love you."

A blue fire ignited in his gaze. He pulled her to him, kissing her soundly. She returned his wonderful kiss, heedless of their public display. Their lips melded together, their breath joining as one. He cradled her head against his arm, and she received the gift of his love.

The train whistled, and the car jerked, knocking Sarah against Luke's injured shoulder. He hissed.

"Sorry." Sarah grabbed his hand, tugging him toward the stairs. "We've got to get off."

He tugged back. "Can't."

"Why?" Surely he wasn't going to leave after her declaration.

"My horse is on this train. You're gonna have to ride with me to the next stop until we can get him off."

"I don't have a ticket."

He bent down and picked up the bag of money she'd dropped. "I've just come into a slew of money. I think I can afford a ticket for my soon-to-be wife."

Grinning, she followed him into the car and sat down beside him as the conductor entered their car. She sidled a shy glance at Luke. "Soon-to-be?"

He smiled and winked at her. "You don't think I'm giving you time to back out, do you?"

He paid her ticket then wrapped an arm around her shoulder. Sarah leaned against him, and he rested his head contently against hers as the train chugged out of the depot.

This was her home. Not a pretty house on a hill. But Luke. And Claire. She didn't know where they would live, but it no longer mattered as long as she had the people she loved near her.

Epilogue

Ten days later

The sound of birds chirping and sunlight shining in the window drew Sarah from her sleep. She awoke cradled in the strong arms of her husband. *Husband.* She smiled. Never had a word sounded so nice.

"Mmm. . .you must be happy to see me."

"Always." She leaned up, placing a kiss on his lips.

Luke growled and rolled over. "You call that a kiss?" Bending down, he proceeded to educate her in an achingly delicious way. With her heart pounding and every part of her crying for him, he pulled back and grinned proudly. "That, my dear wife, is a kiss."

She blinked, giving him an innocent gaze. "I don't quite think I have the hang of it yet. I need more instruction."

Luke's beautiful blue eyes sparked. "I'm more than a little happy to oblige you, ma'am."

An hour later, they stood at the back door of the cabin on Gabe's land, looking out at the horses in the pasture. Luke kissed her head, drawing her close. "Sure was nice of Jack to loan us his cabin for a few days."

"Yes. And I'm grateful to Lara for keeping Claire."

"Me, too."

"But I do miss her."

"Is that a hint that it's time to visit the big house?"

She exhaled a happy sigh. "Not yet. I have something I need to say." She turned to face him, her hand pressed against his chest. "I'm sorry, Luke."

"For what?"

"For wanting a house more than you. I was so foolish."

He cupped her cheeks, gazing at her with the blue eyes she loved so much. "I'm not sorry. I'll admit, there were times I had my doubts that I'd ever win your heart, but I thank God that we're here together." He bent and kissed her on the nose. "You were worth the wait."

She smiled. Her husband was a good man. "Thank you for being so patient." She laid her head against his chest, taking care to stay away from his wound, which was still tender.

She thought of their wedding yesterday in the little church that Jack had returned to pastoring on Gabe's land. It was the most joyous time of her life, pledging herself to Luke and then spending the night together. She trailed her fingers through the hairs on his chest. "Um. . .is it awful of me to say that I'm not ready to share you yet?"

Luke leaned down, his gaze happy. "I feel the same, Mrs. McNeil." He lifted her in his arms, carried her back into the house, and kicked the door closed.

Sarah breathed in a breath of happiness. In a few days, she and her new husband would head back to Anadarko, where the Petersons had already started on the new house. Luke would have his livery, but every night, he'd come home to her and Claire.

She snuggled against him, so glad she quit fighting God and His will for her life.

Surrendering had never felt so good.

About the Author

Bestselling author Vickie McDonough grew up wanting to marry a rancher but instead married a computer geek who is scared of horses. She now lives out her dreams in her fictional stories about ranchers, cowboys, lawmen, and others living in the Old West. Vickie is the award-winning author of forty published books and novellas. Her novels include the fun and feisty Texas Boardinghouse Brides series, as well as *Gabriel's Atonement* and *Joline's Redemption*, books 1 and 2 in her Land Rush Dreams series.

Vickie has been married forty-one years to Robert. They have four grown sons, one of whom is married, and a precocious ten-year-old granddaughter. When she's not writing, Vickie enjoys reading, antiquing, watching movies, and traveling. To learn more about Vickie's books or to sign up for her newsletter, visit her website: www.vickiemcdonough.com.

Land Rush Dreams

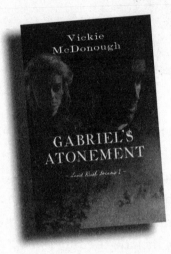

Books 1 & 2
Available Now!